Serving Love

by

Dana Hawkins

The Wild Rose Press, Inc.
PO Box 708
Adams Basin, NY 14410-0708
Visit us at www.thewildrosepress.com

Publishing History
First Edition, 2024
Trade Paperback ISBN 978-1-5092-5510-8
Digital ISBN 978-1-5092-5511-5

Published in the United States of America

Dedication

To My Family. I love you. Thank you for encouraging me, always.

Chapter 1
Today's Special: Sunny Side Up Everything with a Slice of Optimism

"Unless you want a back full of strawberry marmalade, don't stop moving," Holland joked to the hostess in front of her as she scurried to the kitchen, carrying a half dozen dirty dishes. She tossed them on the dishwasher rack and moved to grab a third side of ranch for the woman at Table Thirty. After bumping the industrial refrigerator door shut with a hip, she lifted plates off the warmer. She expertly balanced them—plus the ranch—on her forearms with the smells of toast, sugar, and bacon rising like a hearty fog.

Rushing between one cherry wood table and the next, she hurdled a toddler, who ran right in front of her and flung himself on the floor. *Uff da.* That was close. Before starting at the Salt & Sugar Café in Duluth, Minnesota, almost ten years ago, she would've never considered herself an athlete. Not even really that flexible. But now, her agility was on par with a cheetah.

"So sorry," the mom said. She snatched the screaming, kicking boy out of the way. "Honey, sit down right now. Come, finish your pancakes."

"No worries at all!" Holland flashed her brightest smile and darted to the corner black leather booth near the floor-to-ceiling window. Ever since she'd taken over raising her nephew five years ago, she was often on the receiving end of the look—the heavy irritated one from a bystander who didn't think she was disciplining her unruly child well enough. She was hyperaware not to replicate that expression toward other caretakers. "Here ya go," she said to her favorite residential grandparent regulars, Esther and Dave. "Walnut pancakes for you, and Minnesota wild rice omelet for you." She set down the items on the table, secretly salivating at the cheesy egg concoction. Tomorrow, she'd definitely be getting this after her shift. "Don't worry, Esther. I'm bringing out the pepper sauce and coffee on my next round. Promise me you won't combine the two."

"The only thing I'd ever mix with my coffee is Irish Cream." Esther chuckled before picking up her knife to cut through the pancakes. "How's that sweet boy of yours doing?"

Talking about her nephew always melted her heart. "Riley's such a champ. Growin' like a weed."

Dave grabbed the syrup and pooled extra on the side. "You missed something there, Holland."

"Oh, yeah?" She popped a hand onto her hip. "What's that?"

"Joke of the day."

Of course. "All right. You're gonna love this one. What's a cat's favorite color?"

"What?" Dave asked.

"Purrrrple." She snort-laughed at one of her favorite jokes.

Dave shook his head with a grin and dove back to his food.

She dashed across the rustic hardwood floors to clear off a few plates from another booth, then joined her fellow server, Amanda, on the way back to reload their trays for the next table.

"I'm starving." Amanda pulled her black hair into a messy bun.

Holland walked past the café's bakery and espresso bar with Amanda and pushed through the kitchen's swinging doors.

"Me, too." Holland glanced at her watch. Twelve thirty-five p.m. Two more hours until her shift ended. *Ugh.* Her stomach had not stopped growling since waking up, and she didn't know if she could wait that long to get food into her belly. Normally, she scarfed down something before her shift, but Riley had struggled that morning, and she'd run out of time. "I know what I'm eating after my shift."

"Lemme guess. A chocolate shake." Amanda nudged her with an elbow and shifted plates on her tray. "With a heart attack-inducing dollop of whipped cream on top."

"Wrong." *Right.* "Fine. That's post *post* shift. No, I want to try the new chorizo sandwich. The customers are super pumped about it." She grabbed a cup of lemons for a table.

"Yikes. You sure about that? Chorizo has spice."

"You're so mean. Just because you're used to exotic foods doesn't mean I can't handle it."

Amanda's eyebrow cocked before she scooped ice cubes into the mason jars they used for beverages. "I'll have a glass of milk on standby, in case I need to resuscitate you."

A strand of hair fell from Holland's braid. She pushed it back and reached behind Amanda for a ketchup bottle. "I'm seriously craving some variety."

With Riley's multiple food aversions, eating what he wanted to eat was easier than cooking two meals. "I'm on day one hundred million of chicken nuggets, tater tots, and peas."

Amanda cut the stack of extra napkins and handed Holland half. "Is he with your parents today?"

"No. My parents watching him is a disaster in the making." Holland's parents never properly followed the autism therapist's guidelines the rare times they cared for him. "He's been progressing so much, and I didn't want to screw it up. I swear they do more harm than good." She reached in the mini fridge for a side of sour cream for her next order. "His therapist is helping today."

Thank God. Riley's therapist could hopefully reset him for the evening. Earlier, Holland had failed to calculate the meltdown risk of not restocking the green sticker rewards. The heaviness of her forgetfulness weighed on her. She couldn't make mistakes like that anymore.

"Hey, you're doing great. You know that, right?" Amanda's tone turned soft as she put an arm on Holland's shoulder.

No manual existed for this. Being raised in a house where s'mores were served for dinner, limitless TV time, no curfew, and midnight family dance-offs meant Holland would not offer Riley that subpar parenting. Despite Amanda's attempts to comfort her, she still felt like she failed Riley every day. "Aww shucks." A tight smile shot across her face, and she finger-crossed her bestie couldn't see through her. She popped the tray against her side and double-checked her order slip.

"Holland." Her friend met her gaze. "I'm serious.

You're killing it."

Holland bit back the tears brewing beneath the surface. "Stop getting mushy. Your hair's frizzing."

"This humidity is killing me! Seattle natives are not bred for this kind of weather." Amanda squeezed Holland's hand and grabbed the tray.

Holland took one last sharp inhale before heading back to the grind. And prayed her friend couldn't read the nerves on her face.

****

Several hours later when Holland's shift wound down, she grabbed the half-filled jars of rhubarb jelly to refill and moved to the prep station.

Amanda turned the corner, smirking and holding a utensil bin.

"What's up, Buttercup?" Holland asked.

"New guy alert," Amanda announced. "And ooooh, he is Dreamy McDreamerton."

"Must be James' nephew." Holland remembered the owner mentioned the new chef would start this week. "Didn't realize today's his orientation."

"I'll find out if he's single and report back immediately."

"Um. How would your girlfriend feel about that?"

"Not for me, dork. For you." Amanda folded the cloth napkin around the silverware and ran a palm over it to roll. "Time to dive back into the dating pool. What's it been? Four years now?"

"Five. But nope. Not interested." Holland's voice was tighter than intended. Amanda had good intentions, of course. But the idea of dating was overwhelming at best. A colossal tsunami of a heartbreak in the making at worst. She could barely manage day-to-day anything, much less add a guy to the mix.

"Pass me some of those." Holland wiggled her fingers at the bin.

Amanda sighed and handed her a stack of silverware. She cleared her throat and subtly pointed at James, sporting his lucky bow tie and freshly shaved head while escorting a man around the kitchen. "They're coming."

Wow. Amanda was not kidding. The edgy energy reflected off this man. Inky-black, wavy hair bounced with every step. Muscles articulated against the fabric of his white cotton T-shirt.

"Goodness," Amanda said. "That man is just all…man. I bet he came out of the womb with a five o'clock shadow."

Holland giggled. James was super sweet; perhaps his nephew had a similar personality. Maybe having a friend who looked like that wouldn't be *so* bad.

"Holland, can you come here, please?" James called, motioning her forward.

Oh, no. Had the nephew overheard them? Capital A Awkward.

"I want to introduce you to our newest chef."

Holland smoothed down her shirt and apron, with her heart thumping more than it should. She ignored Amanda's go-get-'em, tiger growl and walked toward the men.

"This is Shane Blackwood." James waved his arms toward the man with the intensely confident stance.

My goodness, he is tall. If she stepped on her tiptoes, the top of her head might graze his chin.

"Shane's my favorite nephew."

"You only have one nephew." She glanced up at

Shane with a smile. He stood with an unreadable expression. Annoyed? Bored? Definitely not loving her joke. *Yikes.* "Nice to meet you. I'm Holland."

She took a moment to study—admire—his features. A playbook of opposites. The stark contrast between his square jawline and full, soft lips. The gentle slope of his nose next to the ruggedness of a five-day-old beard. The thick, almost-jagged black eyebrows above the clearest blue eyes she'd ever seen. He appeared to be her own age of twenty-seven or a little older.

He shook her hand with one firm pump and grumbled something.

"Holland is our resident ball of sunshine and customers' favorite," James said.

"I heard that!" Amanda called from the other side of the kitchen.

"Oh, James. Go on." Holland laughed, but when Shane didn't, she sucked it back. *Dang.* Tough one to crack. Although the first day was intimidating. He was probably just nervous. Even if his stiffened backbone gave off a totally different vibe.

"Can you introduce Shane to everyone and show him the ropes?" James grabbed his cell phone from his pocket and declined a call.

"Should I have him run downstairs and grab something from the basement?"

"Holland." James wagged a finger, then turned to face Shane. "Grabbing supplies from the basement is Holland's version of hazing. The restaurant has no basement."

"You did it to me!" She flashed a smile toward James, remembering her first day ten years ago when she searched high and low for a door that didn't exist. "All right, let's head this way." She gestured like a flight attendant toward the pantry. "I'll introduce you to the pit crew, show you some things in the storage area, and where to add labels—all that good stuff."

He nodded but remained silent, his face devoid of expression.

Geesh. Was it her? They'd met less than five minutes ago, but he clearly wasn't excited James assigned her to show him around. Which was more than a little disappointing, as she lived for orientation days, bursting to give all the tips and tricks she learned over the years. Maybe he just needed a few more reassuring smiles. "A lot of people work here, so don't memorize their names today unless you're good at that kind of thing." She pushed open the swinging kitchen door. "Except for Amanda. Remember her name."

"Amanda?"

He speaks!

"Yeah, the woman I was standing next to with black hair and chunky glasses. She's a force, let me tell you. Totally the one you want backing you up in a bar fight."

"She's like five feet tall," he said in a monotone.

"And still the most intimidating person you'll ever encounter. I met her on my first day of seventh grade. She stomped into the classroom like a confident hurricane, rocking a '90s grunge era T-shirt and combat boots. Like the epitome of cool. I was so jealous, but she chose me to be her bestie." When he said nothing, she tightened her jaw. *Whatever.* He probably just didn't understand teenage-girl angst. She led him past the stainless steel prep counters toward the industrial walk-in fridge. "So, James is your uncle, huh? I love him."

"Yep."

"He takes so much pride in this place. I swear the cafe's like the child he's never had. According to his husband, James devotes more time to this place than to him. But he brings home leftovers every night, so that's how they've lasted twenty years." With a foot, she slid an empty cardboard box out of their way. "Oh, ha. I guess you know that 'cause he's your uncle."

"Yep."

"James said you just moved here, right?" she asked.

"Yep."

Really? The one-word answers were getting old. She exhaled through her nose. Riley had taught her a million things, one of which was patience with people who process new experiences differently than others. Even though he looked like a more confident version of a superhero, maybe he was overstimulated. She used both hands and clenched all her stomach muscles to pull on the fridge door.

He reached above her head and flattened one palm against the door to keep it open.

She sucked in a breath at the refreshing blast of cold air hitting her face, cooling her skin from the brutal humid Minnesota summer air. "Ah, this is the best. I love coming in here when it's so hot outside. With this humidity, you never quite dry off from the moment you step out of the shower. Great for dry skin. Bad for comfortability. Am I right?"

He shoved his hands in his pockets, and the sharp sound of key metal clanged in his jeans. "What's the rotation schedule for the food?" He faced the shelf.

Wow. All business. Okay. She could work with this. As long as she could ignore the tingles shooting to the top of her scalp by being in a small, dark, refreshingly chilly place with him. "Shipments arrive every Monday." She cleared her suddenly sticky throat. "For labeling and rotating stock, James does not mess around. And trust me, he'll check your work. He's super-organized. One day I'm gonna sneak into his home to see if he labels his linen closet. I'll bet you a dollar he does." She showed him the label maker hanging on the rack. "Oh wait, you're his nephew. Bet's off. Unfair advantage." His stone-faced expression made her smile drop.

Flipping his keys through his fingers, he kept his focus on the food. "Where are the Minnesota Department of Health regulations posted? I assume we're following the state statutes for safety and cleanliness, correct?"

Huh? "Um, James is ultra clean, obviously. I've never even seen his clothes wrinkled, much less a dirty prep area." She joked, then swallowed back a cough. "Uh, we have some things posted in the break room." Ten years of doing orientations, and no one had ever asked her about the health codes location. She finished giving him the refrigerator tour.

He pushed the door open.

She walked out under his arm. The steamy kitchen flattened her goose bumps, and she led him toward the customer seating area. "So, what other restaurants did you work at?"

His jaw muscles tightened. "None."

He's never worked at a restaurant but is asking

about health codes? "Did you apprentice?"

"No."

"Are you some sort of food savant? Stalk reality TV chefs' socials and whip up chocolate soufflé in your downtime?"

"Not exactly."

His voice was still gruff but now had a smidge of softness. And he increased to two-word answers. Clearly, her disarming ways put him at ease. Mission nearly accomplished. "I really envy people like you," she said. "My fanciest dish is adding granola to my PB & Js. Don't knock it until you've tried it! You can add it to the chef's menu and take all bragging rights for yourself. Our little secret."

She was met with sustained silence. Again. Was he avoiding eye contact? He wasn't being rude, per se. He was indifferent—a reaction she wasn't used to—and a weight lowered itself onto her chest. "What did the egg say when it walked into the keg party?" Last-ditch effort.

He stopped, darted a glance at her, then put his focus back on the wall. "Excuse me?"

"What did the egg say when it walked into the keg party?" She lifted an eyebrow. "I'm lit!" She threw up her arms and did a little shoulder shimmy. "Get it? Omelet. I'm lit? The egg's drunk. Funny, right?" She bowed. "Don't forget to tip your servers. I'll be back for the ten p.m. show."

Really? Nothing? That was her best joke ever. Oh, well—she tried. He wasn't nervous. His shoulders were back, and his hands were stuffed in his pockets. Nope, nothing but confidence spewed from this guy. He just wasn't very nice. And she didn't like not very nice.

But just like that, a ghost of a grin appeared. "That was a pretty good one."

Score! Her chest lifted, and she bit back a smile.

"Holland, huh?" He scanned the customer waiting area and stared at the hanging artwork. "Is that where you're from?"

Why did the scratchy velvet undertone in his voice when he said her name slide into her ear, race down her neck, and touch every single nerve ending on its way down? A reaction like that was so unlike her. The last time she tingled was probably high school. "No." Her lips grew into a grin. "Holland is where I was conceived."

He raised his eyebrows.

"My parents are hippies." She smiled. "My full name's Holland Blue Mulberry. Nope, I'm not lying. Yep, I should copyright it and put it on jam."

A whisper of a dimple appeared on his cheek.

Her stomach somersaulted like it was auditioning for the circus.

"Thanks for the tour." He shoved his hands back in his pockets, his gruff tone returning. "I'll find James now."

Watching him walk away made Holland's neck warm. Twenty minutes with this guy and she felt a slight void in the space he filled. Twenty freaking minutes.

Goodness…I seriously need to get more sleep.

She returned to the kitchen and joined Amanda at the prep area.

"He's so mysterious, though, right?" Amanda filled her water tray. "What if he's a CIA agent doing undercover work? I mean, look at his biceps. Have you ever seen such defined arms in all your life? I want to squeeze them, but pretty sure I'd break my hands."

Holland shrugged. "I guess I didn't notice."

Lies. But she could never admit the truth out loud.

Chapter 2
Today's Special: Jalapeno Popper Summer Heat

What could he have told her, anyway? *Nice to meet you. Never been a chef before. My current role is perpetual parent disappointer and dream shatterer. And ex-fiancé. But let's not go there today.*

Her smile, though. *Incredible.* And that hair. Shane wasn't normally a hair kinda guy, but Holland's mane lived on a planet of its own. Wrapped in a thick braid that reached to her waist. A perfect combination of fire and sun, such a bright red he would've sworn she just colored it, but her freckles sprinkling, green eyes, pink cheeks, and matching eyebrows made him think otherwise.

He checked behind him to confirm he was alone, leaned against the wall, and pinched the bridge of his nose. Allowing himself a short mental reprieve, he closed his eyes until the muffled sound of approaching footsteps grew louder. "Dang it," he muttered. Releasing a shaky breath, he pushed away from the wall and made his way to the bakery.

Everything about Holland would've normally hit him hard. Her bubbly personality. The coconut scent wafting off her. The beautiful, full, dark-pink lips he forced himself not to stare at and one of the best smiles he'd seen in his lifetime. But no way would he entertain any idea other than appreciating the obvious sunshine surrounding her.

His uncle had given him a fresh start. A place to escape from his failures in the Twin Cities and figure out his life. *Again.* Had he ever thought at twenty-six, he'd be living in the loft above his uncle's garage? Starting a new job in his restaurant? Leaving Minneapolis two semesters shy of graduating law school and running as far as he could to Duluth?

"Want a coffee?" the barista asked. Her name tag read *Maddy*, and she looked like a twenty-something Halle Berry. "Food and drinks are free for employees. They're the biggest perk of working here."

"Coffee's great, thanks. Black." Shane sat on a heavy, chrome-topped barstool and took a moment to admire his new place of employment. He'd been to Salt & Sugar Café when visiting James, but usually to grab a quick bite before they went fishing. Shane never took the time to appreciate the details. James had spent nearly a year converting the abandoned firehouse into a café and maintained several parts of the original structure. White tea-light-wrapped Ficus trees and dark, leather-backed booths surrounded the massive wooden windows nestled among the burnt-orange brick walls. Fire poles remained. The fire station reception area was now a separate bakery and espresso area, with a handwritten chalk menu, rotating cold brews, and an impressive array of teas.

He pulled the recipe book lying on the counter toward him and began reviewing, starting with the house staples for the season. Various local fish—including walleye and bass, multiple corn dishes, wild rice hot dish, and fried chicken. And rhubarb desserts. Too. Much. Rhubarb. Wasn't rhubarb a vegetable, anyway? Whoever had come up with mixing vegetables in desserts obviously lacked taste buds. *Gross.*

The fabric on his shirt constricted him. He hooked a finger in his collar and tugged. After swiping damp hands across his thighs, he flipped through more pages, determined to commit everything to memory. His first day would not be a failure.

Maddy set a mug of coffee down in front of him. "Did you want something else with that?"

"Anything without rhubarb."

She cocked her head to the side. "Huh?"

"Chocolate muffin would be great. Thanks."

A flicker ignited inside him with getting back to the kitchen. Not that he wanted this as his lifelong job, but he used to enjoy cooking. He used to enjoy a lot of things. *Before.* Learning how to live in the after would take time.

"Here ya go." Maddy set a plate next to the mug.

"Thanks. Hey, sorry. Newbie here. Do we tip each other?"

"Nope, another house rule. Besides, you'll cook my lunch on your next shift, and then we'll be even." She grinned and wiped a coffee droplet off the counter.

Shane sipped the surprisingly delicious cup of caffeine. Moving to Duluth was a culture shock, and he thought the coffee wouldn't be as good. The Twin Cities had millions of people, fantastic restaurants, and an impressive nightlife scene. Duluth still had a sort of small-town feel. World-renowned local pie shop. People stopped and chatted on the sidewalk. A festival that had a floating duck the size of a ship. He was in a different world.

Did Holland drink coffee? She probably took it

with extra sugar. Wait—where did that thought come from? Why did he care how she took her coffee?

"Hey." James poked his bald head around the corner. "Give me about ten minutes to finish inventory, and I'll come back and grab you for a deep dive into all things fabulous."

"Sounds good."

"You good, kiddo?"

Not really. "You know I'm almost thirty, right?"

James scrunched his nose. "You know I used to change your diapers, right?"

Shane raised an eyebrow.

James tugged on the ends of his bow tie with a wild grin and sashayed away. He wore a bowtie every day, no matter how humid. The bowtie was his signature look—encompassed who he was and everyone accepted him.

Acceptance. Anyone who said they didn't want their family's approval was lying. When Shane dropped the bomb of a lifetime on his parents—six months after dropping a similar bomb on *her*—the image of his parents' faces killed him. He skipped town right after, like he didn't care. But he cared. Too much, probably. Enough to fill his nights counting the circulating blades on his ceiling fan until the hurt faces of his loved ones vanished.

"Recipes, recipes…." He sunk his teeth into the muffin and flipped the page to the appetizer section. Until he memorized at least half the dishes, he needed to ignore what brought him to Duluth in the first place—the buzz that shot through him when a real estate agent showed him studio space off Main Avenue. An hour after he had toured the space, he drained his savings to plunk down a year's worth of rent. And drove back to St. Paul with his fingers crossed, praying he hadn't made the mistake of a lifetime.

The years' long pinch in his neck loosened when he was in Duluth. Smelling the mineral freshwater of Lake Superior reactivated a tiny blaze in his belly. He spent hours wandering the city that first week, marveling at the lush greenery, endless water, and scenic woodlands. Rolling hills and rushing waterfalls gave off a Pacific Northwest vibe and contrasted with the flattened land of the Twin Cities. Historic buildings with their original brick and woodwork, massive bridges, and walking paths filled him. Finally, he could breathe.

Working at the restaurant was his only real responsibility. Outside of that, he could spend all his time working on The Plan. He had exactly eleven months and eight days to bring his vision, his *dream,* to life. No matter how cute Holland was, he did not want any distractions.

His uncle provided him the opportunity to get out. To be free. A proper do-over. He trailed his fingers over the studio keys in his pocket, the reminder of his purpose. He vowed to put all his effort into the plan. And this time, he wouldn't break his promise.

Chapter 3
Today's Special: Saltwater Dreams Ice Cream

The frayed, yellowed wallpaper with miniature daisies curled in the corner near the kitchen sink. Holland dug around the junk drawer for a glue stick to adhere it to the wall. Gluing wallpaper back up was a bit like chipping at a frozen lake with a toothpick, but she'd never stop. The house had been on life support since the late '80s, but she refused to let her and Riley's home go without a fight.

The timer rang, and she tapped her phone to silence the noise. She shoved the glue back into the drawer, then tussled Riley's flaming red hair. "Hey, Bubby, time for a bath, and then story time."

He stayed seated at the tiny, fake oak kitchen table. The evening sunbeams streamed through the pea-green vinyl blinds, highlighting his cherub face. As he laser-focused on adding a blue bead to the leather strip, the tip of his tongue poked from his plump lips.

"Riley. Bath, then story time."

His tiny fingers clutched the bracelet. "No. No. No."

"Time to be done." Her voice firmed, and her pulse accelerated. "The timer went off. First bath, then story." She took in a deep breath and held it. Some nights were better than others. But she'd made a mistake last month of allowing five more minutes of beading because he was so stinking cute. And she was tired. She'd worked a double that day, and sitting and making jewelry felt good—the one activity she and Riley shared with an equal amount of passion. But that extra five minutes led to a meltdown, tears from both of them, no bath, and a suffocating feeling of failure.

"Okay, Mimi." As he stood, the chair squeaked across the cracked linoleum floor.

She released the air and smiled at the name he'd called her. When his language started growing three years ago, around age four, he called her that name, and she didn't stop it. Rules, therapy appointments, and routines dictated their lives, and he deserved to have control over something. "Show me your hard work."

He fisted the bracelet and held it up high, his smile wide and bright.

"Beautiful! I love it so much!" Of course, it had a perfect pattern of two blue and one pink bead. *Look at him, kicking my butt in the jewelry-making department.*

A year ago, she'd dropped her bead container, and they scattered like cockroaches across the floor. She'd told herself not to cry, knowing it would take forever to reorganize them.

Riley had sat and methodically lined up the beads, one by one.

The process took hours, but she'd been the one holding in the meltdown, not him. He'd taught her patience that day. He taught her something every day. The comfort of a routine. Enjoying simple things like watching a train roll by. Joyfully celebrating differences—not just "accepting" or "tolerating." Goodness, she really loved this kid.

After bath time, Riley's freshly washed apple-scented head and warm cheeks pressed against her chest. She tucked his unicorn stuffed animal into his arms and tugged the purple blankie to his chin. "Which book tonight, Bubby?"

"Mimi! You know."

She kissed his head and snatched his favorite moon story from his shelf. In a sea full of books, he needed this one right before he closed his eyes. She adjusted the weighted blanket on him and flipped the fan one notch higher. The weighted blanket was a godsend, giving Riley the comfort he needed at night to self-regulate. But they lived in hot-as-devil's-breath Minnesota, and she worried her garage-sale-purchased window air conditioner didn't do enough. "Night, Bubby. I love you." She closed the door, and the safety notification bell jingled. She put her ear against the wood to make sure he didn't call out, then tiptoed to the kitchen.

She shoved leftover nuggets in the fridge, scrubbed and rack-dried dishes, and tossed her ripped-off bra down the hall. After sauntering over to her stash, she checked behind her shoulder to make sure Riley hadn't snuck out of bed and reached for it. The Holy Grail. Her freezer. "Ah, come to Mama." She pulled out a chocolate toffee crunch. "Yum."

Gone were the days of tequila shots and margarita happy hours. Replaced by chocolate, peanut butter, or cookie crunch ice cream. One tub was always on hand, even if it exceeded her grocery budget for that week. Sometimes, she missed having a drink. But didn't some rule exist that a parent couldn't drink if they were alone with their kid? If Riley needed her or hurt himself, and she couldn't make a sound decision, then what? She didn't know all the rules about drinking when parenting. Heck, she didn't know any rules about parenting. She made the stuff up as she went along, and she kissed her four-leaf clover magnet she and Riley would survive.

Her parents' unorthodox child-raising methods hadn't set a great example. With all the meals she and her sister ate alone because her parents were traveling—*"living their best life!"*— the girls were also allowed to skip school on randomly warm spring days to go camping. They had impromptu family road trips to a corn maze in Iowa and backyard fires with hotdogs and marshmallows propped on a stick. Her parents passed their free-spiritedness to Holland and their lack of parental skills down to her estranged older sister, Layla.

She eased herself onto the floor next to the coffee table. She lifted the top of the chocolate toffee crunch and stuck one of Riley's coated baby spoons into the ice cream. Yep, she was an adult. But a year ago, when he resisted changing to a metal spoon, she tried his type. And he was right! A smooth spoon against her tongue made the dessert taste better.

Maybe she should make him change to adult silverware. Or maybe not. Was that some sort of requirement? *Nope, not doing this.* Tonight, she was taking off from questioning every decision she made. Tonight, she'd make a gratitude list, not a what-in-the-heck-am-I-doing list. Starting with thanking the heavens Riley wrapped his arms around her daily, giving her more love than she deserved.

Her phone buzzed with Amanda's name flashing across the screen.

"Duuuuude," Amanda said with a growl.

Holland smiled into the phone. "What? What did I miss?"

"DMD."

"What?"

Amanda giggled on the other end of the line. "Dreamy McDreamerton. Just saw him filling up gas. He drives a big-wheeled, convertible-top SUV. You know what that means?"

"That he has a proper four-wheel drive and can get through the hills before the snowplows, if necessary. That he's practical?"

"Buzz. Wrong. It means he's fun. Off-roading. Beach trips. There might be a whole other layer to this guy."

Holland took another bite of the sweet, creamy, chocolate toffee crunch. "We'll see. He's more Grumpy McGrumperton than anything else. Orientation did not go great."

"Aww, come on. If anyone can tame this cowboy, it's you."

"Cowboy? Really? Put down your margarita and chips, call your girlfriend, or take a taxi. In that order."

Amanda laughed. "Ok, love you. Byeeee."

She set the phone down and grabbed her jewelry kit from under the coffee table. She held the charms in the air, and they glinted with the glow from the lamp. Running her fingers through the beading wire, she contemplated her piece. Bracelet or necklace? Green or gold? Comfort or fun?

Several items she made became comfort pieces. The night the social worker rapped on her door with a shy Riley hugging her leg, she'd been in the middle of creating a stacked ring. Twirling that ring every day since reminded her how far they'd come. Even though her dream of making jewelry for the tourists in Maui disappeared after she got custody of Riley, she still stockpiled her inventory and dreamt of the day when she could open a local shop.

Maui. Even if she had to save tips for a decade, she would take Riley someday. After scrounging through the sea glass bin, she took out an aqua piece that matched the Pacific Ocean. The smoothness of the sea glass between her fingers allowed her mind to drift.

Today would go down as her worst orientation of all time. She obviously irritated Shane. Did he retain any information? Would he remember seafood has to go on top and chicken on the bottom? And that James would legit freak out if Shane puts any prepared food below the raw meats. He would know that, right? No one wants chicken-juice-infused cheese.

She molded the wire with her fingertip, then pinched the sea glass to add to the necklace. Maybe if she concentrated on this piece, she wouldn't concentrate on *him.*

Why did she care? Why did this man, who said less than fifty words to her all day, leave such an impression? Sure, he was cute. But she'd seen cute before. He had a portal behind those baby blues, even though he mostly avoided her gaze during conversations. And that gateway seemed to hide something.

Honestly, it didn't matter. She had less than zero time for guy drama. And she and Riley were on such a good path. She wouldn't let a guy ruin it.

Chapter 4
Today's Special: Braised Misunderstandings

Holland's car puttered to a stop in the Salt & Sugar Café parking lot. Her lungs stretched to max capacity before she released a slow, jagged exhale. Riley's therapist, Amy, was taking a two-week long, well deserved, but *holy-cow-this-messes-up-Riley's-schedule* break from behavior therapy duties. No matter how skilled the backup therapist was, having someone new threw Riley for a loop.

Holland dug her buzzing phone out of the console. A text from Amanda popped up.

—*Might want to come in through the fire escape.*—

—*Why, what's up?*—

—*Hottie man has officially crossed into jerkwad territory. He is NOT having it today.*—

Seriously? Shane said less than ten words to anyone during his first week. By week two, he snapped each word like a fire on a log. Now heading into week three, he upped his grumpy ante. Whatever first-day crush she had disappeared by day two. Mostly.

She had no time for this. The bottom of her shirt was still wet, a casualty from Riley throwing his cup of milk against the kitchen wall earlier, and her head throbbed from lack of sleep. She slumped back into the seat and twirled the stacked rings on her finger. After counting backward from ten, she pressed the call button. "Hey, Mom." She propped an elbow on the window ledge and adjusted the air-conditioning vents to blast her face. "Reminding you Grandparent's Day is next Thursday at Riley's school. He's super-excited to see you guys there." *Please, for everything holy, promise me you didn't forget.*

"Holladazzle, I *know*. You've called me like five times to remind me. My cute little worrywart. I have special brownies that can take away your anxiety." Gina's signature singsong voice bounced across the line.

Holland stiffened her jaw. She ignored her stuck-in-the-'70s mother's comment about the pot-laced dessert. "Sorry, I know how sometimes you forget things." *Like my birthdays.*

Gina slurped on her presumable typical breakfast coffee with Irish Cream and smacked her lips. "How's my Riley-bear doing?"

"He's great. A little slip-up this morning when I had to substitute whole milk for his usual oat milk. Let's just say I had to clean cereal off the floor." She left out the part about choking down a cry while wiping the mess, then carrying Riley to the car as he pounded his fists on her back.

"Oh, Holladaisy. You're doing such a good job. I'm sure he'll get over not having cereal. Remember, kids are like fish. They forget everything the second the moment is over."

Not true, but whatever.

"Layla called last night for a check-in," Gina continued.

The sound of her sister's name caused Holland's stomach to tense.

26

"She's loving California. Said the people are totally different from Texas. You know we haven't spoken for—"

"Mom." Holland hated that her mother refused to respect her wishes.

"—several months. She's usually so good about calling every two months. Can you believe—"

"Mom."

"—eight years have gone by since we've seen her! I checked the calendar. Breaks my heart, but I just let you girls live your life. Your grandma was so strict with me, and I promised I'd never be that way—"

"Mom! Enough." Why does her mom tell her these things? Five years ago, when her sister didn't show up to court over Riley's custody—a child she disregarded like trash six months prior—Holland told her parents never to speak about Layla again. Which her mom ignored on the regular. Even if she was a tiny curious about what Layla had been doing, she planted a stubborn stake in the ground and said all Layla conversations were off-limits. "Gotta run to work. Tell Dad hey from me." She threw her phone into her bag and turned off her sputtering engine. "I've *got* to get that fixed," she muttered. Two, maybe three, more paychecks and she'd bring it in to the shop.

Like the sun's stifling heat might not catch her, she bolted between the brick buildings to reach the kitchen alley entrance. Two steps inside and a hand gripped her elbow.

"Thank God, you're here to diffuse the Blackwood Bomb," Amanda said through clenched teeth.

Ugh. What was the deal with him? His face muscles only produced one look: irritated. He had a constant scowl, and chucked food into the compost as if it were life threatening. And she was almost positive he made the line cook cry yesterday after he bellowed about the chocolate sprinkles being too clumpy on a sundae. She rolled her eyes. "What happened?"

"Not sure what the rhubarb did to make him so mad, but he clearly cut it out of his will. Dang."

"Is this different from any other day?" She shoved her purse into her locker. "This is his M.O. Just ignore him. Or punch him in the kidney. Whatever you need to do to get Table Twenty their refills on time."

Shane was cute, although she wouldn't admit that out loud, because Amanda would never let her live it down. He had a sort of movie star quality, a dimple on his cheek that appeared once when he and James talked. But that was as far as any admiration went. He was rude, snappy, grumpy as heck, and she had zero patience for him today.

"Hey, did you get your grades yet?" Holland followed Amanda to the kitchen.

"No. The professor is hella slow. They should've arrived last week. I thought about emailing the dean, but my brain is on summer vibes only." Amanda double-knotted her apron and shrugged. "I think I did okay."

"Ya think?" Holland grinned. A straight-A student her entire life, including so far in her MBA program, Amanda would for sure earn a promotion to CEO of the world before she turned thirty. Holland braked before the kitchen doors and braced herself for The Blackwood Wrath. "All right, I'm going in."

"Don't say I didn't warn you."

The sound of a plate being banged on the counter

echoed throughout the kitchen. *Geez!* Amanda was right.

An orange peel slice met its demise as Shane body-slammed it into the sink. "No!" His voice was low and gruff, and he blasted a heated glare at the second cook. "You layer it like this. Sliced radishes, topped with sliced avocado, topped with a cherry tomato. Red, green, red. Doesn't anyone care what this looks like?"

Yikes. His pickiness about the plates' appearances was ridiculous. *Sure, fine.* Since taking over the kitchen, he elevated the presentation. But people like her regulars, Dave and Esther, didn't care about fanned radishes. Or perfectly crisscrossed icing drizzles underneath the chocolate cake. But this Type-A, frustrated perfectionist acted like he was auditioning for a martial-art-meets-angry-kitchen-guru reality show.

Before Riley came into her life, she was a proud Type-Z'er. Non-existent agendas. No pre-planned trips, just trips. But now her and Riley's mental survival depended on her organizational and schedule-keeping skills. At work, nothing constituted this level of irritation. This fury didn't even happen when the café ran out of walleye on a Friday during Lent, and the only other meatless option was tofu.

A piece of lettuce headed straight at her face. She ducked like a fighter in the ring, and it missed her by an inch. "Really?" She threw her hands up.

Shane's eyes grew wide. "Sorry. I was aiming for the compost."

Was there a hint of remorse in his tone? "Maybe you should take the lettuce to the alley and show it who's boss."

He stared in silence.

"What did it do to you, anyway? Bang on your door saying 'let us in' while you slept?" She grinned. "Get it? Lettuce in?"

His lips tugged upwards at the corners. "Yep. I got it."

Satisfied with his positive reaction, she pushed through the doors to take orders. Gosh, he could be so broody…and moody…and handsome.

Stop that, Holland.

What was his problem, anyway? It was just *food*. He must realize more serious things happened in the world. The intensity was too much. The way his eyes burrowed in fierce concentration while he cooked. His forearms flexed as he chopped and stirred, highlighting every single muscle against his golden skin misted with sweat. *Ack! Enough.*

An hour later, the lunch crowd picked up. The buzz of conversation wafted through the air and mixed with the smell of garlic-and-rosemary-roasted potatoes. While running through a mental checklist, she smiled and scribbled orders in her order pad. Table Twelve—ketchup. Table Fourteen—water refills. Table Seventeen—creamer. She punched the order into the digital ticketing screen, and soon footsteps approached from behind her.

"Two guys on seven. Sorry in advance," the hostess said.

Oh, no. "Got it, thanks." Plastering on her most disarming smile, she hopped over to the table and clicked her pen a few times. "Hey there, can I get some drinks started? Blueberry lemonade? Iced mocha? Italian soda?" With her car verging on a breakdown, she needed to push as many extras as she could.

The sandy-blond haired man with a yellow polo shirt shot her a half-smile. "You got whiskey?"

"Ack, sorry. Nope. Booze-free zone, I'm afraid. May I recommend the vanilla dirty chai? It's chai with a shot of espresso. With all that caffeine and sugar, it'd probably give you the same buzz as a drink," she joked.

"What's the name of the drink again?" The man's gaze trailed her.

She shielded herself with her order pad. "Dirty chai." Her blood turned cold from his gaze. "Would you like me to get one?"

He folded his arms in front of his chest. "Nah. Just wanted to hear you say dirty again."

Ewww. And really? What was he, twelve? "I'll grab some waters and be right back." When she swiveled around, she dropped her smile. She stuffed her pad back into her apron and glanced up at Shane's narrowed eyes. *Great. What did I do now?*

"Lady on Fourteen wants four extra French dressings for her salad." Amanda stacked water glasses on the tray. "What's the point of the salad? People who do that are like those who order a double burger, large fries, and a diet pop."

Holland reached behind her for mustard. "Don't tell Grumperton." She wished her voice didn't sound quite as disengaged. Today was a miserable day. And the last thing she needed was the guys at Table Seven.

"I don't think he cares as much about the taste but more about what the food looks like. His behavior is the weirdest thing I've ever seen with a cook." Amanda whipped her glasses off her face, cleaned the lens with the corner of her shirt, and squinted at Holland. "Hey, you good?"

No. "Yeah, just getting creeper vibes from Table Seven."

Amanda pushed up her glasses with her thumb. "Ugh, I can feel the vibes from here. Those dudes are bad news. Let me know if they hassle you too much. I'll come over there and bust some chops, jujitsu style."

Holland giggled. "I'm like twice as big as you."

"Not true!" Amanda stood on the tips of her toes, bringing her closer to five-foot-two-inches. "But what I lack in height, I make up with my fierce personality."

"Ha. True."

"Order up," a line cook yelled.

Breathing in through her nose, Holland aligned the plates on her tray for her first table and tore out of the kitchen. She tried to release the twisted knot in her belly and failed to shake the feeling of impending doom.

Chapter 5
Today's Special: Anti-Hero Artichoke Dip with Burnt Intentions

Why didn't the people here take presentation more seriously? Would it kill them to care, *just a little*? Shane's need to prove his self-worth shouldn't become the kitchen staff's problem, but here he was being a lunatic because the line cook didn't arrange the steamed asparagus correctly. He snatched the plate off the warmer with an exaggerated sigh and rearranged the veggies.

Bright-green basil accented the red backdrop of fresh cherry tomatoes. Coiled orange peels rested on top of a small bed of arugula. A sprig of mint lay on the berry pie. Plates looked good with the layered colors. Beautiful, even. And not one person in this entire place cared. "Order up!" He returned to serving the next dish.

As he whisked the batter, he saw his parents' disapproving faces swirling in his brain. They both knew he loved art. And he was good at it. No, he was *great*. The studio was where he was the happiest— losing time, mixing colors, working with the medium. But every time he mentioned wanting to be an art major, his parents swapped knowing looks until his dad said, "Art's a fun hobby but won't pay the bills."

Making beautiful plates at the restaurant gave him his daily shot of validation. Slowly evaporating drops from the bucket of doubt. Confirming he didn't throw his life away by following *his* plan, not his dad's. But soon, his thoughts turned into a noose. *Did I make the right decision? What if my plan fails? Will my parents ever look at me the same? Will Cherise find happiness?* Cherise was a casualty of the emotional collateral damage he left behind. And he wasn't sure he could forgive himself. "Grab more capers!" he yelled to anyone who'd listen.

A plate shattering on the concrete floor jolted him from his thoughts, and he nearly smacked his head on the overhead fan. The kitchen went silent.

"Oops," a server mumbled.

The sounds of clanking plates and bustling team members surrounded Shane again. He resumed his duties. He slid two plates of salmon Benedict on the warmer and noticed Holland popping around the corner. Every night, he went home with more questions about her than when he arrived. What did she do outside of this place? Swim in the lake? Hang out with friends? What shows did she binge-watch: zombies or love stories? Why did she look so happy all the time when something else was clearly going on behind her curtain of thick eyelashes? Perhaps this was part of his legal training. Dig deep to uncover everything. Find the answer to why she got him *right there.*

He usually attempted to avoid her gaze when she was looking, but she glanced up and his gaze met hers.

This time, she was the one who shifted her gaze. She yanked down the plates, and her lips formed a thin, straight line. Blotches covered her neck, and a worry crease cut across her forehead.

What happened? *Don't do this.* He didn't care what

happened. At least, not any more than he'd care about anyone. With no reasonable doubt. He certainly wasn't watching her walk away, missing the small spring in her step, wondering who stole it, and how he'd make them pay.

"Grabbing brioche from the pantry. Be right back," the third line cook said.

The second line cook flipped the burgers on the grill, creating a sizzling, meaty smoke in the kitchen.

Shane clapped his hand once to refocus and piled a bowl with orange and mint garnish. He spun the dish around and peeked out to watch Holland on the floor. She was a fascinating case study. Not that he spent any time at all thinking about her. Especially at night when his racing thoughts crowded his mind as he lay alone in the dark. She smiled at everyone. A brilliant, almost-contagious smile that he had failed to ignore these last few weeks. But last week, several times she pressed her thumbs against her temples like she was warding off a demon in her skull, inhaled extra-long, choppy breaths, and maybe even had blinked back a few tears.

He pushed his palm against his chin, and a crack flew up his neck. The circulating fans did little to absorb the heat, and moisture collected on his spine. Great, she'd probably think he was a sweaty monster. *Knock it off. No more thinking about her.*

The kitchen boiled over with conversation.

"Behind you!"

"How much time left on the fryer?"

"Two minutes."

"Where are we at with the blackberries? I needed them ten minutes ago."

"Jack ran to the outside cooler."

"Have him grab an extra whip. We're down to one bottle."

When he watched Holland walk in here today, he couldn't believe he almost hit her with food. She wasn't supposed to turn so fast. And then she cracked one of her nerdy jokes. Man, she was adorable. But his mouth stayed clamped shut. He wasn't tongue-tied around her due to not knowing what to say. He was tongue-tied because of holding it in.

A million words nudged to escape his mouth. Like her cute, little dad jokes and high-pitched giggle were the highlights of his working day. Her smile puts the sun to shame. Speaking to hundreds of customers, while remembering their names and what they liked to drink, was an impressive feat.

He added steamed veggies to a dish instead of fries. "Come on," he muttered. *Focus. Stop thinking about her.* "Order up!" he called.

Holland bolted into the kitchen, with Amanda trailing.

"Holland. Thought you'd want to know the lettuce and I worked out our differences and signed a peas treaty." He tilted up a plate with a side of peas.

She kept her gaze down and slammed the plates harder than necessary. "Good." She pivoted sharply while balancing the tray against her hip.

The queen of cheesy jokes and that's her response? He just handed her an olive branch. Heck, an entire olive tree. After the disaster with Cherise, he wasn't talking to Holland to protect her from him as much as he was to keep all distractions at bay and stick with his plan. Was she mad at him? Wait. He doesn't care. Remember? He inched toward Amanda. "Interesting."

She stared at the food ticket with furrowed brows before she peeked up. "What?"

"Apparently, Ms. Sunshine has clouds once in a while, huh?" *Shoot.* He cared.

She paused and tilted her head. "Yeah, but some guys at Table Seven are giving her a hard time. I think their gross attitudes are getting to her."

The heat spiked straight from his gut to his chest. He strained his neck to look around the corner and watched as Holland placed a plate down.

One guy crossed his arms and said something.

The back of her neck turned red.

Within four seconds, he broke down the case. The cocky grin on suspect number one, who salaciously looked at Holland everywhere except her eyes. The way Holland stepped back like she was avoiding being touched. The loud laugh from suspect number two, who had his arm thrown across the booth's back and his legs taking up as much space as possible.

Shane bolted toward the swinging door.

"What are you doing?" Amanda asked while scrambling to fit eight plates onto her tray.

"Putting an end to whatever the hell's happening." He whacked his dishtowel on the counter. The fire in his belly rose to his chest. He stomped out of the kitchen and marched to the table. "Gentleman, is there a problem here?"

The men glanced up.

He gave them *the look*. His mother called it his "prosecutor look." The one meant to destroy hostile witnesses and force a confession. The one his father said could intimidate even the darkest of criminals. He didn't pull out the look often. But when he did, he normally got what he wanted.

All right, *always* got what he wanted.

The men's faces rotated between white and crimson, and the one on the left cleared his throat.

"Holland, I need you back in the kitchen. I'm taking over this table." He intended every ounce of authority in his voice and leveled a stare. If her face wasn't red before, it now matched her hair.

"Excuse me?"

He softened his expression and pointed a finger toward the kitchen, then snapped his death gaze back to the men at the table. "Did you guys need anything else?"

The one on the right peered down at his plate. "Ah, nope."

She barreled away.

Man, she's fast. He trailed a step behind. Of course, she didn't deserve whatever junk they spewed. But why had the fury rushed through him at that degree? Thank God, her nightmare was over. She'll probably give him an unnecessary goofy dad joke. Better get his poker face prepped, so he didn't bust out some dumb "my pleasure, happy to do it" half-butt response.

She slammed through the swinging kitchen doors.

They ricocheted off the wall and would've smashed his face had he not had ninja-like reflexes.

"What is the matter with you?"

The fire in her narrowed eyes matched her tone. *What?*

"I can take care of myself." She shoved the ice scoop into the bin with such force that a cube flew out. "Been taking care of myself my entire life."

What was he missing here? He listened to his gut, assessed the situation, and saw she was in trouble. "I didn't think you couldn't take care of yourself. I saw how they were—"

"I don't need some wannabe prize fighter coming in and doing this."

What? Was she honestly this upset? He was *helping.* "Sorry, but I thought—"

"Not only did you humiliate me in front of this table, but you also made me feel like some pathetic damsel in distress who needs saving." She slammed her hands on her hip. "*And* I lost out on the tip."

The tip money. It didn't even occur to him. "I'll give you the money."

"I don't want your stupid money." Gripping the tray, she inhaled a shaky breath, her knuckles turning white. After propping the tray on her flattened palm, she froze in front of the doors, plastered on an obvious fake smile, and pushed through.

He scowled at his fellow line cooks.

They shifted their gaze from the drama.

With a dry mouth and a hot chest, he returned to the prep stand. Her reaction was *not* what he expected. But what was he supposed to do in that situation? Let these guys intimidate and harass her? No chance. *I would've done the same thing for anyone. I think.*

Chapter 6
Today's Special: A Sweet Confection Infused with a Hint of Citrus

Holland hated she was relieved when Shane intervened. The guys had hassled her for nearly an hour, and she was this close to either tears or throwing a strawberry shake on their faces. Neither was a good option. And when he stared with so much venom she was surprised they didn't vaporize, she felt supported in a foreign way.

But now, Shane probably thought she was incapable. After an excruciating morning of being an incompetent guardian, maybe he was right. But the one thing she didn't need? Saving—incapable or not. He could keep his stupid savior mentality for himself.

The throbbing in her skull accelerated. She massaged her temples with her trembling thumbs to dull the ache before unloading her plates onto the kitchen rack. "Ugh." She needed that tip for her engine that was so close to dying she said a silent prayer to the car gods every time she turned it over. Shane swooping in wearing his chef jacket like a white knight, with his intimidating stare and imposing voice, killed whatever money the men might have left.

Even though her parents paid for Riley's therapy and school, the expenses were astounding—sensory toys, clothes, haircuts, groceries, an upgrade from his toddler bed. Moving into a more suitable rental than her junky studio apartment and converting it into a kid-friendly space burned through her Return-to-Maui-Dream-Vacation cookie jar fund within the first year of getting custody. And she played catch-up every month since. After rent, his medication, and her jewelry-making supplies, no leftover funds existed. She should probably stop making jewelry. But a sliver of hope still dangled that one day she'd open her shop. Besides, she and Riley bonded the best during this activity. And she really, really needed it for her mental health. A gentle hand tapped her on the back.

"Clocking out. I'm already late meeting Lauren." Amanda swiped her black bangs away from her face. "Don't be too hard on him. He was trying to help."

She added the final plate to the bin and turned. "You saw that?"

"Yeah. I think I inadvertently egged him on. I told him those guys were harassing you." Amanda glanced over her shoulder. "You should've seen his face. He was so protective and sweet."

Holland released a puff of air. "That man is not sweet. He's unbearable. Moody. Arrogant. Annoying." *Gorgeous.*

"Someone's got a crush."

Flames burned her cheeks. "I do not have a crush on him."

"I wasn't talking about you." Amanda waved from behind her head as she sauntered to the door.

Holland grabbed raw sugar and stevia packets off the pantry and stuffed the condiment containers, slamming through her cutwork to pick up Riley by five. Having a backup therapist was enough of a change this week, and she committed to getting him home on time to maintain his routine.

Four-twenty p.m. Already? Her chest heated, and she double-timed her speed. "Do you guys have more forks? I need to finish my cut work," Holland asked the dishwasher, while wiggling her toes to relieve the building pressure. *Come on, come on. I need to leave.*

"Yep, right here."

Thank God.

A blast of steam shot out of the slider, and he slid the tub her way.

She didn't love cut work—*who did?*—but her body loosened after a few moments of repeatedly rolling the silverware into the cloth napkin. Sometimes, she imagined the trip she took to Maui when she turned twenty-one. If she relaxed enough, she could almost taste the salt on her lips from when the wind blew and the ocean misted in the air. She could nearly smell the macadamia nut pancakes with coconut syrup from her favorite little place in Kihei. Although life circumstances deflated her dream of living there, she vowed someday she and Riley would go for a visit. The water and white sand would fascinate him. They could build sandcastles, watch sea turtles, and eat shaved ice. Copious and copious amounts of shaved ice.

"Holland?"

The voice behind her snapped her from her daze. *His voice.* He might have spoken less than ten minutes to her in the last several weeks, but she knew Shane's tone. She scolded her heart for pounding so hard it reached her throat. She turned. "What?"

Shane stuffed his hands in his pockets. "I'm sorry for overstepping today."

Darn his soothing words for making her insides grilled-cheese gooey. Ridiculous.

"I didn't like what I saw and took action without thinking."

That sentence had now practically doubled their talking history. His sheepish demeanor was…surprising. This huge, ripped, beautiful man was apologizing…with sincerity. Her knees turned to liquid, but she stiffened her back so he wouldn't notice. "It's okay." She picked up the silverware again and continued. He needed to step away. The space wasn't big enough for them. She stared at her cut work and reminded herself to focus. She grabbed a spoon, then dropped it. Forks first. Wait, nope, spoons first. *Gah! What's wrong with me?* "A little of me appreciates you stepped in." She glanced at him from her peripherals. "But only a little."

A flicker of a smile appeared before he walked away without another word.

And she finally exhaled. Twenty minutes later, she untied her apron and sprinted to her car. She pulled open the car door, and a gust of air filled with melted crayon and vinyl odors rushed out. Satisfied she wouldn't burn alive inside the car, she flopped down and turned the key. Her car sounded like a lawnmower dying. She cranked it again. *Click. Click?* Ignitions shouldn't click.

Oh no. No, no, no. This is not happening. She repeatedly turned the key, her left two fingers cramping from crossing them so hard. "Please, please turn over." She held her breath. Nothing.

Her parents were out of town and couldn't help. Tapping her hands on the steering wheel, she gnawed on her lower lip. *Think, Holland. Don't cry, just think.* She checked her watch. Four forty-five p.m. Ugh! She needed to leave. Now. She grabbed her phone and dashed a message to Amanda.

—*Hey, you close by?*—

—*Already left and I'm on the highway with Lauren, headed to Gooseberry Falls. You good?*—

She exhaled. *Nope. T-minus twenty seconds before I bawl.*

—*Yep! Call you tonight. Remember skinny dipping is illegal in the waterfalls.*—

—*Only if they can catch me.*—

A ride service might not wait when she picked up Riley. A taxi might take an hour to arrive and would suck up all her tips while the meter ran. And James lived on the opposite side of town.

Deep inhale. Hold. Release. Her parched mouth was hot and sticky, and she turned the engine again. Nothing. After hammering the steering wheel with her palms, she gripped it until her fingers ached. She collapsed her head against her hands before she exited the car and slammed the door shut. The relentless humidity drowned her in moisture as she pressed her thumbs into her forehead and closed her eyes. *Breathe. Think.*

"Car trouble?"

The voice. Again. She wanted to say the engine problem was no big deal. That she had it all under control. That she was sure it'd be fine and would try again in a minute. "Yep." She was sure her face betrayed her attempted confidence.

Shane tilted his head up once and walked to his vehicle.

Really? Whatever. She didn't need his help, anyway.

He tossed his backpack onto his seat and joined her. "Pop the hood and try it again."

The sun's heat sprung off the pavement and hit her in the chest before she sat back in the car. *I don't have time for this!* She opened the hood, and the smell of oil and gasoline filled the air. She tried turning the key. *Click-click-click.*

Four fifty-three p.m. Her leg bounced. Picking up Riley late will throw his entire night off. If he doesn't eat and bathe on time, then he won't get to bed on time, and he'll be tired in the morning, and won't eat his breakfast, and will be off-kilter all day and then won't eat dinner and…and…and… She flung her head against the seat.

Shane leaned his forearm on the top of the car and lowered his head to peer inside.

How, after a full day of kitchen work, did he smell like grapefruit, salt, and soap? An intoxicating combination, and maybe some other time, she could enjoy it. When she wasn't on the verge of ruining Riley's entire next forty-eight hours.

"Doesn't sound good."

"Ya think?" she snapped. "Sorry. I know, I just…I have to pick up my nephew, and I'm late."

His fingers drumming on the roof echoed inside the car. "I'll give you a ride."

"What?" Was he serious? He hardly ever talked to her. What if he was an ax murderer? Or at very least an unsafe driver? "You don't have to do that."

"No problem." He gave her a half-smile and held the top of the door open. "Unless your nephew lives in

St. Cloud."

She bit her lip. Saying *no* was the smart thing to do. Depending on anyone for anything was dangerous. When they stop showing up, they'd leave her unprepared. A solid lesson learned during her childhood. As kind as her parents were, they weren't dependable. When she took dependency out of an equation, it alleviated a heck of an amount of stress. She twisted her wrist. Four fifty-six p.m. She didn't have the luxury of time. Tonight, she needed to depend on someone.

Chapter 7
Today's Special: Getting-to-Know-You Gumbo

Shane wasn't nervous, per se. Nerves weren't the right description. As he watched Holland strap the seatbelt across her chest, a light but definite tugging sensation occurred in his lower abdomen. Probably because at least six months had passed since he had a woman in the vehicle. Or maybe it was because of their encounter earlier in the day with those jerks at the table. Could it be because, against his better judgment, he'd gone home and thought about her every night since they met?

He typed the school address into his map app. As he drove, the wind from the open air whipped through his hair, and his tense shoulders deflated. Bumping along, the mixture of fried onion rings from a nearby restaurant and the hops scent from a brewery flew past. While driving by the old train station, he snuck a glimpse of her. The sun bounced off the stray hairs of her braid, creating a golden raspberry shine. Her cheeks turned a deeper pink. Her lips…

Focus.

He cleared his throat. "Do you normally pick up your nephew from school?"

"Every day." She twirled her stack of rings on her index finger and shifted her gaze between the road and her hand.

"Every day? You're a nice aunt." He adjusted the rearview mirror and stole another quick look. But this had to be his last one. "Do you want me to drop him off at his parents' place and take you to yours?"

She paused before speaking. "No, he lives with me."

"All the time?" He looked at her again. *Ok, fine.* Tomorrow, he'll start on his Holland-free diet.

"Yep." She grinned, then sharply inhaled. "Hey, my nephew is autistic. So, I'm not sure what his reaction will be, having him in this car and introducing him to you. He likes—*needs*—a routine, and this change might throw him off. I don't want you to get offended if he says anything too odd."

Her autistic nephew lived with her. That upped all the typical questions by infinity. Did his mom live there, too? What was the kid like? Was she the sole caretaker? "How old is he?"

"Seven."

"Aren't all kids at that age a little odd?" He thought of some awkward things he did when he was younger. Including the time he mooned his fellow first graders and got sent to the principal's office. "I'm not worried. It'll be fine."

She chewed the inside of her cheek. "Do you have any children?"

"None that I'm aware of." He swiped his hands across the steering wheel.

Her eyes doubled in size at his clichéd joke.

"I'm kidding. No kids. I don't even have any nieces or nephews. I'm an only child, my dad's an only child, and my mom's only sibling is James. And, well, you know his status."

She nodded. "His Saint Bernard could almost qualify as a child. She's like the size of a freshman."

So true.

The car bumped over a few impressive potholes. He drove in silence for several moments. "How long has your nephew lived with you?"

"I won custody five years ago." She flicked her wrist to check her watch for the tenth time.

Won custody means she fought for it. But why? Was it true legal guardianship or something more temporary? And how old was she, for Pete's sake? She appeared to be mid-twenties at most.

He said nothing. She wasn't offering, and her private life wasn't his business. He flipped his blinker on to cross lanes. "I know very little about autism. A couple of movies are the gist of my exposure."

She tucked a loose strand of hair behind her ear. "You've probably had more exposure to people with autism spectrum disorder than you think. The disorder has so many degrees. Autism's not always like they show it in the movies."

Face-palm moment. He really needed to read some articles. *Don't do it. Do not do it.* "So...do you have someone at home who helps you?" *I'm ridiculous.*

Her throat rolled with a swallow. "Nope, just me and Riley."

A tingle flew down his belly, but he pushed it away. As he pulled up to a red light, the wind slowed, and the vehicle filled with the burning rubber scent of hot tar. He tapped his thumbs against the steering wheel, reeling in the questions. His father once told him his inquisitive nature would either make him a lawyer or get him arrested. But he couldn't help it. What was being a guardian over an autistic child like? Does he talk? Was he a genius? Did he like chocolate shakes as much as her? "Can I ask you something?"

She held his gaze. "Sure."

He knew she had green eyes. *Obviously.* Next to her hair, her eyes were the first physical feature that stuck out. But being this close as the sun cast rays on her face and the reflection of the sky highlighted the irises, he realized he'd never seen that shade of green before. A spectacular mixture of turquoise and jade. If it wouldn't seem creepy, he'd ask to take a photo so he could recreate the hue for the canvas. "What's the best part about your nephew having autism?"

Her eyes softened. "No one ever asked me that before."

Too much? He purposely said next-to-nothing for weeks, sticking to his vow of minimal distractions to focus on his plan. And now he might need to clamp his tongue between his teeth to stop him from asking any other invasive questions. "You don't have to answer. I was just curious."

"No, it's a good question." The wind started again, and she tucked a piece of hair behind her ear. "He has a phenomenal memory. Almost photographic. If he likes a movie, he can repeat every single word."

His insides were too warm. The navigation app showed two minutes to the school, but he wasn't ready to leave this conversation. "That's amazing. I bet he has a vivid imagination."

"Definitely. And he's the best hugger," she continued.

He perked up at the gentleness of her words, and he thanked the universe that driving occupied his hands, so he didn't reach out and touch her arm.

"But I think one of the best things is he almost never feels the negative stuff neuro-normative people feel. Like, he doesn't feel sadness, regret, guilt, or shame...his brain just operates differently."

What would it be like not to let a dark shame cloud follow him? Disappointing his parents. The situation with Cherise. Constantly questioning his decisions. Sleepless nights worrying he'd never make enough money to support a family with his *hobby*. "I didn't realize that happened with autistic people. Can you imagine how much better off as a society we'd all be if we didn't experience shame?"

"Right? Probably happier and healthier." She relaxed into the seat. "If I got hit by a car tomorrow, I know he'd adjust fine to a new guardian. He might miss me a little, but not the way other kids would. As long as he kept on his routine."

The map app announced he'd arrived at the school. He clicked on his blinker to enter the parking lot.

She pointed toward the side door. "Right over there." She unbuckled her seatbelt before the car stopped. "Thanks. I'm really sorry I might be five minutes or an hour. I totally understand if you want to go home, and I'll call a taxi."

No way would he leave anyone in this situation. Especially her. "I'm good waiting. It'll give me time to catch up on the news." He couldn't decode the look on her face before she sprinted to the door. Relief? Sadness? Combo of both? *Snap out of it. Stop breaking her down like a case.*

Ten minutes later, Holland stepped outside, holding a child's hand. His hair was the same flame-red as hers, and he was sporting a superhero T-shirt, shorts, and a lopsided grin. A newfound lightness reflected from her, and they bounced down the paved steps toward him.

Shane hopped out and took a step in their direction but stopped. He'd been told in the past his six-foot-three frame could be intimidating, and he didn't want to freak the kid out. Maybe he should sit. But that might seem unwelcoming. Crouch? That'd look too bizarre. He finally curled his shoulders, leaned against his vehicle, and waved.

"One, two, three, eyes on me," the boy said.

Shane dashed a glance between the child and Holland.

"That's Riley's greeting." Holland grinned. "He says it the first time he sees someone that day."

Ah.

She squatted to meet the child at eye level. "Riley. This is Mimi's...um...friend, Shane. He's bringing us home tonight. We're taking his SUV."

Mimi?

Riley scanned the vehicle and lifted a chubby finger toward the door. He poked at it a few times. "Where's the top?"

Fair question, kid. "I took it off for the summer."

"Why?"

"Because I like feeling the wind in my face." It also provided a sense of weightlessness he didn't experience anywhere except while he painted. The breeze calmed the spin cycle of tormenting thoughts and let him forget his past. But he refrained from divulging that to a child. "Would you like to take a ride in the—"

"We're *going* to take a ride." She stood and tugged Riley closer. "You need to get in the back seat. Like Mimi's car."

Riley stood quietly for several long seconds until his eyes grew at the same speed as his smile. "Okay." Still holding her hand, he pulled her to the side of the car and pointed above the door. "Ooooh. No window, Mimi. No window!"

"Come on, Bubby. Hop in the back." She looked at her watch and frowned.

"Like a boat, Mimi. A boat on the street!"

Huh. Never thought of it like that, but he's right.

"Boat!" He thrust his arms out, then curled his fingers into a fist.

Shane thought the kid's face might crack from smiling so broadly. *I feel ya, kid. I had the same reaction after I bought this a few years ago.*

"What's this?" Riley pointed at the front of the vehicle.

"That's called a grill." Shane rapped his knuckles on the hard plastic. "It helps protect the SUV."

"Why are the tires so big?"

"In case you get stuck in the snow or mud, they'll help you get out."

Riley's mouth twisted. "I like mud."

Me, too. As a child, Shane sculpted with mud in the yard, sloshing in buckets of water from the house into his sandbox. As an adult, squishing his hands through clay was therapeutic. Once he released the fear of getting messy, his tension melted, and his creative energy spiked.

Riley jerked on Holland's arm.

She glanced at her watch and flicked her fingers on

her purse.

"Why do you have stairs on your car?" Riley asked.

Shane looked at the step outside of the passenger door. "Because some people are little like Mimi and have a hard time getting into tall cars."

"Hey!" She nudged him with an elbow and wandered a full lap around the vehicle with him and Riley. She peeked at her watch again, and her face dropped. "Riley. You need to get in the back. Now. We're going home."

Why was she so upset? The kid seemed to enjoy it, and he was, too. For the last ten minutes, he hadn't thought about failures or regrets or plans. It felt...*nice.*

Her cheeks flushed, and her eyebrows scrunched together. "Riley, back seat. Now." All warmth disappeared.

Riley didn't respond. Instead, he played the grill like a piano, the thudding sound of his fingers on plastic ringing out.

The car wasn't holding anyone up in a carpool line, and the kid looked content. Holland, who normally skipped around carefree at work, had the rigid posture of a robot. Maybe she was worried he had to leave. "I've got no place to be right now," he offered. "No big deal to stay here as long as you guys want."

She inhaled a jagged breath. "It *is* a big deal, Shane."

Wow. Not fun to be on the receiving end of that tone.

"I'm sorry. I just...he's hungry and not showing it." She bit the side of her lip. "And we're already way behind schedule. I need to get him home and feed him

54

some food. If I wait any longer, I know he won't feel good, then I won't feel good."

Ah. He didn't irritate her. And he needed to analyze later—not now—why his belly relaxed so much. "There's a restaurant a block away. Want to go there?"

She shook her head. "No, restaurants have too many noises. Besides, he has a really limited diet."

"Picky eater?"

She tightened her jaw. "He's not picky."

Huh?

"Sorry, I'm being a jerk, and you're trying to be helpful. His food issues are deeper than being picky, but we don't have to go into that."

She must've read the confusion on his face. Tonight, he'd forego painting for research. Was there a link between autism and food? How would the kid not know if he was hungry? Riley seemed to be in a different world right now, his eyes barely blinking as his fingertips traipsed across the grill. "What does he like to eat?"

She sighed. "Chicken nuggets."

"Drive-thru? Not sure about your rules with him, but I don't mind."

Creases developed on her forehead.

He wanted to take those creases away. Do everything he could do to never see those creases again. "My treat."

She lowered herself and eased Riley's face up to meet hers. "Get in, seatbelt first. Then, we'll ride in the wind."

His fingers halted against the grill for several long moments. "Like a boat."

"Yep, like a boat." She released her stiffened

shoulders. "Seatbelt first. Then, car-boat ride." She gripped Riley around the waist to boost him to the back, then tugged on the belt multiple times. After strapping herself in, she locked her gaze with Shane. "Please go slow."

"What do you take me for?" He winked. *Did I just wink?* It was nothing. A friendly gesture meant to diffuse the growing tension. Obviously. "Wait, don't answer that."

A soft giggle escaped her mouth.

He committed that sound to memory. No other sound in the world existed that traveled from his ear to his chest.

The nearest drive-thru was less than ten minutes away. He adjusted his mirror to see both the road and Riley. The wind was a welcomed breeze, but the backseat took more air than the front, and he wasn't sure if it'd be too much for Riley. But his closed eyes and wide grin indicated he was perfectly happy. He rolled up to a red light, and a few rocks crunched under the tires. "Do you like the truck-boat, Riley?"

"Yay!"

Soft fingertips touched him.

"Thanks for this ride." A small smile tugged at the corners of Holland's mouth. "I seriously appreciate it so much."

He shrugged and ignored the shivers running up his arm. "Fuggetabout it."

"That was the worst mobster impression I've ever heard. And trust me, I've seen a million of those movies." She twisted her neck to look at Riley and relaxed into the seat.

After making his way through the drive-thru,

Shane inhaled the savory scent of fried chicken and French fries circling them. He handed Holland the food and rolled the vehicle into a parking spot.

"I can't believe I succumbed to the pressure of getting him a cherry icee. They're so bad for him." She popped the drink into the console. "Icee's have so much sugar."

He lifted an eyebrow. "Says the woman who has chocolate shakes for lunch every day."

Her mouth dropped open, and she broke into a smile. "That's fair."

That smile. *Good Lord.* The federal courts should register it as a secret weapon used for negotiations and de-escalation.

"Want to eat in here or grab a spot on the lawn?"

"Lawn. Definitely." Anything to elongate whatever was happening to his insides. He hopped out and grabbed a blanket from the trunk.

Holland flipped down her seat, took Riley's hand, and led him toward the massive oak tree at the slope. "Do you always keep an emergency blanket in your car?"

He shook out the soft flannel blanket, then spread it on the ground. "You never know when you might want an impromptu picnic."

"The girls must really like you." Her mouth snapped shut.

If she only knew what he did to Cherise, she wouldn't think that. The shaded spot under the tree took the edge off the heat. As the leaves rustled in the background, Shane laid out the food.

Holland cleaned Riley's hands with a baby wipe.

The salty fries tingled his tongue. He was a sucker

for a mom-and-pop drive-thru. But, sitting under the tree with the two of them, the pop was colder, the burger juicier, the shake sweeter. New goal—eat more fast-food.

"Icee, Mimi." Riley reached for the drink.

Holland held him by the wrist. "First food. Then icee."

"No."

"First food. Then icee." She released his wrist and ripped off a piece of the nugget. "Here, take a bite."

Riley's legs banged against the earth and guttural sounds erupted. An ear-piercing shrill flared from his tiny body, echoing across the parking lot. A fist pounded the ground before he ripped up the blanket and rolled himself into it.

Shane winced. Riley would hurt himself but couldn't blame him for his reaction. At Riley's age, a cherry icee sounded better than dinner. Heck, at any age, a cherry icee sounded better than food.

Even though Holland's reddening neck hinted at stress, her calm voice didn't. Fifteen minutes later, after more coaxing with hushed, firm words, Riley finished a partial dinner.

Shane shook the blanket out, and grass blades fluttered to the ground. He grabbed the garbage, crumpled the bag in his hand, and reached for the drink.

Riley twisted his body. "I hold the icee."

"Let's throw that in the trash." Holland dusted off the seat of her pants.

His red eyebrows crunched together. "No. I hold it."

She pressed the back of her palm into her forehead and shrugged at Shane.

He leaned toward her ear and cursed that her coconut shampoo affected him as strongly as it did. "Fine with me, if it is for you."

Ten minutes later, as the vehicle bounced over potholes, Riley held the drink in his hands with a wide grin.

Shane turned down a dead-end street lined with older homes, mature foliage, and a few kids playing a fierce game of tag through the sprinklers.

Holland tapped him on the shoulder and pointed toward a small, weathered house, probably over one hundred years old. "Over there. White house on the right."

All the bumps and dips of the gravel driveway were no match for his oversized tires. The porch appeared to be on the cusp of collapsing with gouged-out chunks of wood and flakier paint than the rest of the house. But it had a cozy swinging bench nestled among vibrant flowers and, amidst the overgrown grass, lay a small strawberry and snap pea garden.

He pushed the gear into Park. Something sounding like *gurplup* happened behind him. And cherry icee scent filled the vehicle.

"Oh no! I knew this would happen. Shane, I'm so sorry." Holland whipped off her seat belt and hopped out of the car. The front seat dropped forward, and she caught the cup before more liquid spilled. "Let me get some towels."

"It's okay. Seriously." He used this vehicle for camping, fishing, and off-roading. People had sloshed mud, dirt, fish guts, and who knows whatever else on the floor over the years. Cherry drink was nothing.

She fumbled getting Riley out of the car, and her

face turned redder than the cherry icee. "Riley, come on. I need to grab paper towels."

He ripped his arm away from her grip. "Mimi, no!"

"Inside. Now."

Riley stomped a foot into the ground like he was made of cement.

"Holland, seriously. I'll clean it out. It's no problem." Shane opened his door. "Now, if it were spilled milk, I might force James to give you a Monday afternoon shift."

Her head bobbed up, and she paused her frantic flails. "Did you just tease me, again?"

"Maybe."

She grinned for a split second. "I'm so sorry. I have to get him inside and settled."

Already? His chest fell. Would it be too weird to ask to sit on the porch swing? Or maybe, he could bring dessert back to their place? Good plan. Or maybe, he should stop intruding. Better plan. "Why don't you throw me your car keys? I can look at it tonight."

Her mouth cracked open for a moment before she spoke. "I can't ask you to do that."

"You didn't ask me."

Riley gripped the lower corner of her shirt.

"I don't know." She shifted between her feet. "I think I'll just have it towed."

He leaned against the hood. "Let me work on the car. I used to fix old cars with my dad, and I miss it. It'll give me something to do."

"A 2008 is not *that* old." She smiled and tossed him the keys. "Really, thank you."

Backing out of the driveway, he had only one thought cross his mind. *What in the world did I just get myself into?*

Chapter 8
Today's Special: The Nosy Uncle Cocktail: Crisp Apple Wine with a Splash of Motor Oil

The multiple keys hanging from Holland's ring clanked together in his pocket. As Shane made his way toward Holland's broken-down car in the café's parking lot, he dug out the keys and twirled them on his finger. He opened Holland's car door and smiled at the sheer amount of *stuff* in her backseat—crayons, cups, paper, toys, books. The car looked like a daycare center.

The engine barely turned over but sounded more like a belt or cylinder issue and less like the transmission. He popped the hood and studied wires and tubes. The evening sun warmed his back while he poked around in the engine compartment. After a few minutes, he slammed the hood shut. Nothing he could do about the car here.

He dragged the tow gear out from his trunk and drove the four miles to James' place. *Oh, no.* James was on the porch, drinking white wine. Which meant Shane needed to get his game face on to avoid questions from his uncle, who was like an emotional K9 dog—able to sniff attitude changes from a block away. He stepped out of the vehicle and slammed the door.

"Do I even want to ask?" James asked with a grin.

"Probably not." Shane released the car from the tow hitch. "Where's Mateo?"

"Why? He has fewer mechanical skills than me."

"Funny. No, just wondering."

"Work party. Won't be home until late." James stood and leaned against the wood railing. "Is this Holland's car?"

"Yep." He stepped into the garage and returned with a box of tools.

"Why is it here?"

"Wouldn't turn over earlier, so I offered to look at it." Shane prayed his poker face and even tone masked the desperation to make Holland's life a little easier.

James took a sip of his drink and narrowed his eyes.

Shane turned his back and braced for the onslaught of questions.

"You know I'm too pretty to help, right?"

Whew. "I do know this." He fumbled inside the toolbox and pulled out a rag.

"You're not working at the studio tonight?" James asked.

"Nah, not tonight. I needed a break." Not entirely true, as every hour away from the studio was one less hour working on inventory. And time evaporated at an expedited rate. But tonight, Holland's glow and her nephew's smile muted the anxiety of not painting.

Shane checked all the standard fluids and pulled the cables from the spark plugs. One by one, he examined the tip for corrosion, checked the ceramic wasn't cracked, and confirmed a suitable gap.

An hour in, James tapped him on the shoulder with a cold bottle of local IPA. "Want to take a quick break?"

The condensation from the glass bottle dripped on

to his arm. "Sure." He settled in, and the porch steps creaked underneath him. The citrus-laced hops cooled his throat and counteracted the muggy air.

James planted his feet on the floor and rocked himself on the swing. "Watching you reminds me of when you and your dad used to work on that old sports car."

A mental picture popped up of Shane working with his dad in their garage—twisting metal, tinkering with gaskets, and changing upholstery. When he was younger, he'd receive a forbidden caffeinated soda from his dad after laboring for a few hours. They'd click their pop bottles together and look over their shoulder to make sure his mom wasn't watching. During college, especially during anxiety-ridden exam time, his dad would call, and say he needed help with Red Banana—the nickname Shane gave the sports car when he was five. His dad didn't need the help. But Shane needed relief. For hours, they'd crank on wrenches and yank on bolts, until his tension vanished.

"Have you talked to your parents since the incident?" James asked.

During the first good day this month, *the incident* was the last thing Shane wanted to talk about. When he said he was dropping out of law school, he was all but thrown out of his parents' house. "But what about the family legacy," his dad had yelled right before Shane slammed the front door and stormed off. "Why do you ask a question you already know the answer to?" Beads of sweat pooled on his forehead from the humidity, and he lifted his shirt to wipe them off. "Remember, I went to law school. That's lawyer tactic 101. I'm sure Mom told you."

The swinging stopped. "Well, she hasn't talked to me, so I don't know."

His stomach clenched. "Really? Why?"

Inhaling deeply, James crossed his legs and fixated his gaze on the lawn. "She blames me for you dropping out of school. Thinks I'm a bad influence."

Shane's heart sank. "No. Did she actually say that? I never told Mom about our conversations for this exact reason." His mom and James were always close. He had no idea they stopped speaking after he and James had The Talk. Another sip of IPA didn't relieve his dry mouth. "I'm really sorry. Truly. I didn't think this would blow back on you. Is there something I can do?"

"Listen, kid." James inched closer. "I've never been more honored to be considered a bad influence in my life."

Shane scratched at the label on his bottle. As the buzz of dusk mosquitoes commenced, he flipped on the electric citronella candle, and the flame cast a warm, flickering light across the porch. "Do you ever regret dropping out of your Ph.D. program?"

"The only thing I regret is not doing it earlier." James dug a toe into the railing. "The restaurant is where I'm meant to be. Not in academia. I know things feel off right now, but I already see a positive shift in you."

Maybe James was right. If Shane could crawl past the guilt and focus only on his physiological sensation of being away from law school, he was feeling lighter. And, if he got the shop going and sold a few pieces, he'd show everyone—including himself—he made the right call.

"Here's a question," James said. "Are you happier

now?"

He focused on his bottle. After considering, he shrugged. "I think I can be."

James nodded. "Have you talked to Cherise at all?"

"She's called and texted a few times, but I've ignored them. Probably not the most mature way to handle it, but I've got nothing left to say." *What else can possibly be said when you've told your fiancée the wedding was off, you're moving out, and it was me, not you?*

"At some point, you might need more closure. For what it's worth, you did the right thing." James opened his mouth but then closed it. He grabbed the wine bottle next to him and topped off his glass.

Deep down, Shane agreed with James. Breaking up *was* the right decision. Confirmed by what she did a week after he called off things.

Silence filled the muggy evening air. He stared at the perfectly manicured grass and reviewed the playbook of his last year. Proposing to Cherise while ignoring the dread. The cold, callous way he broke it off. What his parents said that final week in Minneapolis. Moving here. The restaurant. Holland.

"So, Holland," James said.

Did he just read my mind? "What about her?" He snapped, too quickly.

"If you have her car, how did she get home?"

"I gave her and her nephew a ride." He swallowed back a grin.

James lifted his head in a slow nod and focused on the grass. He draped an arm across the back of the bench and pushed his legs into the porch to swing. "She's worked for me for almost ten years now.

Changed a lot from when I first hired her. Still has spunk, though, a perpetual sunshine around her."

Yeah, she does. "How's she different?"

"Those first years, she had such life. A free spirit. She bounced in for her interview—this seventeen-year-old kid with the confidence of a thirty-year-old, seasoned server—and said, 'I've never served a day in my life. But I promise I'll become the best server on your staff. And your favorite by the end of summer.' " He twirled the wine in the glass. "She used to sing in the kitchen, play '80s pop music after hours, and drag the busser away from his dishes to do the tango."

Shane smiled at the visual. He rolled the torn-off bottle label between his fingers. "She probably threw in a terrible joke while dancing."

"Ha, yes. She's still got that joy, but now there's a weight attached to the spark." He set his empty glass on the table next to him. "A lot of responsibility got thrown at someone so young. At anyone, really. Gone are the days of her taking an impromptu road trip to Chicago to find the best hot dog."

Shane was naturally inquisitive, but he swallowed back the near obsession of finding out every detail. What other road trips did she take? Which hot dog was her favorite? "How did she end up with custody of her nephew?"

"I only know bits and pieces," James said. "Sounds like her sister just didn't want to be a mom anymore."

So much there to unpack.

"She took some time off when it all went down." James tapped his knee with his fingertips. "I'd ask her how it was going. She'd always smile and said things were fine, but once I found her crying in the cooler."

Shane's stomach dropped at the image.

"She laughed it off and said she was a walking cliché and was crying over a spilled milkshake," James continued. "I knew it ran deeper but didn't want to pry." He stood and stretched his arms, then squeezed Shane's shoulder. He grabbed his wine glass and moved toward the house.

Shane returned to diagnosing her engine trouble and attempted to be as nonchalant as possible, so James couldn't decode his mannerisms. "Hey, do you have Holland's number?"

James raised an eyebrow and smirked.

"Don't look at me like that. I need to talk to her about her car." *Mostly.*

"I'll text it to you," James said. "Goodnight, kiddo."

Five minutes later, Shane typed out and erased his fifth message. The dusting of butterflies in his belly was totally unwarranted for a text.

—*Hey, it's Shane. James gave me your number. Do you need a lift in the morning to bring Riley to school?*—

The dreaded three bubbles appeared, disappeared, and appeared again. Finally, his phone vibrated, and he exhaled his trapped breath.

—*You don't have to do that.*—

—*It's no big deal. Your place is on my way.*—

—*It's literally the complete opposite direction.*—

—*Don't tell James, but I stop at a bakery near your house for breakfast sandwiches.*—

Why did he just lie? Okay, the text wasn't *exactly* a lie. In the court of law, the statement would pass. Truth was, he only went there once. The sandwiches were not as good as at Salt & Sugar Café, and he planned on never going there again. But she didn't need to know that.

Holland's name appeared on the screen.

—*I really appreciate it.*—

He poised his fingers above the screen.

—*All good. Sleep tight.*—

Sleep tight? His mouth curled into a grimace. He sent that message with twitchy thumbs without thinking.

The summer sun lowered and disappeared, inviting a slight breeze. He worked on her car, cleaned the spilled icee from his vehicle, and broke down his feelings. She was incredible—sweet and funny. He had this same feeling in the beginning with Cherise. A sort of prickle beneath his skin. A touch of an increased heart rate. One too many thoughts of her funneling into him.

Ultimately, Holland was another person to disappoint. Besides, he had nothing to offer. *Yet.*

An hour later, he lay in bed, and a heavy stone sank to the pit of his stomach. After reviewing all the evidence of his failed engagement, his parents hating him, and breaking of every vow he made, he settled the case. Verdict: *I can't get close to Holland.*

Chapter 9
Today's Special: A Bowl of Cereal Sprinkled with
a Pinch of Pride

"Good morning, Bubby." Holland sat on the corner
of Riley's bed and inched the covers off him. A purple
stuffy fell onto the floor. She scooped it up and
playfully buried the toy in the crook of his neck.

"One, two, three eyes on me." He yawned and
stretched his arms over his head, his belly button
peeking out under his dinosaur pajamas.

She tugged on the window shade to roll it up and
clapped her hands. "Let's get dressed. Then breakfast.
Then we get to ride with Shane, again, today."

He rubbed his eye with his knuckle. "The car-
boat?" He leapt off the bed and raced down the
hallway. The sound of his feet pounding against the
floor echoed off the walls.

Whew. With a different morning routine, she
eliminated as many triggers as possible that might cause
a meltdown. Full box of cereal—check. Oat milk
delivered last night—check. Favorite T-shirt and
matching underwear, clean and ready—check. But with
his regular therapist still gone, and Shane driving them
to school, she'd have to be on her toes for transitions.

She suspected Riley would have a great morning,
knowing Shane was picking him up. When Riley
returned home yesterday, he didn't stop talking about

the car-boat and spent the rest of the day sketching an impressive replica of the vehicle. And she spent the rest of the evening thinking about Shane.

After breakfast, she grabbed his backpack and motioned him toward the door to put on his shoes. Tonight, she had to search online for a new laceless pair. Riley grew so fast, and his current ones had one, maybe two, weeks of life left. With Riley being so tall for his age, strappy shoes were hard to find in his size. But Riley struggled with laces, and Holland didn't foresee a near future where he'd tie independently.

"Put your jacket on for the ride. The air's a little chilly." She fetched her purse and apron from the kitchen and opened the cabinet to grab a few extra granola bars. A small plastic toy tripped her in the hall, and she swallowed a choice word. She toed it to the side, then stopped in her tracks. "Riley! Did you zip up your jacket?"

"Yay!" He clapped.

Tears sprang to her eyes. Did that just happen? "You zipped your jacket!" She swooped in and squeezed him tight against her. He might as well have said he developed the cure for some obscure disease. He. Zipped. His. Jacket. Why did she step away at that precise moment? Was this how a parent felt after they missed their kid's first steps? Sure, she practiced with Riley. But things like zipping a jacket or tying shoes might never be possible. And yet, he did it, all by himself. "Mimi's so proud of you!"

Moments later, her cheeks burned from smiling so long. She gripped his hand and went outside to wait for Shane. The heat index broke yesterday, thankfully, and the crisp air held the scent of freshly cut grass. She inhaled a breath and tussled Riley's hair. Soon, the growl of Shane's SUV approached from the end of the block, and he pulled into her driveway.

Oh goodness. He looked like he just stepped off the big screen with his white T-shirt, jeans, and aviator sunglasses. She didn't know what to do with her hands, so she squeezed Riley's hand and gave an awkward, lopsided wave.

Shane hopped out of the vehicle.

"One, two, three eyes on me." Riley beelined and wrapped his arms around Shane's waist in a hard hug.

Shane's arms tensed for a second before they loosened, and he hugged Riley back.

"Riley, some people don't like being hugged like you do." She didn't want to ruin the jacket-zipping triumph, but she needed to constantly reinforce the message of personal boundaries. More than once, Riley embraced a stranger in the grocery store, and Holland cringed. At his age, he got a free pass. But people would not be as gracious as he grew older.

"It's okay. Hi, Buddy." Shane patted him on the back until Riley released.

His gaze met hers, and the softness in his face hardened.

"Morning," he said.

His tone was not even close to as friendly as it was yesterday. Was he mad he had to drive them? Maybe, he wasn't a morning person...which shouldn't be a surprise. For weeks, all she saw was this cranky face. She forgot about his normal demeanor with the friendly reprieve.

Riley tugged on Holland's arm. "Mimi! Show the picture."

Shoot. The jacket-zipping excitement made her forget about the picture he drew. "The picture's on the kitchen table. Come with me."

"No." He swept his hand across the grill, his gaze narrowing on the plastic.

Her current choices were potential meltdown, leaving him out of eyesight, or giving in and reinforcing defiant behavior. She checked her watch. *Dang it.* Right now, defiant behavior won. When she had more time, she'd return to proper parenting. "Can you keep an eye on him for a second?" Her pulse increased.

Riley had grown and stretched these last few years but was still a major elopement risk. He'd wander off much like a toddler would without realizing the dangers. Unless Riley was with Amy, or another therapist, her heart raced with every horrible scenario of him getting kidnapped, lost, or drowning.

"Sure thing." He joined Riley.

She glanced between the two, then sprinted back into the house. When she returned, she stopped to enjoy the scene.

Riley was sitting in the driver's seat. His tiny fingers gripped the steering wheel, and he bounced like he was going over speed bumps. "Vroooommmm.... Vroooommmm."

A real, full, dimples-on-display smile spread across Shane's face. He pointed at various things and called out "gauge," "shifter," and "hazard lights."

Watching Shane interact with Riley—*uff*— kicked everything up a notch. Her belly flipped and turned on itself, and she shook off the urge to snap a picture. "Here's the drawing." When she handed Shane the paper, it flapped in the breeze.

As he studied the image of a red vehicle, huge black tires, and a sun, his eyebrows lifted. "You drew this, Riley?" he asked. "Great job! Can I show you my favorite part of the picture?"

Riley nodded, and he tightened his grip on the steering wheel.

"Here." Shane pointed to the top left corner. "The smile on the sun."

Riley clapped. "You keep the picture."

Huh. Riley often held on to toys, pictures, and blankets like a pit bull. She'd have to mention this to Amy.

"Really?" Shane's gaze flickered from Holland to Riley. "Thank you. I know the perfect place for it." He set it in his backpack and ushered Riley into the back seat.

Seat belts snapped, the engine started, and soon, the neighborhood was in the rearview mirror.

Riley tapped Shane on the shoulder. "Why do you smell like oranges?"

He wasn't wrong. Shane had a distinct scent that drifted off him. Like a citrusy raindrop, bright and strong.

"Hmm." Shane glanced at the rearview mirror. "I don't know. Must be the soap I use."

"Why do you have big muscles?" he asked. "Mimi says I need apples and veggies for big muscles. Do you eat a million apples?"

"I do like apples." Shane glanced through his side-eye and shifted closer to the door. "What's your favorite fruit?"

"Peas."

He chuckled. "Good choice."

The blur of houses, trees, and cars rushed by them on the drive to the school.

Riley closed his eyes and lifted his face to the wind.

Shane was quieter than yesterday…and further away. The need to fill the silence was unbearable, but she kept her focus on the road and not his stiffened posture. After what felt like an excruciating ten-minute drive, Shane pulled into the school. Once she noted Riley finished a little fussing, she squeezed one last hug, left him in the classroom, and returned to the vehicle.

Now, Shane was squished so tightly to his door it looked uncomfortable.

With his eyebrows drawn together, he exited the parking lot in silence.

Heat crept up the back of her neck. A couple miles in, she cleared her throat. "Thanks for chatting with Riley. Sometimes, his questions are a little socially off."

"I'm socially off sometimes, too." His forearm muscle tensed, and he focused on the road. "Don't think twice about it."

His voice was kind, yet more aloof than yesterday. And not even close to the warmth it had with Riley. The tingles from yesterday flatlined. She fidgeted with her bracelet and bit her tongue not to be a pest and ask about the car. But this whole standoffish vibe confirmed she would never ask him for another favor. After work, she'd ride a banana boat bike if she had to. "Did you have a good night last night?"

He was silent for several moments. "It was fine."

Something in his tone, tight-lipped expression and

how he avoided her gaze made her stomach coil. Clearly, he was not happy he had to drive her to work. *This! This is why I don't depend on people.* Because they'd always let her down or make her feel like junk. When she arrived at work later today, she'd tow her car to the shop. She could pick up extra shifts to cover the costs, or maybe ask her parents to borrow their car. Although asking her parents for anything was a truckload of good intentions mixed with bad executions. But, it'd be better than sitting through the mother-of-all awkward mornings with a brooding Shane.

The second he rolled the vehicle to a complete stop, he jumped out of the car. He reached for his backpack in the trunk, then thrust her car keys into her hand. "Your car's fixed."

Wait, what? "It's…fixed?" She palmed the keys and skip-jogged to keep up with his hastened strides.

"Yeah, just needed a new spark plug."

The weightlessness in her body outweighed her negative sensation with his indifferent tone. "I-I don't even know what to say. You did that?"

He gave her a clipped nod and kept walking.

"I can't even…I don't…Thank you." He fixed the car. Just like that. But why? She almost didn't care *why*. For the last month, she'd wondered every day if that day would be the one she'd have to choose between supplies for Riley or a car bill.

A wave of relief washed over her, and she ran to Shane with arms outstretched in a hug.

His body went rigid against her touch. He patted her once and stepped away.

The flush of joy she had disappeared in a snap.

This is what Riley feels like when he hugs a stranger, and they don't want the touch! Flames shot to her face. She dropped her arms, and her chest muscles tensed so much she thought she might faint.

Without uttering a single word, he increased his speed and stormed into the kitchen.

And she bit back the tears brewing beneath the surface.

Chapter 10
Today's Special: Espresso Shakes with a Heaping
Scoop of High School Nemesis

Holland plowed through the kitchen doors with a tower of stacked, dirty dishes.

"Stop sliding the plate! The strawberries are shifting. Grab the whipped cream. No! Seriously, just move. I'll do it. The flow's messed up." Shane's voice boomed through the kitchen, competing with the silverware clanging, the hum of the ice machine, and swearing staff.

"Go, go, go! I'm twelve orders deep!"

"Where's the extra aioli?"

"Who took my spatula?"

"Come on, man. I'm dying here!"

"Out of my way! Move, move!"

The lunch rush hit Salt & Sugar Café fast and furious. Sweaty servers shuffled around, juggling plates, glasses, and silverware like circus performers.

Holland gratefully accepted the straw Amanda shoved in her face and gulped the ice-cold water to counteract the sweltering heat. The air-conditioning struggled to keep up with the one-hundred-degree temperature, and the high humidity turned the kitchen into a sauna. Her skin was sticky, her mouth was dry, and her nerves were shot.

"What got into him today?" Amanda brought the

straw back to her lips and jutted her head toward Shane.

Holland watched Shane crack an egg with so much fury, she was pretty sure the cook next to him caught shrapnel. She threw crushed nuts and cherry fixings on top of a sundae and shrugged. "What gets into him every day? Not swirling the whipped cream right. Not adding berries right. Not *breathing* right." Her unusually cranky voice surprised herself.

"If he thinks we do it wrong, then why doesn't he just do it himself?"

"Why servers have to put the finishing touches on plates is a timeless question. But, if he doesn't lighten up, he's about four seconds away from getting a pie in the face."

Amanda chuckled. "Give me a fair warning if you do it, so I can film it." She grabbed a side of salsa in the mini-cooler. "Maybe we'll go viral."

After plating her tray, Holland used her butt to open the kitchen door. Two weeks had passed since Shane fixed her car and the awkward hug in the parking lot. And two weeks since he said no more than a couple of words to her. Obviously, she overstepped and was self-conscious for a solid week about the inappropriate touching. Which then morphed into annoyance that he *clearly* couldn't get over it, as he'd all but ignored her since then.

But she couldn't shake the image of him acting so differently with Riley. He allowed a portal into himself that showed a soft spot, and she stewed on it for days. Ultimately, his kindness must've been a momentary lapse, and he reverted to his natural, jerk state. "Dave, you braved the heat today." She set a plate of waffles with droopy whipped cream in front of her favorite regular.

"Well, the waffles aren't going to eat themselves." He unwrapped the silverware from the napkin. "Don't let me eat them all. I promised Esther I'd bring home leftovers since she had her knitting club today."

"I'll grab a box immediately, so you won't be tempted. You want extra strawberries?"

"Only a Neanderthal would have them any other way."

Grinning, she refilled his coffee. "What do you call a sad strawberry?"

"What?"

"A blueberry."

He peeled back the top of the coffee creamer. "That might be your worst one yet."

"I'm too hot to remember any others." She wiped the moisture gathering on her upper lip with the back of her sleeve. "After work, I'm jumping into the lake, full uniform on and everything. I feel like I'm melting."

Dave laughed and cut into the waffles.

She shifted to clear plates from a different table, when a woman's voice sounded behind her.

"Excuse me, miss? Can you refill my lemonade?"

The woman was on lemonade number five in less than twenty minutes. Holland crossed her fingers that the customer didn't go into a diabetic coma. After shift, she was telling James he seriously needed to rethink his free refill policy. "Of course!" Walking back to the kitchen, she blew air up through her bottom lip in a sad attempt to fan her face. She grabbed a glass of water and checked her next order.

"Holland! Table on Five," the hostess called out behind her.

"Be there in a sec."

Amanda burst through the doors. "Run for your life."

"Why?"

"The Three Bs." Amanda tossed dirty dishes onto the rack.

Holland stopped filling waters. "Noooo."

Brooke, Britni, Bree—although she could never tell who was who. The girls from school who took pleasure in others' misery. Traveled in a trio, like a weird, alpha-female brat pack. Looked almost identical with their shiny, glass-like, straight blonde hair. Gossiped next to lockers. Loved teasing Amanda when she first arrived as a newbie in junior high, until Amanda told them where—and how hard—to shove it. The ones at prom who ganged up on Holland in the bathroom and touched her dress while saying, "Oooh...is this...*vintage?*" knowing dang well she got it at the secondhand store.

"Want me to take their table?" Amanda said. "I promise I won't spit in their drinks."

"I don't believe you." Holland reached for the water pitcher. "Nah, I can't ask you to do that."

Amanda lifted the corner of her lip. "Oh, I *want* to do it."

"That's what I'm worried about."

"Amanda," the hostess called from the front. "Group of ten on Tables Twelve and Thirteen."

"Dang it." Amanda grabbed her pen from her apron and put a hand on Holland's shoulder. "Call me if you need backup. I'm armed with a decade of subtle insults and passive-aggressive comments."

"Don't worry. I got this." *I don't got this.* Why did

81

these women make Holland nervous? Ten years had passed since she graduated, and a low-level rumble in her stomach grew for having to converse with them. She stretched her arms, grabbed the lemonade for the table, then pushed through the doors to approach the table. "Hi, ladies. What can I get you to drink?"

Maybe they won't remember me.

"Heidi, no way! How are you?" the shortest one of the three women said.

Shoot.

"No, her name's *Holland.* Like the *country*," another one of the women said.

Holland could hardly tell them apart in high school. Now, as adults with same inverted bob haircuts, identifying them was impossible. Did they coordinate their spaghetti-strapped sundresses today, too? "I'm great. Good to see you. Hot day, am I right?" Small talk was normally Holland's expertise, but today her tongue felt sticky and uncoordinated. "Can I get you started on blueberry lemonade, pop, or an iced mocha?"

"I had no idea you still worked here," the one wearing pink said. "Didn't you work here in high school?"

The words made Holland's throat tighten. "Yep, sure did."

"Well, you must really love this place," the one wearing the green dress said, flatly.

"I sure do." Not that Holland thought she'd still be working here ten years after graduation. But, even the worst days at the café were probably better than being stuck in a stuffy office with gross communal coffee, sending emails all day.

"My parents never let me work in high school," the

one in the blue dress said. "I was always so jealous of girls who could."

Liar.

"So, Holland, where do you work during the week?"

I'm so over this small talk. Hurry up, ladies. Orders are piling up. "Ah, here."

The three women simultaneously raised their eyebrows and shuffled in their seats. "Oh, this is your regular job?"

"Yep." Why was she embarrassed to say this? The flexibility with the job was everything with her and Riley's chaotic schedule and provided them enough money. Not to mention, she'd never find another boss as wonderful as James. Holland cursed the heat rising in her cheeks.

Pink Dress leaned back to look past Holland. "Well, I imagine the job has perks with eye candy like that."

Holland turned and saw Shane at the open counter, organizing plates.

"My goodness, girls. Don't tell my Scottie, but that man makes me want to fan my face."

The other woman looked behind Holland like she was invisible. "Oh, Bree, you're not kidding. What's his story, Holland?"

"Too long to share and probably not my place." Holland masked her clenched teeth as a smile. She had no idea what Shane's story was, but holding this information was a delicious, tiny power trip, providing her with some fuel to get through this painful conversation. "Why don't I start with a round of waters?"

"He must be new in town," the third woman chimed in. "I'm sure I would've remembered if I saw him at the grocery store."

"Move back, Brooke. You're blocking my view." Blue Dress giggled. "Holland, tell me he's single. I can think of twenty girls who'd line up to date him."

"I call dibs!" Pink Dress raised her hand. "Too bad I'm married."

Shut. Up. Holland clicked her pen multiple times. "Today's specials are a strawberry-stuffed waffle served with a side of…"

The women bounced their gaze between Shane and the menus.

"Hey, Holland." Pink Dress lowered the menu. "I heard you took in a special needs child."

She did *not* just bring up Riley. These women have no right to know anything about Riley.

"Bree, don't ask about that," Green Dress said in a hushed tone.

"Oh, sorry. Is that the wrong word?" She gritted her teeth. "Delayed? *Autistic?*"

The heat from Holland's face exploded to the rest of her body. Did she really say the word "autistic" like that? Lower her voice and whisper it like she was swearing? The pen gripped in her fist cusped on breaking.

"Bree!"

"Sorry, yikes! I'm not trying to offend anyone. I try to keep up with all the changing terms for…*special* children." She drummed her fingers on the table. "I heard he lives with you?"

"Not sure that's your business." Blue Dress laid down the menu.

Darn right. Not that Riley's diagnosis embarrassed Holland. Autism was a badge of honor, and every day he filled her with pride with his accomplishments. But Riley's autism was her story, not theirs. They didn't want to celebrate his growth. They didn't care he zipped his jacket on his own or got dressed *all by himself* this morning. They just wanted gossip. Holland's intolerance level rose to an eight. "Um, yep. My nephew lives with me."

"And, he's...special, right?"

"Aren't all children special?" Holland clapped back with a sugary smile. "You have kids, right? I bet you think they're special, too." *Take that.*

"Oh yes, of course. I just mean, if he's challenged, that'd be so hard. I can't imagine not having a...normal child."

Her knuckles now turned white. She wasn't hiding Riley's diagnosis, but the barrage of invasive questions needed to stop. "He has autism, yes. And he's amazing." And challenging, and she was constantly terrified she wasn't doing enough. But no way in heck would she say that to them.

"Ah, he *is* autistic. Is he high- or low-functioning?"

Enough! Holland was five seconds away from belting out a throat punch. The words "high or low functioning" needed to be slammed into the trash, never to be spoken of again. This woman just wanted to know if Riley was verbal, probably because that was how she equated function. Which was *none of her dang business.* Riley had speech delays, sure, but he could also recite the alphabet backward. He created worlds in his head better than any Hollywood producer. He could zip up his own jacket!

"Well, bless your heart," Pink Dress said.

Pink Dress just threw a punch. *Bless your heart* was *never* a compliment. "I really love the dresses you all have on. Did you match your outfits today just like in high school? Even at our age? So cute!" Gloves removed. Holland braced for the comeback but was met with silence. *Checkmate.* "I'll give you ladies a minute with the menus."

Holland sucked in gulps of air, attempting to lower her heart rate to something that wouldn't cause paramedics to drag her out of the restaurant. How dare those women make Riley seem less than? Like a charity case or like someone they could gossip about over their Sunday coffee. Riley was *amazing.* Getting custody of him was the best thing that had happened. With all the challenges and struggles, her life exponentially changed for the better when he arrived.

A drop of sweat rolled down her spine. She stomped into the kitchen, her chest on fire, and threw the silverware into the bin. Hard. She shifted her gaze and saw Shane's furrowed eyebrows. "What?" she snapped.

He shook his head and walked away.

Enough. Enough of Shane making her feel bad, these women making her feel bad, everyone in the entire planet making her feel bad. Time to take matters into her own hands.

Chapter 11
Today's Special: Mortified Mocha Shake with Sweetened Savior Complex

Holland stood in front of the kitchen door and counted down from ten. Taking her ex-classmates' lunch order was, quite possibly, the very last thing she wanted to do in existence. Cleaning up after Riley last month when he caught a stomach bug was more appealing. She pulled up her chin, exhaled, and pushed through the door. From here on out, she vowed to use all her training on redirection if Riley came back up in conversation.

"Holland, tell us you're going to the high school reunion next month," Pink Dress said. "We're all on the committee, and it'll be so much fun. Everyone's going to be there."

Being on a college frat party cleanup crew sounded better than a reunion. "Not sure I can make it."

Green Dress folded her hands in her lap. "Are you going to be catering it? We're all on the board and hired this restaurant to do the catering."

She filled each glass with water. "I'm not part of the catering team."

"Well, great, then you have no excuse," Pink Dress said with a smile before her face dropped. "Unless finding babysitters who take autistic children is too hard."

Holland sucked her lips into her mouth and exhaled through her nose. "I imagine everyone has trouble finding good babysitters these days." *That's it.* The final thing she'd say about her personal life. Why did she still let people like them affect her after all these years? She was an adult. School's been out for a *decade.* And they weren't even being inherently awful. Yet, their words cut deep. Blinking back the hot sting of tears, she took their orders and returned to the kitchen.

"Order up!" Shane's eyebrows drew together.

Holland fumbled while adding plates to her tray. With shaky hands, she grabbed a sourdough toast and a side of pancakes. Shoot! Did Table Five order wheat or sourdough? She flipped through her order pad to confirm. How did she enter the order into the ticketing system wrong? Or maybe she had it right and wrote it wrong. Ack! She snatched the white bread, then swapped it for the wheat instead. Her cheeks burned from Shane's intense stare. "Why do you keep looking at me like that?" she snapped.

He flinched, then softened. "You, okay?"

Really? Two weeks of no talking, making her feel horrible, and creating a gargantuan distance between them, and he was asking if she was okay. "What do you care?" The anger in her body reflected in her tone. Storming out of the kitchen, she shook off an avalanche of negative feelings and flipped her scowl to a forced smile. After clearing a table, she joined Amanda who was walking down the hall.

"How's it going with the Three Bs?" Amanda balanced multiple glasses in her hands.

Holland pushed open the door and stacked her dirty dishes onto the racks. "One of them said bless your heart."

Amanda gripped her arm. "Oh no, she didn't. Want me to spike their lemonade with a ghost pepper? I swear I'll do it."

"I love you for offering. But no." Holland sighed and loaded her tray. Ten minutes later, she stopped by to check on the women. "Anything else I can get you?"

"Nope. Just promise us you'll be at the reunion. We bet the twenty-year reunion class we'll have a bigger showing." Green Dress wiped her mouth with a napkin. "Catching up when you're not so busy will be amazing. Right, girls?"

The other women nodded and smiled without emotion.

"And you can bring your significant other!"

Holland's chest fell.

"Wait, you're not single, are you?" The bless-your-heart one leaned in and touched Holland's forearm. "Such a pretty girl like yourself? No way."

"No, I'm not single." Why did she lie? Holland had never once thought she needed a man to feel complete.

Pink Dress smacked a hand on the table. "Tell me you're with that beautiful man in the kitchen. I'll never believe it!"

Flames flew up from her neck to her scalp. Why would she never believe it? Was she not good enough for someone like him? Holland reached her breaking point. Either tears, a throat punch, or water thrown in their faces would commence in less than five seconds. She glanced behind her shoulder and lowered her voice. "We are together, but keeping it quiet. We're not wanting the staff here to know about our relationship. You know, drama in the workplace. Who needs it, right?"

The women released a high-pitch squeal.

Holland swore a dog on the sidewalk barked from the noise.

"Eek!" Green Dress shimmied her shoulders. "I had no idea you could land such a fine man."

This woman sucks.

"Whoa, I didn't mean it like that." Green Dress held up her hands. "I, ah…I cannot wait to meet him at the reunion."

"Hopefully, we can make it." Holland's stomach coiled so tightly from lying she thought she might throw up. She pivoted sharply without another word and returned to the kitchen.

The lunch crowd thinned, the hum of chatter slowed, but the burn from the interaction with the women rose. Holland refilled sides of ranch dressing and thoughts assaulted her. What if the women saw Shane somewhere and said something? Duluth was not a small town, but it wasn't huge, and they were totally the type of women to bump into him in the produce aisle and strike up a conversation. They'd probably lean in with a hushed voice and say some variation of *cat's out of the bag*, or *secrets safe with me*, or the ultra-cringe-worthy *spill the beans*. Holland would be humiliated, Shane would be angry, and the women would be satisfied. She pushed her thumbs into her temples and exhaled.

James popped into the kitchen with a clipboard and pencil, his bald head glistening with moisture. "Holland, did you take your break yet?"

Perfect timing. She needed to get out of this place. The sweltering heat outside might melt her, but she didn't care. After filling a superhuman size glass of lemonade, she grabbed her cell. Her belly sank when she saw Amy's name.

—*Riley's having a tough day. When you pick him up, let's chat about some ways we can help eliminate a few of his triggers.*—

Her chin dropped. She blinked back tears, threw her apron onto the table, and slammed through the exit door. Protected by the seclusion in the alley, she unleashed her tears. She slid down the brick wall to the pavement, drew her knees to her chest, and buried her head.

She didn't know how long she sat in that position. Something wet and cool brushed her arm, and she jostled from her thoughts. She shielded her eyes against the sun, and an outline of a milkshake squinted into focus.

"You looked like you needed chocolate relief."

Shane's voice was soft and hesitant. She kind of hated him for his sweet gesture. She wanted to say something snappy—tell him where to shove the shake, or ask why he hadn't said a word in weeks, and now held a chocolate peace offering. Instead, she wiped her eyes with the back of a hand and grabbed the glass. "Thanks."

He paused for several long moments. "Can I join you?"

She shrugged. "Sure."

He sat next to her and stared at the brick wall.

The coolness of the ice cream was a stark contrast to the afternoon heat. She appreciated he didn't ask questions. Normally, she'd rather slip on a pancake and do a swan dive face-plant on the floor than be caught crying. But today, she didn't care. She drank the shake in silence and sniffled. "This is really good." She stirred the shake with the straw. "What did you do differently?"

"I added a shot of coffee liqueur."

She whipped her head around. "What? You can't do that! I can't drink on the job."

He let out a chuckled puff of air through his nose. "I'm kidding. I added heavy cream and a shot of espresso."

"Ah." The tears stopped, and she continued sipping on the melting drink. For the next several moments, the only sounds were slurping, the faint beeping of a garbage truck, and her heavy sighs.

"Tough day today."

He said it like a cross between a statement and a question. She needed to tell him what she told the women. That, as ridiculous and juvenile as it sounded, she couldn't let them win. They stereotyped and dehumanized Riley, and Shane was caught in the anger crossfire. Maybe a sinkhole would magically appear and suck her into the abyss. "Sure is." She tapped her fingernails against the milkshake glass. "I had a table I really could've done without."

"Oh yeah? More rude guys?"

"No, rude women." She wiped off a dribble of ice cream from her hand. "A group of girls I graduated with who were miserable then and are miserable now."

He swirled his shake that had transformed into the consistency of milk and took long sips. "I'm always shocked how some people don't evolve. When people think of high school as their glory days, and hang on to toxic relationships because of legacy, I think of it as

Social Darwinism."

That's freakishly insightful.

He tilted down his chin. "Sorry, today sucked."

Her body turned warm, and not just from the heated pavement seeping through her pants. Maybe she didn't have to tell him what she told the women. They were rude, but the chances of them bumping into him and saying something were nil. She could bury this whole thing and pretend it never happened. "I need to tell you something." What if he stormed out of the alley? Humiliating. Or, what if he had a girlfriend, and Holland's words got back? *Great.* Now she can add home wrecker to her list of failures today. Without warning, the slow roll of another tear fell.

"Whoa. What's happening?" He inched closer.

His signature citrus scent filled her nose, disarming her at a startling rate.

"I promise I won't yell if you forgot to add the rosemary arrangement for Table Twelve," he said.

She dropped her head with a small grin. "No, it's not that. Those women grilled me on so many things. They have a way of making me feel bad. A lot of history exists between us. And they asked me if I was single, like feeling all bad for me and—"

"Slow down here." He set down his empty glass on the pavement. "What happened?"

Crystal-blue eyes caught her gaze, and she hated that she melted as quickly as the shake in her hand. "I told them you were my boyfriend." *Oh, God.* The searing heat that hit her face was intense enough to cook a steak. He needed to say something. Tell her she's a jerk, laugh, be mad...*something.* Not sit in silence with an unreadable expression. "I'm seriously so sorry. The words just slipped out, and it's unfair to you, and you probably have a girlfriend, and she'll hear this, and I ruined things and—"

"I don't have a girlfriend," he said in a matter-of-fact tone. "No worries."

The relief in those words was more than vindication she didn't ruin a relationship, but she didn't want to dissect that right now. "Thank God." Now her chest was hot. Any more of this conversation and she'd implode on the spot. "I mean, thankfully, I didn't cause trouble. But, really, I'm so sorry. Super uncool thing to do. I can't believe I even said it."

"Seriously, don't sweat it." He nudged her with an elbow. "Stuff like this is small. You're all good."

She bit back a grin. "Coming from the man who murdered a head of romaine yesterday because it lacked the proper shade of green."

"That's different." His lips twitched up. "It's all about presentation."

She set down her empty glass, and her stomach uncurled for the first time all day. She glanced at her watch. Two minutes left on her break, but she wanted to elongate the moment for as long as possible—the kindness in his voice, the sensation of his shoulder brushing hers, *the confirmation he was single.* Not that she'd do anything with that information. Probably.

"So, does this mean I need to take you out for dinner now since we're fake dating?" The dimple in his cheek deepened with his smile.

"Gosh no!" She'd already done enough damage. A pity date was the last thing she needed to add to her list of failures today. "Absolutely not."

His lips pulled into a straight line.

Probably from relief.

"My break's up. I better go back." He stood and held out his hand.

As he helped her up, she did her best to ignore the tingles that shot up her arm.

Chapter 12
Today's Special: Awareness Angel Food Cake

I can't believe I asked her out, and she shot me down.

The words slipped out of Shane's mouth. Granted, his fumbled request wasn't the smoothest way to ask Holland on a date. Not that he had a lot of experience—the last woman he asked out was Cherise in the eleventh grade. With his thoughts racing, Shane tied his apron and headed to the café's kitchen.

For the past six weeks, he had the terrible idea of asking Holland out. When he fixed her car the other week—and she had hugged him—he had used a herculean amount of strength not to scoop her up in his arms. But she deserved someone who had their life figured out...someone who didn't disappoint everyone they love.

Even though he didn't mean to ask her out, and the rejection stung, he was relieved she turned him down. The idea of him dating Holland was ridiculous. She was *amazing*—smart, funny, kind. Skillfully maneuvered a challenging situation with her nephew and excelled beyond all measures. And, when he heard she told her former classmates they were together, his insides did jumping jacks. Despite the fact she probably just panicked and picked the first guy within sight, her words sparked hope.

His phone vibrated against his leg. He grabbed it, and his gut sank.

Cherise. She was a bulldog—a fighter to the end, regardless of the consequences. Seven months ago, he never intended their relationship to end the way it did. He thought he'd reminisce with her for a while, share a few tears, and part amicably after hugging. For the previous year, he'd been planning to leave. So, the day he walked out, he was prepared...healed, even. And she was shattered.

He knew why she was calling—she needed her final say. Sure, he had logistic meetings with her after the split. He paid the rest of the lease and gave her the furniture and appliances. Then, he took his coffee mugs, clothes, and a painting he'd purchased from a Minneapolis artist and packed his vehicle. But she didn't have her day in court, so to speak. She never argued her case.

He sent her call to voicemail, and a minute later, a text appeared.

—I'd really like to talk. Just for a few minutes. Can you call me?—

Why was he such a jerk? Was he incapable of taking his lashings like an adult? He snuck out to the alley and hovered his fingers over the call button.

"Shane."

Cherise's tone was void of all emotion. *Shoot.* Now, he couldn't gauge how this conversation would go. "Cherise." A thick silence followed. He fanned the bottom of his shirt and paced the pavement. "You asked me to call. What do you need?" A bead of sweat formed on his temple. Definitely from the sun. Definitely not from the fear of facing his failure. He didn't want to be mean. But this was unchartered territory.

A million excruciating seconds passed.

"How are you?" she finally asked.

He blew out a breath and turned his face toward the sun. After nearly a decade with someone, he now felt like she was a stranger. He opened his mouth, but no sound exited. *Just get it over with already.* "You didn't call to chitchat about how things are going. I doubt you care. What do you need?" He winced at the harshness in his voice.

"Wow…" A low whistle echoed through the phone. "I didn't want this conversation to be hostile."

"What did you expect?" Did she think he'd be happy receiving a verbal beating? Of course, he deserved it, but he'd had enough of those in his life from his parents and law school advisor. The list was long and tired. "Seriously, what do you want? It's coming up on what…six, seven months since we last spoke. Why are we doing this, now?"

"Let the record show I tried communicating with you multiple times over the past several months."

He tightened his grip on the phone. "We're not in the courtroom. There's no record being entered into evidence." *Thank God.* Because he proved he was a total jerk. "Just say it."

"You know what? A conversation right now is a bad idea. I'd really like to talk when you've calmed down."

He slapped a palm against the side of the building. "Calmed down? Are you serious? You're the one who's upset and keeps pestering me. Time to move on." He hated himself, right now, right here. She didn't deserve his terrible behavior.

"Time to move on? Get over yourself."

He leaned against the brick wall. "Then why are you calling? Seriously, just say it, or stop contacting me. It's not doing anyone any good."

"Because I—" Her inhale was loud through the receiver. "Never mind. This was a mistake."

The phone went dead. He swallowed hard, tried to untwist the coil in his stomach, and returned to the kitchen.

Later that afternoon, once he finished cooking the last meal of his shift, he grabbed the sanitizing spray and wiped the counters.

James strolled in and patted Shane on the arm. "Good work today." He leaned closer to his ear. "But you have to be nicer."

Shane stopped mid-wipe to look at his uncle. "I am nice."

"You scare the servers." James' voice had a playful touch.

"Are you serious?"

James nodded.

While he worked, Shane purposely kept his head down. He took breaks by himself, cleaned in silence, and clocked out every night without incident. "I've never once said anything bad. I hardly talk to anyone."

James drummed a pencil against the clipboard held to his chest. "You get mad at how things look."

Shane balled the rag in his hand. "Of course, I do. But I don't think messy plates are a moral failure on their part or anything." Proper aesthetics were crucial, but he'd never degrade a person. He only made comments on the way things *looked*. His stomach turned sour. *Did I turn into my dad?* Ignoring signs, pushing agendas, and expecting things outside what people wanted to do?

James rapped a knuckle against the stainless steel counter. "You really are an artist, aren't you?"

The words lingered, even after James left. Shane ran his cloth across the prep table and breathed through the pit growing in his stomach. He clocked out and trudged to his vehicle. The heat had barely broken after work, but the breeze picked up and offered a bit of a reprieve during the drive to *his spot.* After stepping into the studio, Shane inhaled the deeply gratifying smell of fabric, canvas, oils, and paint. He tossed his bag onto the couch and put on his smock, the ritual immediately sending a calming antidote through his veins.

Adding paints to the palette brought a wave of relaxation. Picking up the brush kissed him with serotonin. Swiping the brush across the canvas injected him with dopamine. He layered colors, stepped back, admired his work, and got lost in the rush of creating.

His phone buzzed, jolting him from his trance. At seeing his mom's name, he inhaled, his chest constricting.

—*Hi, honey. You, me, and your dad need to talk. It's been almost two months, and I think everyone has calmed down and hopefully come to their senses.*—

He didn't *not* want to speak to his parents. He loved them. But their condemnation of his decision gutted him, and he held on to stubborn hope that they needed to reach out first—which she just did. The heaviness in his body lifted.

—*Sounds good. We can talk on the phone or meet in person?*—

—*That'd be wonderful! And great news...your*

father chatted with the Dean at the Law School. They said you can enroll again in the fall, even though the registration deadline passed.—

All lightness dropped like a cinderblock. His parents would never respect his decision. And maybe, they were right. Maybe, he *should* return to law school. But his insides spiraled with thoughts of exams and papers and lectures. He was happier here, in Duluth. At least, he thought so. He was certainly happier painting than prepping for the bar.

As his mind raced, he scratched his palm with the dry, brush bristles. Did he make the right decision? Should he follow his mother's advice and look at re-enrolling? If his plan wasn't successful, he'd be lost. He couldn't support a family on a paycheck of broken dreams.

His phone buzzed, and he was ready to turn it off for the night to avoid any other conversations with his mom. Instead, Holland's name flashed across the screen, and his pulse skyrocketed.

—Hey. Hope it's okay to text you. I had a quick question.—

His heart should not be thumping this hard.

—Sure, what's up?—

He held his breath and waited for the three bubbles to appear.

—What do you call a cow trapped in an earthquake?—

His smile should not be this pronounced.

—I don't know. What?—

—A milkshake.—

And his urge to hug her was borderline illegal.

—That was really bad. Might be your worst one

yet.—

—It was really bad. Ha! Actually, that's not why I messaged. I just wanted to thank you for being so cool about what I said today. I'm seriously so embarrassed. Thanks for not throwing raspberries at my face.—

A minute passed before he decoded the undeniable tingle festering inside his stomach. Excitement? Nerves? Whatever the feeling was, he didn't want it to stop.

—Raspberries. Never. They're too messy and delicious. Now rhubarb, on the other hand...—

A shocked emoji popped up on his screen.

—What do you have against rhubarb?—

He smiled at the message and tapped his thumbs across the screen to respond.

—The sheer amount of sugar needed to offset the bitterness is such a waste. They're like a tart weed Minnesotans put in everything. And they're hard to make beautiful.—

He pushed a palm into his forehead. *I can't believe I just wrote that. She'll think I'm a total food nerd.*

—You have a point. The way you showed us how to lay the berries with the rosemary twigs was pretty cool.—

He typed out the next message before he lost his nerve.

—What are you doing right now?—

—Waiting for the chicken nuggets and tater tots to be done in the oven. Riley's watching a train video.—

—You up for a visit? I read this article and had an idea for Riley.—

Three bubbles. Stop. Three more bubbles. Stop. He couldn't breathe. The air officially deflated from his lungs. Why was it taking so long? A simple *yes* or *no* was all he needed. Was she writing a thesis on how to turn him down? *Again.*

Finally, a message appeared.

—Sure, as long as I can get him into the bath at 7:30.—

He nearly sprinted out of the studio. After starting the car, he whipped a U-turn in the middle of the road, then floored the gas. He had to make a quick stop, and then he'd see her and Riley—outside of work and without distractions. He didn't remember the last time his heart danced like this.

Chapter 13
Today's Special: Chocolate Cupcakes Frosted with the Possibility of New Beginnings

He's coming over. He's. Coming. Over.
Holland meant to say no. She read Shane's text, her body turned to liquid, her insides turned on themselves, and she *meant to say no.* Holland scurried into the living room to pick up a few toys scattered across the floor, then swung by the bathroom to look at herself in the mirror. Her hair was still wet and in a messy bun from her after-work shower, and her shirt was moderately wrinkled.

She studied her face—dark circles lined her eyes, cheeks pinked from the humidity. Should she wear makeup? Wait, why would she wear makeup? She hardly ever wore makeup. *Breathe.*

The timer on her phone buzzed, indicating dinner was ready. She followed the familiar scent of baked chicken nuggets and tater tots down the hall. She grabbed the potholder Riley made for Christmas last year and opened the oven.

After downing nuggets and peas, Holland heard knuckles rap against the door. Her heart leaped from her throat to her brain, constricting both her breath and thoughts. *Holland, stop. Maybe he's just bored.* She opened the door. "Hey!"

The sound of Riley's bare feet slapping against the

hardwood floor approached from behind. "One, two, three eyes on me." He tugged on Holland's shirt.

"Hi, Riley." Shane smiled, then shifted his gaze to Holland. "Hey, you."

Gah! Why, when he sounded like *that,* her heart did *this?* The palpitating needed to calm before she checked herself into the E.R. She held the door open and waved him inside. "Come in. Riley, let Shane come into the house."

Shane toed off his shoes at the doorway and scanned the room. "Can we talk for a second?" he whispered and glanced at Riley. "Privately."

Gulp. She brought Riley into the kitchen and pulled up a train video, before returning to Shane. "What's up?" She tucked her hands into her pockets, trying to keep her stiffened arms relaxed.

"I want to be respectful of your rules. But I read an article that sometimes kids who are autistic like following a recipe and baking. So, I brought all the ingredients to make chocolate cupcakes." He held up a bag. "But I'm not sure if Riley can have sugar before bedtime."

This is really thoughtful.

"In case you say no to the cupcakes, I brought backup watercolor paints and paper." He held up a different bag.

Ok, this is really, really thoughtful. "You're sweet for doing this," she said. "I think he'd love to bake. We tried it once, but I didn't know you couldn't swap butter for olive oil in brownies."

He shook his head. "You didn't."

"Oh, I did." She laughed and escorted him to the kitchen, where she lifted Riley's headphones off and lowered herself to face him. "Bubby, Shane is here to make cupcakes. Let's go wash our hands first, then we can bake."

Riley climbed on the stool next to the sink and pumped vanilla soap into his palms.

Shane laid supplies on the counter. "Do you have a spatula, spoon, and bowl?"

"Yep." She opened drawers and pulled out utensils.

Shane reached into the third bag and paused. "Riley, do you know what every chef needs?"

Riley's eyes grew wide, and he shook his head.

"A chef's hat and apron." Shane rummaged through the bag with a broad smile and pulled out three matching aprons and chef's hats. "One for you. One for Mimi. One for me."

Holland giggled. "They're pink."

Shane settled his mouth close to her ear. "It's all they had left at the store."

His breath against her cheek made her heart flutter. She took a step back. "They're perfect."

"Chef's hat! Chef's hat!" Riley wildly clapped his hands and plopped on the fluffy, pink hat.

Shane gripped the apron. "Want to put on the apron yourself, or do you want help?"

"Help me. Then help Mimi." Riley hopped off the stool and opened his arms.

Shane wrapped the string multiple times around Riley's waist, then tied it in the back. "There ya go, Bud."

Gentle flutters in Holland's chest transformed into something indefinable. But the feeling was warm and buttery, and she wanted more.

"Help Mimi with apron." Riley pointed at her

shoulders.

She shook her head. "Riley, I can do my own."

"No!" Riley smacked a hand against the kitchen counter. "Shane help Mimi."

Her gaze locked with Shane's.

With a hint of a grin, he nodded.

She flattened the apron against her chest and reached the ties over her shoulders. A moment passed before his fingertips brushed the tiny hairs that fell from her ponytail away from her neck. The zings swished down her spine, touched her toes, and flew back up. She prayed he couldn't see the goose bumps on her arms.

With a delicate touch, he slowly tied the string around her neck and reached to tie the other around her waist. He cleared his throat and stepped aside, his cheeks pinker than a minute ago. "All right, now the hats."

"Say cheese!"

Riley used those words to ask for a photo. "Shane might not want his picture taken." She reached for Riley's hand. "Let's get started on baking."

"Say cheese!" Riley repeated and stomped his left foot on the linoleum.

"I don't mind. We can snap a pic." Shane handed Riley a spatula and held a spoon for props.

"Mimi, too," Riley said.

She darted a glance at Shane. "Selfie time." She tilted the phone up, with Riley in the middle, and Shane at the end. "Say cheese!" She held the phone out for them to peek at the picture.

Shane grinned at the phone, then he showed Riley the recipe card and pointed at the measuring cups. "This says one cup. Let's scoop out the sugar until it reaches the very top."

Riley scooped the sugar and dumped it in the first bowl.

"And this says two eggs." Shane pointed to the next line. "Let's get two eggs."

Riley held the eggs in his hands. "I want to crack it."

"Bubby, I don't think that's a good idea." Holland approached and peeked above Riley's head. "Shells might break in there."

"We can crack them in a separate bowl. I brought a dozen, so he has ten to work with. I'll do the last two if it gets down to the end, and we haven't successfully cracked one without shells." Shane searched her eyes. "Is that okay?"

Pretty sure at this point Shane could ask her anything, and she'd agree. She was a terrible cook and even worse baker, so she stepped back and took a voyeur view from the corner—Shane explaining how to use each utensil, Riley's enormous hat slipping on his forehead, and Shane waiting until Riley destroyed all ten eggs and cracking the last two.

"Time to put the batter in the oven." Shane held out his arm toward Riley's chest. "Step back so you don't get burnt, okay?"

Soon, the deep, warm scent of flour, butter, and chocolate permeated the kitchen. Holland sat at the table with Shane and Riley.

Riley described trains, meticulously breaking down everything from the locomotive, caboose, baggage car, and air brake.

Like a natural, Shane filled him with praise and

peppered him with questions.

By the time the cupcakes were cooked, cooled, and frosted, Holland wasn't sure if Riley or she beamed more.

"Ready to taste our creation? Cheers!" Shane tapped each cupcake overflowing with frosting and enough sprinkles to feed a herd of unicorns and took a bite. "So good. Great job, Riley. You're an excellent chef."

Riley licked the chocolate from the top of the muffin. "Yummy!"

"These are delicious." Holland took a second bite of the creamy dessert. "I'm totally over my chocolate quota for the day."

Shane narrowed his eyes. "You actually have a quota?"

She nudged him with her elbow and noticed the clock. Seven twelve p.m. *Ugh.* Why was she worried she'd be lonely the second he left? She and Riley had lived alone for five years. The only other people who visited her house were Amanda or her parents. Her heart shouldn't be clenching like this at the expectation of a void. But Riley needed a bath before bed, and she couldn't break routine.

"I'm full." Shane patted his stomach. "I'll clean up, then take off."

She gathered the spoons into the mixing bowl and moved to the sink. "You don't have to clean. I got this." *But if he cleans, he can stay a little longer. Which sounds…kind of amazing.*

He joined her at the sink. "A gentleman never makes a mess and leaves."

"Very funny." She removed the chocolate-smeared

apron from Riley and set the timer. "You can watch screens for ten more minutes until bath, then it's story time."

Riley pressed Play on his screen and continued licking his treat.

She returned to the sink, savoring each time Shane handed her a dish and his fingertips touched hers. Looking down, she bit back her smile. How did it feel this good...this *natural*...standing in her kitchen washing dishes with *him?* Her feelings didn't make sense. None of this evening made sense. But right now, she didn't want anything from tonight to make sense.

Shane put the leftover dry ingredients in the cabinet and stuffed his hands into his pockets. "I should get going. Bath time's important."

"Sure is." Her stomach flipped. "Thanks for tonight. We had a lot of fun."

Shane stepped over to Riley. "Thanks for baking with me." He looked at Holland, then back toward Riley. "Maybe we can do it again, if Mimi says okay."

"Yay!" Riley licked his fingers.

Holland peeked at her watch. *Two minutes until the timer goes off.*

"See you tomorrow?" Shane swung his keys around his finger.

The tiny hairs standing up on her scalp nearly made her dizzy. "I'll walk you to the door." The front door was like a dark-doom abyss, and the second he stepped through it, the magic from tonight would disappear.

He pulled his hands from his pockets and reached toward her. Color shot to his face.

She waited for his skin to touch hers again, and her breath hitched.

Instead, he pivoted and gripped the doorknob. "Goodnight."

No!

His footsteps creaked against the wooden stairs with every step.

Don't leave! "Shane?" What was she going to say? She wasn't prepared. But she hated knowing whatever this swimming, warm sensation funneling through her would stop the second he left.

"Yes?"

He stepped one foot back on the step and held the railing like he was ready to sprint into her house. "Do you want—" *Ding-ding-ding!* She flinched at the loud timer and tapped it off.

"What were you saying?" he asked.

I can't do this. "Oh, um. Do you want to bring cupcakes home for you and James?"

"Nah, I'm good." He stepped back onto the gravel and waved. "Goodnight."

As her heart thumped so hard it reached her neck, she leaned against the door. She exhaled a ragged breath and headed to the kitchen. "Okay, Bubby. First bath, then story."

A half an hour later, after she tucked a purple stuffy under Riley's arm and read his favorite story, Holland plopped onto the couch and checked emails. "Dang it." Riley's school accounting office notified her about a delinquent bill. Her parents forgot...*again*...to pay the therapist. Pressing her thumb into her forehead, she blew in and out five times. She couldn't afford to cover the bill on her own and was grateful her parents picked up the tab. But this was the third time this year, and anytime she had to apologize to the school and text her mom, she got heartburn.

She reached for her phone.

—*Did you send the check to the school for Riley's therapy last month? They emailed me a delinquent bill.*—

Her phone buzzed.

—*Oh shoot! Sorry, forgot. I'll do it tomorrow. And you reminded me, too! Brain fog, too many trips. LOL. Sorry, Holladazzle.*—

Holland switched to her photo app, and her chest moved from tense to fuzzy. Scrolling in on Shane and Riley's faces, she decoded their expressions. Riley seemed happy, excited even, to bake. And Shane looked…peaceful.

She rested her head on the coffee table. *What am I going to do?* Was there even anything *to do?* For the first time in forever, she didn't want ice cream. She didn't want to make jewelry. She didn't want to binge-watch anything. She wanted her insides to keep dancing and stop all this nonsense at once.

Nothing could ever happen between her and Shane. Her life was complicated and messy, and she barely held it together as is. Adding a man to the mix, messing with their routine, dropping her defenses…a disaster in the making. Even if she could've sworn a small spark ignited between them. But maybe she made up the magnetism? She had less-than-zero experience with men. Never had a serious boyfriend in her life. But now, her inexperience probably meant she read into every exchange with Shane. She flew off a message.

—*Here's the picture from tonight. It was a good night.*—

A message popped up.

—It was a *great* night.—

The tip of her fingers carried so many more words. The patience Shane had for Riley made her want to dive in headfirst and never come up for air. But he was a friend. Nothing more. People were unreliable, messed with routines, and continually let her down. Her mom forgetting to write the check was proof of that theory. Bringing someone into Riley's life, or hers, and making her depend on them wasn't fair. But friends...friends she could do.

Chapter 14
Today's Special: Apple Bobbing Pie

Shane shielded his eyes from the sun, and his ears from the sonic boom exploding from James' voice.

In the employee parking lot of Salt & Sugar Café, James paced with his clipboard and a creased forehead. Sweat beaded under his golfer hat while he reviewed inventory for his booth at the Solstice and Shenanigans Festival.

For the third time.

James poised his pencil like a dart. "Do we have all the preserves?"

Shane tapped the side of the van. "Check."

"And extra cotton cord?"

"Check."

James drew a slash mark through a line item and tugged on his lucky magenta bowtie. "Cash, scissors, gift bags, boxes?"

Shane raised his eyebrows. "Check, check, check, and check."

"And all the cinnamon rolls, scones, and cookies?"

"James. We're good." Shane slapped a firm hand on James' shoulder. "We've run through the list twenty times already. We have everything. Your restaurant is less than ten minutes away, if we need to come back."

James hugged the clipboard to his chest and exhaled through his nose. "This is *the* festival of the year. It's my name. And my reputation. And my—"

"Good looks on the line?" Shane shut the catering van's heavy doors holding the precious cargo of miniature pies, cookies, and jams. "Things will be fine." He trotted back to the restaurant and flipped over the *Meet Us at The Festival!* sign on the front door. He pulled on the handles to confirm the door was locked, then returned to the van. He drove caravan-style with James and three other staff who were working at the booth today. After navigating to their area, Shane unpacked and set up the canopy and tables.

James arranged the treats and jams on the cedar display shelves.

Within minutes of Shane's arrival, a near-giddy anticipation developed. Festival, farmers' markets, fairs…being surrounded by energy, sounds, and unique foods forced the grizzly bear in him to smile. People were always happy and relaxed at festivals.

"Damn it!" James snapped as he knocked over his liquid chalk menu and muttered several other choice words under his breath.

Okay, *most* people were happy and relaxed.

James readjusted the sign and walked around the table to double check the placement.

The scent of sunshine on dewy grass mixed with kettle popcorn and mini-doughnuts filled the air, and soon the area came to life. A few hours later, after the booth was assembled, Shane itched to look at the other vendors before the crowds arrived. He strolled by the apple bobbing, gluten-free cookies, corn on the cob, and face painting booths, and took a mental inventory of all the places he could sneak away later for a snack. He pulled out his phone and reread the text exchange with Holland from last night. Treating himself, he scrolled over all the messages from her this last week.

As if the universe read his thoughts, his phone buzzed with a message from Holland.

—*What makes a joke a dad joke?*—

—*What?*—

—*The punch line is apparent.*—

He chuckled and cleared his throat.

—*Solid. Eight out of ten. You and Riley gonna make it to the festival today?*—

The idea of seeing her today made him want to do a backflip next to the cheese curd stand.

—*Hopefully. So far, Riley's having a good morning. P.S. How's James? During the festival, he's legit possessed by the ghost of a '50s housewife.*—

—*I did hear some creative spins on a few swear words. But he seems to be doing good.*—

—*Ok. I gotta make like a tree and leaf.*—

—*Pretty sure it's leave.*—

—*Let's leave the comedy to me, big guy.*—

—*Ha. All right, chat later.*—

The pavement was warm beneath his feet, and he picked up his pace. He moved through the festival until he stumbled upon a large booth with artwork tucked under a white canopy. If he allowed himself to dream, maybe next year he'd have a booth of his own. "Beautiful work," he said to the artist and continued to study the realistic portrayal of trains nestled among various landscapes. *I bet Riley would like this stand.*

As he walked toward James' booth, he let his mind drift to the time he spent at Holland's place last week. The hollowness in his chest filled during those few brief hours of mixing batter and sampling frosting. He had wanted *so badly* to wrap his arms around her and tell her goodnight.

But, at work, a sort of...*flow* traveled between him and Holland. When Amanda wasn't there, he'd coordinate his breaks with her. Sipping on a chocolate shake, she'd talk about her favorite movies, the worst foods she ever ate, or argue with him about which '90s group was the best. He ducked behind the rope and joined James under the tent.

"Glad to see the prince returned to his castle. I was about to send the search party after you." James narrowed his eyes in an exaggerated glare.

James' largest competitor broke the invisible hospitality code by incorporating cookies and homemade jam into his menu this year, which was James' festival claim to fame. The competitor started a "friendly" competition on social media, betting on who'd sell out first. James was in a tizzy ever since. "Ten minutes, James. I was gone ten minutes."

"This is your first festival. You don't know how ferocious people can get. Last year, when two suburban moms with straw hats and acrylic nails both reached for the final blueberry pie, a fistfight broke out."

"Is that true?" He raised an eyebrow.

"No." James chuckled and patted him on the back. "But I love thinking my food is so good someone would throw punches for it."

Shane finished premixing the lemonade, scooping ice from the van into their cooler, and realigning the pies. He breathed in the perfect, eighty-degrees, Lake-Superior-mineral-scented air.

James cut pieces of cotton cord for the gift bags and lined them in a row. "Are Holland and Riley coming today?"

Shane remained silent, focusing on the scones and nothing else.

"Don't play coy, Scooter. I see how you two make all sorts of hetero love gazes at each other."

Shane opened his mouth to deny it but snapped it shut. He puppy-dog eyed Holland every time she entered a room. James might have said it with a wink, but his uncle was the most perceptive human on earth. "I'll give you a thousand dollars to never say my childhood nickname again."

Not thinking of Holland every free moment was increasingly difficult. Shane only recently lifted from the self-disgust fog for what he did to Cherise and wasn't sure if he was in the right headspace to start anything. He'd be lying to himself if he said he didn't want to be more than friends, but she was frustratingly hard to read. Sometimes, she looked at him from the corner of her eye, and her face lit up. That must mean something. *Right?*

He poured himself a glass of lemonade and internally shook his head. He was in no place to offer her stability. And she needed more than someone who she could banter with. If he painfully swallowed his pride, he really wanted her to find someone amazing. Someone who could give her and Riley everything they deserved—everything he couldn't give her. No matter how much it killed him, she was worth it not to pursue.

Within an hour, the festival filled. The swarm of people laughing while eating cheese curds and deep-fried candy bars was the exact energy he needed to keep up with the insatiable crowd. Who knew this town loved scones *that much?*

"Lemonade, please, and a chocolate chip cookie," a woman in line said. "And what jam do you have?"

Interacting with customers, rather than working in the kitchen, felt different. The pressure to validate his artistic talents vanished, replaced by the need to perform for the crowd. "Blueberry, strawberry, and rhubarb." He motioned toward the shelf. "Would you like a sample?"

He exchanged cash, wrapped frosted pastries in bags, and chatted with folks. When he glanced up, he caught his breath in his throat. He should not have this intense of a reaction when he simply noticed Holland.

She navigated through the crowd, holding Riley's hand with a balloon tied to his wrist. He held a half-eaten, half-smeared-across-his-face, dripping vanilla ice cream cone. And she *glowed.* Seeing her outside of work pants and shirt was a rare treat. Everything about her long, yellow sundress, sunhat, and relaxed smile took this day to the next level.

Holland approached Shane from the side, away from the customers.

"Hey, Riley." Shane set down his pen on the table. "How's your ice cream?"

Vanilla dripped from Riley's face, and he swiped his cheeks with his sleeve. "One, two, three eyes on me."

Holland waved a hand in front of Shane's face. "Nice to see you, too."

"Where's the car-boat?" Riley glanced behind the canopy.

Shane softened at the term. "At the restaurant. I had to drive in a van today."

"No fun." Riley frowned.

"You're right. Not nearly as fun." Shane shifted his focus. Holland in a dress should be illegal. His insides flushed with heat, and he seriously struggled with being respectful and maintaining eye contact. "Having fun?"

"Definitely." She wiggled her index finger.

He obliged at the indication to come closer and dipped his head. The customary coconut shampoo scent, now mixed with sunscreen and ice cream, lingered around her. Goose bumps popped on his arms, and he clasped his hands behind his back to hide his reaction.

"I have some seriously juicy gossip," she whispered and looked over her shoulder. "About the butter."

Shane took a half-step back. "Huh?"

"But I don't want to spread it." She snort-giggled.

He sucked in his cheeks so a laugh wouldn't escape and shook his head. Not that the joke was that funny, but few things in life brought him as much joy as watching Holland cracking herself up. "I'm rating that a six out of ten." He poured water onto a napkin and handed it over for Riley's sugar-coated hands. "Did you guys just get here?"

She swiped the moistened wipe across Riley's fingers. "We've been here since it started. I wanted to get here early, before the crowds got too big. Riley might get a little overstimulated."

James approached behind him, wrapping a paper bag with a ribbon. "Hey, guys."

"One, two, three eyes on me." Riley dangled his other sticky hand out for Holland to clean.

James smiled at Riley. "Are you having fun—"

"Excuse me! Are you out of chocolate chip

120

cookies? I see a sign for chocolate chip cookies, but none on the shelf," a woman with a tote bag the size of a Great Dane said.

"Oh dear, let's hope not." James probably knew only Shane could detect the sarcasm in his tone. "See you later, Riley. Oh, and Holland."

She twisted her mouth. "Very funny."

"What are you wearing?" Shane asked Riley, peering at what looked like a security badge around a necklace with a superhero logo on the front.

"My superhero badge. I'm famous." He held it out for Shane to read.

My Name Is Riley Mulberry and I'm Autistic. If I'm lost, please contact my auntie on the back. Shane flipped it over and saw Holland's name and number.

"Riley's therapist recommended him wearing it at places like this. Just in case…" She swirled a wrist in the air. "We're gonna keep moving. Can you grab me some water? We already finished one off."

"You bet." His hands brushed against hers, and he scolded himself for the warm sensation in his stomach. "Want a cookie for the road? It's on the house."

"I heard that!" James called from the opposite side of the canopy.

Shane hoped his face masked his intention to elongate their time at the booth. He already knew when she turned to leave, he'd be counting the seconds until he saw her again. Which competed against all logic, and wreaked havoc in his brain, knowing full well he was in no position to ask her out. "You guys have plans after the festival tonight?" He tried to sound casual, not hopeful.

"Just the usual."

She either ignored his tone or didn't pick up on the intention of his words: *please ask me to come over.*

She pulled her beeping phone from her purse. "Riley, Grandma's here. Time to go."

Riley shook his head. "Play."

"Riley, no. Not today." She rested her hand on Riley's arm.

He planted a foot into the pavement. "I don't want to go."

"We'll meet Grandma, and then play more games. Time to go." She readjusted her bag and tugged Riley closer. "Good luck today. Keep James under control."

The disappointment he felt watching her walk away was more than what he should have for a co-worker. Or a friend.

She took a bite of the cookie and wiped off the chocolate that dripped on the corner of her lip. The midday sunshine followed her with every soft footstep.

He held his breath, hoping she'd return.

"Holland, huh?" James' voice snapped him out of his daze.

"What about her?" He averted his gaze and replenished the cookies, feeling James' gaze searing into him until he raised his eyes.

James cocked his head and studied Shane's face before he returned to rearranging pies. "She's a special one, isn't she?"

Shane didn't answer him and refused to look up. But he was sure his uncle read the answer on his face: *she sure is.*

Chapter 15
Today's Special: Festival Favorites Seared with a
Flash of Fear

Gina Mulberry was a hard one to miss. As a fan of
bright colors, enormous hats, and screaming loud
designs, Holland could spot her mom through the
crowd of festivalgoers from a block away.

"One, two, three, eyes on me!" Riley picked up his
speed.

Holland reluctantly dropped Riley's hand in the
middle of the crowded festival.

He rushed toward his grandma and wrapped his
arms around her neon-orange dress.

"My sweet boy!" Gina squeezed Riley and kissed
his head before pulling back and pinching his cheeks.
She adjusted her peacock-feathered hat and dug into her
tote. "Grandma brought you a surprise." She pulled a
root beer out of her bag.

At the sight of his favorite beverage, Riley's face
lit up. "Pop! Yummy. Pop, pop, pop, pop."

Holland sighed. "Mom, it's too much sugar right
now."

Gina swooshed her words away with the back of
her wrist. "Holla Kitty, you've got to live a little."

Fingertips pressed into Holland's cheeks with a
little pinch, and Holland groaned.

"You know stress is the number one cause of

premature death, right?" Gina grinned and nudged Holland with her elbow.

Holland rolled her eyes. "That's not actually true."

"A little root beer never hurt anyone. Besides, look! I brought the mini-cans. *See.*" Gina dangled the can in front of Holland's face.

She said it like she deserved a reward for not bringing a two-liter. "That's still too much—"

"Come on, little man. Grandma's got a purse full of dollars that need to be spent on games." She patted her bag and planted a sloppy kiss on Holland's cheek. "I brought your favorite, too, princess." Items clanked together in her purse until she pulled out a small bag of salted chocolates.

Grr. Those *were* her favorite. The crux of their entire relationship was things like this. Good intentions followed by negative consequences. Especially when it came to Riley—missed transitions, lack of routine, not adhering to guidelines. Holland begrudgingly popped a half-melted chocolate in her mouth and welcomed the sugar relief.

"Mimi, the circles." Riley pointed toward the ring toss game. "Please?"

"Absolutely!" Gina grabbed his hand.

Holland breathed through the annoyance at her mom for never checking with her if things were okay. The hum of the crowd surrounded her, and people passed with cotton candy and basketball-sized salted pretzels. Scooting past a couple of teenagers playing ring toss, she found Riley a spot to play.

Gina dug out several dollars and handed them to the man behind the counter, then linked her arm with Holland's.

"What's Dad up to today?" Holland kept her focus on Riley.

He tossed the ring overhead. The metal clinked against the glass and fell. A deep scowl and reddened cheeks accompanied every missed bottle.

"You know him." Gina shrugged. "Tinkering in the shed."

Over and over, Riley threw the rings. One hit the worker, at least a dozen hit the floor, and by some carnival miracle, he landed one on the bottle.

The attendant handed him a prize.

"I won!" He clutched the blue stuffed duck which boasted a human-sized head.

"So proud of you, Bubby." Holland squeezed him and gripped his hand. The crowd grew. Weaving through the people, she dodged elbows, strollers, and running children. Following the hearty, buttery smell of roasting corn on the cob, she led Riley and Gina to a nearby food vendor.

Riley dove into the cob, butter dripping down his face. He didn't seem interested in eating the corn, as he rotated the cob in his hands without biting it and instead licked off the butter and salt.

She continuously patted his face and chest with a napkin until she surrendered to the mess.

"Why didn't you work at the booth this year? Don't you normally work it?" Gina ripped open a second packet of salt and doused her cob.

Holland rested her plate on her lap. "Yeah, but every year I think of how much Riley would love coming here. So this year, I told them I couldn't work."

Gina sunk her teeth into the corn and wiped the corner of her lip with a thumb. "I would've brought him."

Heck to the no. Holland opened her mouth to reply but pivoted and took a sip of pop. The idea of her absentminded mom in a public place with Riley shot her anxiety through the roof. On the rare occasions Gina watched Riley, Holland forbade her from leaving the house, unless her dad was with them. He was no better, but two sets of eyes were better than one. Besides, her father hated festivals except Oktoberfest. Gina wouldn't have been able to drag him here.

Riley handed Holland his cob and waved both hands. "Shane at the booth."

Holland's back straightened.

"Who's Shane?" A devilish grin spread on Gina.

Riley kicked his legs under the bench. "With the car-boat. He's got the big muscles!"

Busted. By my seven-year-old.

"Oh, *reeeeeally*?" Gina sucked in her cheeks. "Tell Grandma more about Shane."

"And I got an icee, and he has a bumpy ride." Riley shrugged. He stood and wiped his greasy palms off on his shirt. "Come on, Mimi."

Holland tossed the cobs into the garbage and dug out baby wipes from her purse. "Let's go look at the pictures. And people are bobbing for apples. We can watch. So fun, Bubby. Tell Grandma about school yesterday. Remember the song you sang?" *Help me out, here. Grandma needs a distraction.*

Riley bent to pick a rock instead and studied its features.

No such luck.

Gina zeroed-in on Holland's face. "Shane, huh?"

"Mom, don't." The very, *very* last thing Holland

wanted was to talk about Shane with her mom. Her feelings were already more complicated than she wished, triple-pancake-stacked on top of her already complex life. And her mother had a way of clawing out information.

"And we make cupcakes!" Riley said.

Holland resisted the urge to shush him.

Gina leaned toward Riley. "He made cupcakes for you all?"

"I'm not doing this," she said to her mom, then tugged Riley toward the apple bobbing.

He wrapped his arm around Holland's elbow and watched people ducking their heads and biting their way to an apple.

"Big muscles, huh?" Gina wiggled her eyebrows and flexed her grandma muscles.

Holland couldn't help but let out a small giggle. "I don't want to talk about it."

"Oh, Hollaberry." Gina weaved her arm between hers, giving her a love tap on the side of her head. "Nothing wrong with a little hanky-panky now and then."

"Mom!" She dropped her head but cracked a smile. Not that she hadn't thought about it. "By the way, no one says that anymore."

"Necking?"

"Seriously, gross. Enough." She laughed and wrapped an arm around Riley's shoulder. "Come on, Bubby. Let's go to the next booth before Grandma has to leave."

For the next hour, Riley putted at a mini-golf stand, threw bean bags into a wooden clown mouth, and watched an artist make animal balloons. When it was time for Gina to leave to meet her travel agent, he gave her a lopsided hug and stomped toward the crowd.

Earlier in the week, the humidity had lifted. The sun now shone like a cozy blanket, and a light breeze carried a whiff of Lake Superior along with fried funnel cakes. The sounds and smells of the festival had to be a lot for Riley, but he didn't ask for his headphones or to leave.

Holland kissed him on the head. "Oof, Bub. You're a sweaty monster." She buried her nose in his neck. "And a stinky one, too!"

He squealed with a giggle.

"We're leaving in ten minutes to go back home."

He jerked her arm. "Mimi, no. Stay. Please, please, please."

She bit the inside of her cheek. Getting out of the house, away from work and therapy, was everything she needed. And seeing Shane working his dimpled magic with the customers was a delicious treat. She didn't want to leave, but Riley had too much sugar and stimulation. His increased arm flailing warned her of an approaching disaster. "Today was fun, Bub. I know. But I'm setting the timer for ten minutes and then—"

"Watch out!"

Flying apples and arms and the hard thump of someone hitting the pavement exploded next to Holland. She stumbled on a rogue apple and grasped at the air to hold her balance.

A kid on roller skates sprawled before her on the sidewalk.

A woman frantically gathering scattered fruit blinked into focus.

"Oh my gosh, are you okay?" Holland crouched

next to the crying, bloodied kid. Another apple rolled by, and she snatched it and set it to the side.

The boy sniffed while holding his knee. "Yeah, I'm okay." He swiped his tears on his sleeve, plopped on his butt, and dabbed at his knees with his wrist.

She dug in her bag for a half-drunk bottle of water and handed it over. "Here, ya go. Why don't you pour this on your leg? It might help."

As he dumped it on his wound, the kid winced. After lying back, he grabbed his cell phone from his pocket. "I'm gonna call my mom."

She stood and dusted her hands. "Riley, time to—" Her neck hair shot upright. "Riley? Riley!"

The surrounding space blurred. She spun, and her voice detached from her body as she screamed Riley's name. *No, no, no, this isn't happening.* He was right here. A minute ago, he was right here! Her heart throbbed in her ears. A hallow, pounding sound drowned out the surrounding voices. "Riley!" Spots filled her vision. She looked at every passing child, parent, and stroller.

Riley was gone.

Chapter 16
Today's special: Baked Rutabaga with Oil Paint Relief

Shane's day at the festival flew by as quickly as the strawberry jams flew off the shelf.

With a massive smile, James created a *Sold Out* sign on his chalkboard for the scones and raspberry preserve. "I never know year to year how many we'll sell. The crowds fluctuate so much." He tossed the liquid chalk marker on the table and pulled up a chair.

Shane lifted a lemonade to his mouth and glanced into the crowd. Holland was speed-trotting toward him with creases cutting across her forehead. Even from a twenty-yard distance, he spotted her wrinkled brows and flushed face. He leapt from his seat and ran to meet her. "Are you okay?"

"Have you seen Riley?" She spat out, breathless. Her glance dashed behind him as she hurried down the pavement.

He jogged to keep up. "No. Is he lost?"

"Riley? Riley!"

The shrill in her shaky voice sent a spike of shivers down his back. He swept his gaze across the crowd. "How long has he been gone?"

"About five minutes. I turned only for a second...Riley!... A woman collided with this kid, and he was bleeding, and apples went everywhere and...Riley!"

Faces blurred. Voices and music blended. "We're looking for a boy, seven years old. Red hair. Superhero T-shirt on." He repeated it to everyone he saw, and every vendor he passed, while matching her frantic steps.

"Riley!" she yelled.

Her voice was louder now with a sharp, guttural tone. Fire ignited in his belly. He gripped her shoulder. "Let's split up. Where did you last see him?"

She clenched her eyes shut for a split second and pushed a palm against her forehead. "Um, the apple bobbing place. Near the...the face painting area...Riley!"

"I'll head that way. You go to the security desk and show them his picture on your phone. We'll find him." His calm voice masked the tension in his stomach. He turned back the way he came, breaking up his speech between calling Riley's name and giving his description to everyone he passed. Balloons, strollers, and shoppers with canvas bags whizzed by him, and tunnel vision took over.

Picking up his pace, he looked under tents, across the street, and in store windows. Each second repeating Riley's description to bystanders strangled him a little more. His heart pounded and thudded in his ears. He turned to the booth with the train paintings he had admired earlier in the day and stopped like he ran into a brick wall.

"Riley!" He sprinted toward him but froze before he reached him. The trapped air in his chest released, and he wiped his forehead off with the back of a palm. Riley looked like he was in a different world. His gaze didn't move from the painting, even when Shane called his name three more times. He stretched to touch Riley's shoulder but retreated. Would that scare him? Without shifting focus, Shane retrieved his phone from his pocket and tapped the screen. "I found him. He's safe."

"Oh my God!"

Holland sounded like she exhaled lungs full of air.

"Where are you? Is he okay? Is he hurt?"

"He looks completely fine." He scanned Riley for any marks or signs of distress. "We're over by the paintings, near the festival entrance on the north side."

"I'm on the total opposite side. I'll be right there. I was so worried...thank you so much...I can't believe this happened. Please stay with him. Don't look away, not for a second."

The shaky relief in her voice simultaneously filled and broke his heart. "I won't. I got him." He slipped the phone into his pocket and approached Riley.

Riley started walking away.

"Hang on there, Riley. We need to wait for Mimi."

"No."

Shane seized Riley's hand with a gentle, yet determined, grip.

Riley ripped it away and made a break toward the exit.

Oh no. Chasing a kid in a public place was unchartered territory. Should he just pick him up and throw him over his shoulder? What were the rules about picking up kids who weren't yours? That seemed unethical. Maybe he should follow Riley until Holland arrived? "How about we look at more pictures while we wait for Mimi?"

Riley balled his fists. "No, no, no, no, no, no, no!"

More than a few people tossed Shane a questioning look, like they were deciding if he was a threat to Riley or a dad who couldn't control their kid.

Riley knocked into an easel.

Shane grabbed it before it hit the ground. "Sorry," he muttered.

The artist shot daggers from under his thick-rimmed glasses.

"We need to move from here." *Before the artist calls the police.*

"No!" Without any warning, Riley spun and took off.

"Riley, stop!" Shane's footsteps pounded against the pavement until he caught Riley by the shoulder and held tight.

Riley's tiny fingers curled, and he swung, his knuckles landing square on Shane's bicep.

Dang, that kid has a left hook.

While waiting, Riley rocked on his toes. His piercing screams ripped through the crowd.

Sweat gathered in the lower part of Shane's back, and his heartbeat pounded in his ears. He looked into the crowd of smiling faces and cotton candy, but no Holland. He rested his palm on Riley's shoulder and cleared his throat to soften his voice. "Mimi's almost here."

Riley's pained, scrunched facial expression didn't change at all.

Maybe he didn't hear Shane? Could he hear anything?

Riley rotated between rocking and hitting Shane.

Shane's air constricted as much as when he looked

for Riley. What if someone thought he was kidnapping him? *Think, Shane, think.* He scanned the festival. James' competitor was one booth away. "Let's get a cookie. Chocolate." He held out his hand. *Please, kid, take it.*

Riley's fist paused midair before he landed another punch, and his rocking slowed.

After an agonizing ten seconds, Riley grabbed Shane's clammy hand and tiptoed a few steps with him toward the booth. Gripping Riley like he was drowning, Shane grabbed two cookies, threw a twenty on the table without waiting for change, and steered them to the lawn. "We're going to sit on the grass and eat the cookie."

Riley's spine stiffened. "I want the cookie."

"First, sit on the grass and then eat the cookie." Shane mimicked how Holland spoke to Riley.

Finally, Riley softened.

Shane led them past a bench and sat. *Please eat slowly.*

Riley scarfed down the cookie, minus a few escaped crumbs that fell onto his shirt.

The kid clearly liked chocolate as much as Holland. And later, maybe, Shane would chuckle about that. But right now, his body was on fire. He swiped his palm across his forehead, his mind turning into a black hole of nothingness. *Now what?* "I see pictures in the sky."

Riley cocked his head.

"Let's lie down and look at cloud pictures." He eased himself onto his back without removing his hand from Riley's. Blades of grass tickled the skin under his shirt, and he thanked the universe the sun had dropped behind the buildings.

Riley's chocolate-smeared face was void of all smiles, and he stood with his feet cemented into the earth.

"What does that look like?" Shane pointed to the cloud and held his breath. And held it a little more.

Riley lowered himself to the grass and put his shoulder next to Shane's.

Thank God.

"A circle."

"Very good." Shane's body slowly sunk into the ground. "What about that one?"

Riley shifted against him and stared. "A boat."

He texted Holland their location and pointed back at the sky. "And that one?"

"Upside-down cow!"

Shane tilted his head. *Huh.* The cloud *did* look like an upside-down cow. After several minutes of naming clouds, Shane's heartbeat slowed.

"Riley!" Holland's voice thundered through the crowd. She sprinted to them with flushed cheeks. "You scared, Mimi! You can't leave Mimi." She collapsed to her knees and hugged him.

Like a boulder-ton of weight had lifted, her chest rose and fell with every breath. She pulled back and shifted his face side-to-side, as if she were inspecting it for damage.

She peered at Shane and dragged trembling hands down her face. "Thank you. I was freaking out."

The quivering mixture of pain and relief in her voice gut-punched him. "I was scared, too."

"Riley elopes...wanders...he doesn't understand the dangers." Her eyebrows drew together. "How did I let this happen?"

The self-blame in her voice was one he knew well.

"I know better than to let him out of my eyesight, even for a second." Her voice shook. "I dropped his hand and…and it could've been so much worse."

Her deflated shoulders, scrunched forehead, and deep frown made her seem older than she was. He needed to take away her guilt and somehow put it on himself. "You're not the first person to have their kid run off. You won't be the last." He reached over and touched the top of her hand, trailing a thumb across her porcelain skin before whipping it back. *Great.* Now, she probably thought he used this moment of weakness to hit on her. "Have you two been here all day?" He cleared his throat.

"Yeah. He was having so much fun and didn't want to leave." She looked at her hand. "So stupid. I had a balloon tied to his wrist this morning, but he wanted to take it off. I do that in places like here for this reason, so I can spot him if he walks off. And I should've made him, Shane. I took the balloon off…I lost him…I just…" Her chin trembled, and her eyes turned glossy. She buried her head in her hands.

"You can't blame yourself. It could've happened to anyone." He reached out to rest his hand on her arm but pulled back before making contact. "You're incredible, seriously. Watching the way you are with him…I would've given anything to feel that kind of support from my parents."

Her shoulders shook.

His need to comfort her overtook any rational thought about maintaining healthy physical boundaries. He pulled her into his chest.

She went stiff for a moment before she crumpled.

The warmth of the sun, her body, and his relief mixed, and he could've stayed enclosed in this blanket for eternity.

"More cookies, Mimi."

Riley's voice interrupted his thoughts.

She shot up and swiped her eyes with the back of her hand.

He felt an inexplicable emptiness.

"Absolutely not," she said with a sharp tone.

"More cookies!" Riley screamed.

She crossed her arms. "No."

Riley's legs pounded the ground like a swimmer kicking away sharks.

"More cookies, more cookies, more cookies!"

"I need to get him out of here. He's gonna lose it." She breathed through her nose. "I knew it was a bad idea to stay here this long. Why didn't I leave when my mom did? I should've listened to my instincts and left then."

Seeing this side of a normally spunky Holland made his gut ache. As someone who did the same, he suspected her internal condemnation had risen to an unholy level.

"Riley. Time to go." She dusted off the seat of her dress and reached for Riley's hands.

He stayed firm. "No."

She lowered herself to pick him up.

His arms flailed, and his feet made direct contact with her shins.

Her cheeks turned red, and she sucked in her lips.

Shane should leave and let her handle this in private and definitely not do what he was thinking of doing. *Don't do it.* "Riley, do you want to paint a picture?" *Too late.* He shot a look at Holland. "If that's all right. Sorry, I should've asked first." *What am I doing?*

Riley halted his movements and stared at Shane. "Paint?"

"Is that okay?" he whispered to Holland.

She glanced between Riley and him and gnawed on her cheek. She checked her watch, looked at Riley again, and nodded.

His stomach flexed and chest relaxed, the mixed physiological response confusing the rest of his organs. Well, he just did that. No turning back now. He shot James a text.

—*Sorry, worst employee ever. I'm leaving with Holland.*—

—*Raising my eyes but remaining silent.*—

—*And Riley! Found him. Going to take them to the studio. I can come back and help clean.*—

—*You're good. Maribelle's teenage sons offered to help in exchange for cookies. It's cheaper than your salary.*—

"Follow me for painting." He tugged on his jeans to shake off the grass clippings, then waved his arms toward the street. "First walk, then paint."

Holland wrapped her cross-body purse around herself and grabbed Riley's hand. She followed Shane down the tiny slope to the pavement.

Shane walked next to them with Riley in the middle when he felt Riley's little fingers push against his palm. He held Riley's hand, and another feeling took over. But he didn't want to dwell on the emotion—he *shouldn't* dwell on it. His heart filled with the longing for a family. *Must be the adrenaline talking.*

When reaching the intersection, she paused. "Stop. Look left, look right, look left again." She moved her head side-to-side. "Safe?"

Riley mimicked her movement. "Safe! No cars."

With each step, Shane's stomach twisted tighter. Holland was about to see *him*—who he was and what he loved. In the last couple of months, he slowly lifted from the fog of doubt on his life decisions, but at this moment, the dark cloud was heavy over his head. He had grown to admire and respect her, and what if she thought his stuff wasn't good? Or thought his dream was ridiculous? He was now less than two blocks away, and his mouth grew parched.

"Where are you taking us?" she asked.

"It's, ah…" He rubbed the back of his neck with his free hand. "Kind of like my second home." No one knew about his sanctuary except James. The place where he fed his soul and *breathed.* He had a flash memory of showing Cherise several pieces years ago. She had known he loved to paint but never seemed interested in looking at his work and instead focused all their conversations on the law.

One night, she finally flipped through the paintings with an uninterested gaze. "They're really nice. This'll help you unwind between cases," she said.

Her words had gutted him.

The cars lined Main Street with busy shoppers and tired festival goers heading home. As he meandered down the sidewalk with Holland and Riley at his side, he was surrounded by the sounds of engines and a few honks. He led them to the left and stopped in front of the studio. "Could you wait here for a second?"

Once inside, he leaned against the door and took a few heavy breaths before he grabbed his in-progress canvas, covered it with a tarp, and set it inside the closet. He shoved the framed photo on his desk upside down and secured it in the drawer. No one needed to see those items. He rested his forehead against the cool, wooden frame of the front door. *Deep breath. You can do this.*

Chapter 17
Today's Special: Open Faced Vulnerability Topped with Rich Artistic Layers

Holland held Riley's hand in front of paper-covered, glass double doors of a massive brick building. Closed blinds covered the windows. Was this place a vacant office? She trusted Shane, but her intuition hinted whatever was inside, he'd worked hard to keep secret. He'd been so talkative with Riley until he'd gotten closer to this building. Once Shane approached the door, he went silent, his face turned pale, and he rubbed the back of his neck. What was behind these walls that changed his demeanor so much? Her throat turned sticky, and she firmed her grip on Riley's hand.

The door opened with a rosy-cheeked Shane behind it, who looked at her only for a split second, before he faced Riley.

"Ready to paint?" He held out his hand for Riley.

Holland stood in silence as she looked around the space. What was this place? The scent reached her first—a warm, inviting smell wafted in the air, almost like clay dough mixed with oil and lavender. The room was the size of a coffee shop and had a couch, a couple of chairs, and several tables. A huge, rustic wood shelf bolted against the wall held dozens of paint tubes and brushes, and thick paper lined the shelves. Canvases in various stages of completion covered the walls.

Was this an art museum? An art classroom? She stepped into the well-lit room and was at a loss for words. Her heart had finally stopped racing from losing Riley. But now she was in an unfamiliar, yet beautiful, place and didn't know how Riley would react to his new environment.

"All right, let's set you up." Shane, still holding Riley's hand, escorted him to a table. "What are your favorite colors?"

"Purple! Purple, purple, and purple." Riley clapped. "And blue and green and orange."

Shane squeezed colors onto the palette. "Those are my favorites, too. All artists wear aprons. Just like chefs." He wrapped a smock around Riley. "Let me lower the height on this chair so your feet touch the floor."

Holland grabbed Riley's bright-red chewing necklace from her bag. "Do you want your gum-gum?"

"Yep," Riley said.

Once she placed the chewable necklace around Riley's neck, she watched as he popped it into his mouth and gnawed on it like candy. Riley had a massively stimulating day, and even though he couldn't articulate it, his body craved downtime.

Several of the hanging paintings captivated Holland. How did someone create such masterpieces? The landscapes and portraits were so detailed they looked like photographs. An oil painting of a woman— a grandma, maybe, with curly, gray hair and soft wrinkles—hung in front of Holland. The woman was laughing with her arms spread, and a smiling child in front of her swung on a swing. Every strand of hair was highlighted, every wood grain from the swing set articulated. Holland moved her head to the side and focused on the light from the grandma's eyes. How does someone paint joy? The corner had a signature. *S. Blackwood. No way.*

Shane approached from behind.

Her skin prickled. She slowly ripped her gaze from the painting. "Are these yours? Did you paint these?" Unlike anyone she had met, Shane reeked of confidence and usually stood straight with his chest out, his shoulders back, and a smirk. But now, he shoved his hands in his pockets and stared at the floor before pulling his head up, his throat bobbing with a heavy swallow.

"Yeah," he said.

"I had no idea you painted." Her brain fired off mixed messages. Weren't artists sensitive, emotionally intelligent, and in tune with the environment? Granted, she'd become friends with him after he shed his cranky exterior. *But this?* Painting beautiful portraits was a whole new level. Slowly, his intense attention to detail for plate presentation made sense. "They're incredible. Absolutely breathtaking."

"Yeah?" The rigidness in his chest released, and he exhaled. "Thanks."

She leaned back for a better look at the woman in the painting. "I feel like I'm right there with them. The painting's beautiful."

A smile crossed his lips. "I painted this from an old photograph of me and my grandma."

"That's you?" She leaned closer, the warmth in her heart building at a slow but steady rate. "Cute kid."

His eyes softened around the edges with something deeper brewing, like he was fighting back a blush. She studied the wooded landscape. "I don't understand how you captured light this way. I can't get over the details. The painting is so realistic I can almost hear the waterfall. Does it sound weird I feel like I can hear something in a painting?"

"Not at all." He inched toward her with a smile and touched the outside of the rustic wooden frame. "It's actually a huge compliment."

She glanced at Riley.

He chomped on his necklace while painting long, broad strokes.

She circled the room. Joy was the central theme of the paintings—nothing dark, wild, bright, or abstract, which surprised her. The soft palettes featured landscapes or faces, wrapping her in an almost familial hug.

The hug from earlier. *Uff.* How did he know what she needed when she needed it? An hour ago, when she was angry with herself about losing Riley, Shane's embrace was everything she craved. Everything she needed at that moment. His strong, powerful arms held mystical powers, making her fears and self-doubt fade. She couldn't remember the last time she felt so...*safe.* And if the timing was different, and her life was different, she would've begged him not to let go. "You're seriously gifted." She focused back on the wall. "I'm completely blown away."

He smiled but remained silent and turned to look at Riley.

Riley circled his brush in the purple color and swiped it across the paper.

"How many times do I need to thank you for everything today?" Holland asked.

He shrugged. "It was nothing."

"Don't say that. It was everything." She stopped herself from saying anything more, and a heaviness built in her chest. When he held her on the grass, something shifted. The walls between them slowly disintegrated for weeks, but his touch was different—comforting but electric. More than friends?

Stop it. Now was not the time to decipher why, after five years of being happily single, one hug sent her into a tailspin. Her life was just too much. No matter how comfortable he made her feel, he was not the calm to the chaos. Altering her focus, she faced the next wall, and her breath caught at an ocean scene. "Oh my." She wanted to touch it but refrained. The painting looked so *real.* "The ocean water against the horizon...so beautiful. It's like I'm literally standing in a different world. I swear if I had an ocean sound on my headphones, I'd be right there." She looked at him. Was he blushing? "Reminds me of Maui."

The corners of his lips turned up. "That's amazing. Maui inspired the work."

"What?" Her chest lifted. "Maui's my happy place. I visited there once years ago, and it totally became my dream home. But with Riley and things, Maui evolved into my dream vacation." She tilted her head and continued studying the colors.

He cleared his throat. "Ah, do you want something to drink? I've got cold water and probably warm pop in the back."

"Tempting choices." She grinned. "Water's great."

He grabbed two water bottles from the mini-fridge, handed her one, and then checked on Riley. "Wow, great work! Let me grab a little more purple."

"Monster train!" Riley cheered and swirled the colors.

"It's a perfect monster train." Shane motioned Holland toward the couch. "What's your favorite part about Maui?"

She sank into the squishy cushions and pulled a pillow onto her lap. "Everything—the tropical landscaping, the white beaches, the bluest ocean I'd ever seen. Oh, the smell. The combo of the saltwater and flowers in the air…I swear I walked into paradise." She cracked open the water bottle. "Oh! And the food."

"So, basically, you love everything about Maui." He lowered himself into a wooden chair next to the couch. "What's your favorite dish?"

"Without a doubt, macadamia nut pancakes with coconut syrup. Eat. Die. Go to heaven." She licked her lips and rolled her eyes. "For years, I had this fantasy I'd move there and open a little jewelry stand."

"You make jewelry?" He lifted his eyebrows. "I'd love to see it sometime."

A tingle flickered in her belly. "Sure. I mean, my pieces are nowhere near what you do." She waved her hands at the wall. "I used to dream I'd wake up in my tiny hut right off the water, eat some pancakes, and sell a few necklaces on the beach to tourists. Maybe fish in the evening."

He took a swig of water and brushed the droplet off his lip with a thumb. "That sounds incredible."

"Things changed, obviously." She glanced at Riley. "But I wouldn't change anything for the world."

He picked at the label on his bottle. "But you still make jewelry?"

"I make jewelry!" Riley shifted his gaze as paint

globs plopped on the desk. He poked at it with his fingertip. "Necklaces and bracelets and necklaces and bracelets."

"You sure do, Bubby." She beamed. "Riley loves making them with me, too."

Shane stood and grabbed a towel. He wiped Riley's fingertips with it, then cleaned the spatters off the desk.

Her insides warmed. "I mostly do beads or sea glass work. I used to be really into it. My free time still goes to creating, but now I have less availability."

He returned to the couch. "Is creating pieces relaxing? Or was it a way to get to Hawaii?"

Hmmm. She thought this over. "A combination of both, I guess. Making jewelry fed into the dream of moving there. But now, I use the time to relax." Glancing between Riley and Shane, she filled with a sense of contentment. A few hours ago, she would have never thought she'd be sitting in this beautiful space chatting with Shane while Riley painted.

Shane twisted the towel in his hands. "Same. I'm most relaxed when I create."

"And you're not yelling at servers." She grinned.

"Hey! I stopped that weeks ago." He laid his arm on the back of the couch.

She swore he inched closer. The bottle in her hands accumulated moisture, and she placed it on the floor. "Are you grateful for your talent?"

He sucked on the side of his cheek. "Hmm. I guess I never thought of the gratitude part of it." He picked at the water bottle label. "Yeah, I am. Even if it created issues in my family."

"How could your talent create issues with your family?"

147

He abruptly stood like he'd been burnt and straightened his jean legs. "I'll check if Riley needs more paint," he said.

The sudden shift in his demeanor made her stomach sink. She studied his back, as if that would clarify why he shut down so quickly. Blinking back the sense of rejection—which was ridiculous because they were just friends—she stood and joined them.

Chapter 18
Today's Special: Gratitude Pie Topped with a Nutty Surprise

Holland woke after a fitful night's sleep, the fifth one in a row after the festival. The fear of Riley wandering off drummed up sweat-inducing nightmares. He couldn't understand the dangers of leaving her side. He didn't have the natural fear of strangers other kids did, remember he needed to look both ways while crossing a street, or that water could be fatal. And she failed at keeping him close.

She stepped into the shower. Her thoughts moved to Shane and what slowly churned between them since the day she met him—how her heart palpitated when he entered a room, the way her skin sparked when she made physical contact, and her inability to not laugh at their text exchanges. As warm as he made her feel, she turned cold, thinking of being more than friends. She couldn't manage a relationship. Depending on the morning she and Riley had, sometimes she could barely get to work on time. Besides, what could she possibly offer him? A smile with a truckload of baggage?

Getting dressed, she looked at the clock—six fifty-five a.m. Today, she had a meeting with the school about pretend play curriculum. She needed to work with Riley more at home to elevate his social skills. Amy told her Riley's intolerance for sharing had grown. Being an only child, he had free rein at home, meaning play-share practice fell to the bottom of the list. When she read the meeting agenda last week, she had swallowed back a bitter taste. Last week, she forgot twice to work on fine motor skills and ran out of time practicing his breathing exercises. She had to figure out a plan tonight so she didn't keep failing him.

She buttoned her shirt and quietly tiptoed down the hall to wake Riley. He was such a good sleeper. Leaning against the doorframe the same way she did most mornings, she marveled at the angelic creature.

A rosy-faced Riley was on his back with an arm over his head, his chest rising quietly with each breath.

He was her *everything.* "Time to wake up, sunshine."

Beneath the weighted blanket, he rustled and gave her a sleepy smile. "One, two, three, eyes on me."

The sun peeked through the window, and she crawled into his bed. "Setting the timer. Then we get dressed, eat, and go to school." Five minutes was the sweet spot for cuddle time in the morning before life began. The best part of her day when she soaked in the snuggles and mentally reviewed a daily gratitude list. Today's list: Riley still has his cute, chubby cheeks, her landlord had not raised the rent in four years, the heat index broke, a buy-one, get-one ice cream coupon arrived in the mail, and Shane. The timer went off, cutting through her thoughts. She blinked and shook her head. "Time to get dressed."

Riley's lower lip curled down. "Video."

"Get dressed first, then video."

Riley stared for a few seconds, then kicked off the covers. "Okay."

Years ago, when Amy suggested Holland combine an unwanted task, like getting dressed, with a desired activity, like screen time, their life improved dramatically. She even used this trick for herself—dishes first, then ice cream. Because if she had the ice cream first, a rom-com movie would be second, and she'd leave dishes in the sink until the next day.

An hour later, as she flew by signposts and lights on the way to Riley's therapy session, Holland let her mind wander back to when Shane met Riley and gave them a ride. Whatever hesitation Shane had that first day with Riley seemed to melt shortly after. Shane mentioned he'd never been around anyone with autism spectrum disorder, but he interacted with Riley with such ease that Holland could've sworn he had a family member with ASD. And her gratitude bucket overflowed that he kept Riley calm at the festival, which made the conflicting feelings more intense. Because not only was Shane seemingly not scared off by her and Riley, he genuinely appeared to enjoy them.

She arrived at the school with Riley and escorted him up the stairs.

Amy was waiting at the door of her private therapy room. "Good morning. Both of you have a seat." She pointed to a small table that held Riley's favorite toy—kinetic sand. "Riley, show Mimi how you build a sandcastle. I'll set the timer for two minutes."

"Sandcastle!" He beamed as he dove into the sandbox, dragging his rake across the sand before letting it squish through his fingers. He molded it into a ball, and a few minutes later, the timer buzzed.

"Great job." Amy silenced the buzzer. "The timer went off, which means it's my turn to play."

He stopped squishing and straightened his spine but didn't back away.

"Riley." Amy placed her hands in her lap. "You may look at a book in the quiet corner or play with trains until it's your turn again."

Waiting for Riley's response, Holland held her breath.

He clapped his hands and skipped to the train table.

Holland exhaled. Last year, he would've dragged his feet when leaving his preferred toy. *This child is incredible.*

For ten minutes, Amy practiced interval play with Riley before free-choice time. After watching him connect the wooden tracks, she faced Holland. "Riley's doing great after a couple of regressions last week. We'll keep stretching and growing him. How's share play going at home?"

The familiar tightness in Holland's chest intensified. There was always *so much*—timers, schedules, certain foods, therapy, school. As if Amy could read her mind, she laid a warm hand on Holland's forearm.

"I see your dedication, and I know you've been doing your very best," Amy said. "His progression is remarkable. You've got this."

Holland swallowed. She wasn't so sure. But she'd keep trying.

After the weekly meeting wrapped, she drove toward work and transitioned her thoughts from Riley to Shane. A solid friend boundary line with him blurred. Sometimes he seemed interested, but those times fluctuated, leaving her heart and head in a hot mess.

Stop it. Shane and I together is unrealistic. He was a talented, gorgeous, and sweet college graduate—even though he hid that part of his personality. She was a single parent with a high school education, wearing the same clothes for the last decade. He deserved someone sophisticated and successful.

She pulled into the parking lot ten minutes early and checked her social media. The devil and angel on her shoulder played a fierce game of tug-of-war. *Don't do it. But really, who's it hurting?* "Gah," she muttered and pulled up Shane's profile.

He didn't seem to use social media during the last few years. She swiped through pictures of coffee mugs, a sunrise over a lake, and him in a graduation gown. She scrolled through a few more when her breath caught in her throat. Shane stood behind a woman, his palms flat against her hips, both beaming into the camera. She took about two seconds to figure out this was an ex-girlfriend. And she was *stunning*—a tall brunette who was wearing the heck out of a pencil skirt with a crisply-ironed shirt. Everything about her was so...polished.

She pulled down her rearview mirror, poked a few rogue flyaway hairs back into her braid, and lathered on pomegranate-tinted lip balm. Showing up to work with makeup or perfume would be out of character, but after seeing that photo, she had the urge to step up her game. *What am I doing?* She snatched the apron from her passenger seat and bolted to the kitchen.

Shane was at the prep table, whistling.

Whistling?

"Morning." He locked his ocean-eyed gaze with hers.

She cursed her pulse for thumping so wildly. "Morning." She inspected the massive pile of vegetables laid out on the table. "What time did you start today? You look like you're almost done with prep work, and it's not even ten."

He tossed the end of a carrot into the compost. "Mateo and I cheated on James and went for the early-bird breakfast at Grummie's."

"Oh, no, you didn't. Mateo's gonna be sleeping on your couch if James finds out. He hates the owner of the restaurant. He's convinced he was the one who wrote the anonymous negative review online."

"I know, but he has better biscuits and gravy, and so far, I can't replicate the recipe." He plucked the next carrot from the batch. "But if you tell James, I'll deny it until the day I die."

She pulled the strings on her apron tight around her waist and headed toward the door when she pivoted. "Oh, I forgot. Quick question."

He lifted his head. "What's up?"

"What do you call a guy with no shins?"

He stopped mid-peel. "What?"

"Tony." She slapped a hand against her thigh. "Get it? Toe. Knee."

He cracked a grin and shook his head. "Hey, Holland?"

"Yeah?"

"Nine out of ten."

Satisfied, she shuffled to the locker area as her stomach flipped. She really needed to pull herself together, but having a silly crush was pretty delicious. *It'll fade. Someday.*

"I don't understand how you do it." Amanda

opened her locker door and inspected her hair in the mirror.

"Do what?" Holland pulled out her order-taking supplies.

"You're like the grumpy whisperer."

"What does that even mean?" Holland scribbled in her order pad, confirming each of her pens had enough ink.

"You turned Mr. Grumpy into Mr. Loveable." Amanda brushed her bangs to the side and applied a coat of lip balm. "I even saw him smile at someone. *Smile*, Holland—with teeth. I didn't even know he had teeth."

"Oh my gosh, stop." She glanced over at Shane. Her gaze met his for a moment before she diverted her attention back to Amanda. "Maybe we didn't give him enough credit."

Amanda slammed the locker door shut. "Maybe."

A shift in Shane occurred since he first started at the restaurant, but Holland refused to take the credit. Nerves probably overtook him initially, and now, those nerves had settled. Holland strolled to the hostess stand with Amanda. While waiting for tables, she pinched Amanda's forearm. "I hate you forever."

Amanda poked her in the side. "What did I do now?"

"You and Lauren are going on vacation this weekend, leaving me hanging for the reunion."

"No chance in h-e-double hockey sticks you could force me to go to that vomit-fest." Amanda gurgled her throat with a fake gagging sound. "I'm serious. You know they won't take attendance, right? I don't understand why you're going." She reached for the stack of menus. "You won't wind up in the principal's office like when you skipped class to maintain your thumb war reigning championship."

"Pride is pride. No way was I giving up my title to Derek Dingmen." Holland grabbed a towel to help clean the menus. "Erica Ellens DM'd me last night and said she's flying in for the reunion."

"Erica? From the yearbook committee? Love that girl. Haven't seen her in forever." Amanda slumped against the table with a frown. "Darn. Erica being there almost makes me want to stay back from vacation."

Erica was one of the few people Holland still spoke to from high school. Tight schedules meant Holland could only see her at the reunion—the only reason she was dragging herself to her living nightmare. "My parents begged to take Riley for the entire weekend."

Amanda pulled out the next menu. "Yikes. How do you feel about that?"

"Mixed emotions, honestly. I need a break. But it might take two weeks to get him back into a routine." Holland reached for the paper towels and spray. "They promised to stick to the schedule and use the timer, so I should probably just let it go."

She grinned. "And make sure they have Amy on speed dial."

"For sure." Holland chuckled. "What are the specials today?"

Amanda cocked her head. "Wait. You don't know?"

"What do you mean?" Holland's eyebrows scrunched. "We don't keep the same specials every Friday."

"Wow. I really thought you knew." Amanda set her

towel on the counter. "I thought the menu was a joke at first, like you made James or Shane do it."

Holland shook her head. "Huh?"

She jutted her head toward the daily menu stand. "Go look."

Holland dashed to the lobby and took several moments to absorb the words.

TODAY'S MENU
Holland Special
Macadamia nut pancakes
Topped with whipped cream, coconut shavings
Served with your choice of coconut or maple syrup
Side of eggs and ham

She blinked multiple times, then reread the menu. Shane remembered her favorite meal from Maui and turned it into the daily special? A flock of butterflies in her belly set off in full flight. She strolled back into the kitchen with her lip caught between her teeth. "I've never been more excited for my lunch break."

Dimples appeared on both of Shane's cheeks. "The pressure's on to perform."

She scratched at her apron with a thumb as her insides melted. "You know, there's a rumor on the street about you."

"Oh yeah." He rested the spatula into a bowl. "What's that?"

"Sounds like you've been smiling at co-workers this week."

He flinched with a wide grin. "Yikes. I don't want people to know I have a heart. It'll ruin my cover."

She stepped onto a landmine of zings and zaps. He was just being friendly, *right?* Maybe this was recipe testing? Or was this something more? She leaned in, close enough that his citrus scent met her nose. "It'll be our little secret."

****

After Holland's shift, she read a message from her mom letting her know they'd picked up Riley from school. With rare time to herself, she took the long way home. She drove by Lake Superior with her windows down, and the smell of the lake water permeated her car. She almost asked Shane for a ride so she could feel the sun on her skin while riding with the top down, but she didn't. He'd already done enough this week.

She returned home, and her house was eerily quiet. Even though the time was barely after seven p.m., she eased into pajama pants and grabbed her leftover box. Yep, this was her third serving of pancakes today. Nope, she didn't feel bad about it. Shane captured the authenticity of pancakes from Hawaii, and her toes practically curled with every bite.

Containers of beads, gems, glue, and wires topped the coffee table. The urge to create itched at her fingertips. She had a quiet house, time on her hands, and a pile of leftover macadamia nut pancakes. Smiling, she reached for her cell and snapped a photo to send to Shane.

—*If I fall over with a heart attack, tell the paramedics this is my third serving of macadamia nut pancakes today.*—

—*So, you're on your ninth pancake?*—

—*Nine sounds like a lot. Over-indulgent. Someone not in control of their sugar intake. Let's say the third round of three. That sounds nicer.*—

—*Did you remember to bring home the syrup?*—

She grinned at the message, unable to read his tone.

She typed out her response.

—*What do you think this is? Amateur hour? Of course, I did.*—

—*Did you share any with Riley?*—

—*He's at my parents for the weekend.*—

Several minutes passed before a message popped up.

—*What does an evening alone for Holland look like? Bar-hopping? Shaking down dudes playing nine-ball? Texas Hold 'Em poker?*—

—*Do I really seem that exciting? I'm sitting on my floor in my PJs, about to throw on a sappy but satisfying romance movie, eat pancakes, and make a necklace.*—

—*Movie, food, and a creative outlet. Sounds like a perfect evening.*—

She hovered her thumbs over the phone. *Don't do it. Do it! Ack.* Why was she texting him? Because she was lonely?

—*If you want to come over and join me, you're welcome to. I'll save you a pancake.*—

The minutes clicked by, each one more excruciating than the last. Finally, his name flashed on her screen.

—*Thanks for the offer. I'll have to pass.*—

In a snap, her heart fell into her stomach, and the pancakes looked so unappetizing that she tossed them to the side.

Chapter 19
Today's Special: Self-Doubt Soufflé and a Glass of
White Wine Wisdom

I'll be right there. Shane wanted to say that to Holland's text inviting him over. But he didn't. He tossed his phone to the side and drug his hands down his face, ignoring the paint he had added to the brush earlier when Holland first texted. Thoughts of her had preoccupied him since he first met her, but now, she assumed world domination of his mind after he brought her to his studio. He couldn't remember ever feeling as vulnerable as he did when she observed his artwork. Her interest in his work filled a piece of him he'd been missing for months or maybe even years. He felt *validated.* For the first time since leaving law school, he tasted closure.

After that day, a new realization hit him. If his heart skipped like this after that moment, what would happen if he completely opened himself up? He'd fall in love, for sure. And his commitment wouldn't be fair to either her or Riley until he was confident he could be the person they deserved.

He dipped the drying magenta-filled brush in water to rehydrate and tapped it against the glass. Could he ever be what Holland needed? His dad spent a lifetime pounding into his head that Shane had to follow in his footsteps—pass the bar by twenty-eight, become a partner by thirty-five, and take over the family law firm by forty. Stability and financial security make a good husband. Living with your uncle and spending your free time chasing a dream, not so much.

Re-angling the framed photo on his desk allowed him to study the details from a different side. The sharp, broad strokes against the canvas turned fuzzy. What if the gallery failed? After using most of his savings to pay for the lease, he couldn't stay open if he didn't sell any pieces. His salary at the café was not nearly enough to support a family. The idea of finishing law school and becoming a lawyer made him sick. He had zero options. And Holland and Riley deserved a man with options.

Focus vanished. The wooden handle of the brush tapped against his restless legs. He paced the studio, took gratuitous sips of water, and ran a finger along the framed edge of a painting when his phone rang. His heart raced. He had zero willpower. If he read another message from Holland asking him to come over, he'd leave mid-paint stroke and drive directly to her place.

He snatched the phone off the desk, and his gut dropped. Cherise. *Again.* He declined the call. "Back to work," he muttered to the canvas. Working his flat brush in yellow number five, he refocused. Short, delicate swipes slid across the canvas. Slowly, the form took shape.

A knock from outside made his heart jump. *Holland?* He put his mouth to the door. "Who is it?"

"Your favorite uncle."

"You're my only uncle." He flicked his gaze to the desk. "Give me one sec." He flipped over the framed picture and faced the painting to the wall before he opened the door.

James held up a bottle of wine and two glasses. "Care to indulge?"

"No. But you're more than welcome to." He opened the door wider and stepped back.

"Oh, thank God." James dropped his shoulders and beelined for the couch. "My stress level is at an all-time high."

Shane wiped his hands on a rag and tossed it onto the counter. He grabbed a water bottle from the cooler and pushed the chair from the desk against the sofa. "You know alcohol will make it worse, right?"

"Yep." James pulled a wine opener from his back pocket. "Tomorrow, at the reunion catering gig, Joey and Kianna will be assisting, and Tanner will be the lead. You'll be the runner."

"Wait, I thought Kianna was the lead and Tanner was the runner." Shane narrowed his eyes. "You could've texted me these changes. So, why are you really here?"

"Nothing gets past you, huh?"

"You have the worst tells. Painfully obvious. Promise me you'll never go to Vegas."

James poured a glass and sunk into his seat. "Fine. I need to know how you're doing. Sometimes I think good, sometimes I think not good, sometimes I think it's none of my business."

"All the above." Shane settled into the chair and exhaled.

James folded his eyebrows. "Talk to me."

Multiple thoughts swirled, and Shane struggled to articulate them. He should pretend to prep for a case and write everything down. Draft a timeline of when his feelings shifted so drastically of wanting to be around Holland all the time mixed with the fear of being around her. He needed a proper verdict. At the bare minimum, he needed to reach a settlement so he could focus. Because now, his concentration cracked, and it threw his plans into mayhem. "How did you know you and Mateo were meant for each other?"

James halted his sip and lowered his drink. "Wow. That's not what I thought you'd say. I can't believe you're asking me for love advice."

"Now you made it weird. Never mind."

"Sorry, sorry. No, let's do this." He stared at a fall-themed woodsy painting on the wall for several moments before speaking. "When we were dating in grad school, Mateo always supported me. We had so many plans. I'd earn my Ph.D. and get a fellowship at Berkley or Stanford. He'd finish his MBA and become a financial planner for one of the big firms. But then I became miserable and told him I wanted to drop out and open a restaurant in Duluth. He told me to do it. He did this without a hint I'd disappointed him, or failed, or anything."

Shane tugged on the edges of his smock. "Did you feel bad, like he gave up his dreams for you?"

"I asked him that question, and he said his dream wasn't where he worked. His dream was marriage and sharing a life—whether that was in LA, Minneapolis, or Duluth. Didn't matter as long as we were together."

This detail pushed Shane's admiration of Mateo to a new level. He rocked back on his chair and let the words settle. "What about the money? Did you worry you were giving up a more financially stable lifestyle?"

James rubbed the top of his head. "Part of me did.

But I knew if I believed in myself only half as much as he did, then I'd make my place a success. And I did. I make more here than I ever would as a professor. But the money's inconsequential. In terms of happiness, my choice paid back in dividends."

Happiness. Joy. No longer a foreign concept.

"You can tell me to buzz off, but I gotta ask." James clicked his finger against the glass stem. "Were you happy with Cherise?"

Shane marinated on the question. Memories of studying over pizza, late-night TV, and the law library flashed by, along with pictures of screaming matches and a feeling of emptiness. "For years, I wasn't *unhappy*, per se. We lacked joy, I guess." He stopped rocking on the chair and stared at his hands. "We were so focused on school. Every conversation surrounded the law, grades, or applications. Nothing was in the present." He never created, enjoyed nature, or *laughed* alongside Cherise. After nearly a decade as a couple, complacency turned into golden handcuffs. Staying together was easier than breaking up.

"That makes sense." James sipped the wine. "Does your mom ever talk about Grandpa?"

Shane shrugged. "Not really. I don't remember a lot about him."

"Do you remember him smiling?"

Shane reached into his memory bank and came up blank. "I remember Grandma smiling, but not him."

James nodded. "He was a great provider. Your mom and I had everything we needed, materialistically. But you know what we didn't have? Laughter. Family game nights. Our dad at home for dinner. A dad who wasn't always stressed out." Drumming his fingers on the couch, he studied the wall. "They didn't talk about anxiety the way they do now. He concentrated so much on providing that he worked sixty-to-seventy hours a week. He was never happy. We were never happy and he died before he reached sixty."

The words' heaviness lingered. What James said made sense, of course. Shane didn't want to be the type of dad who wasn't present for his kids. But he also wanted to give them everything. "What happened was awful, but in a sick sort of way, I get it. Being a good partner is all about providing security and stability, right?"

James cocked his head to the side and narrowed his eyes. "Maybe. But that's not synonymous with finances." His gaze drifted, and several moments of silence passed. "With my dad, I always felt like a burden. I think your mom did, too, like we caused his anxiety. He worked so hard to give us all these things."

Remaining silent, Shane twisted and untwisted the bottle cap.

James leaned forward. "I know it's tough with your mom right now, but she's doing what she thinks is best. I'm confident she'll come around."

"Maybe." He crossed his arms and tapped his fingers against his biceps, wondering how two people raised by the same people could be so vastly different. "Our last text exchange was that my dad talked to the dean at the law school. Seriously, James, I'll be thirty in a few years—and they're calling the school." At some point, he'd need to confront his parents and have a genuine conversation. When he told them he was dropping out, they blamed it on stress and anxiety and ignored the simple truth—he did not want to be a lawyer, and art made him happy.

James topped off the wine. "No doubt about the fact they've overstepped on occasion."

Shane chuckled. "Observation of the century. Did you know when I was a kid my dad had this little plaque that said *Shane Blackwood, Super Junior Partner*, on the bottom? He kept it on the small desk in his office. They always expected me to be a lawyer." Maybe they were right—his stomach knotted at the thought of his shop failing. "I don't know…maybe I didn't give my parents enough time to sit with my decision." He spent over a year contemplating and processing his choices. His parents had less than ten minutes before he stormed out of the house because they didn't instantly support him.

"Is that what you think?"

"I honestly don't know." Shane shrugged. "I hope I did the right thing."

James twirled the wine in the glass. "In ten years from now, will you regret doing it or not doing it?"

How did James know the exact questions to ask to make his brain twist even harder? "I think I made the right decision to move here."

"I *know* you made the right decision. You're lighter. Smiling more. Happier."

He flicked his fingers against the bottom of the chair. "I have to smile 'cause you told me I scared the staff."

"True." James laughed. "Proud of you, kid."

James might be right. Before moving to Duluth, he didn't remember the last time he smiled out of happiness—not the need to schmooze. Since his arrival, he had smiled more than in the last several years combined. The reason why wasn't lost.

"So, you want to talk about Holland?"

Seriously, does he read minds? "Why would I want to talk about her?"

James dipped his chin. "You think you're clever, but I was with you when you were born."

"Is that true?"

"No, but it makes for a better story." James set the glass on the side table. "Your relationships are none of my business, but you aren't fooling me. I mean, The Holland Special? Macadamia nuts pancakes. Really?"

Heat flushed his cheeks. "Maybe I'm planning on doing that with all the staff."

"Bull." He slapped his palms on his knee with a grin. "I'm not one to judge, and the customers loved it. You're obviously fond of her, and I don't blame you. She's pretty special."

Of course, she was. But he didn't want to admit it out loud. He pulled in a breath. "Well, my feelings don't matter, anyway. Timing isn't good."

"Timing?" James cocked his head. "What does that mean? Because of Riley?"

"What? No. Not at all. He'd be a bonus. Timing because of *me*." He wrapped his fingers around the edge of the chair. "I'm a law school dropout living above my uncle's garage. Not the most attractive offer for a woman." Saying the words was a tiny knife slice in his gut. Maybe next year, if by some miracle she was still single and the gallery was successful, then he'd ask her out. Until then, he had to keep her at an arm's distance.

James crossed his arms. "You aren't giving her much credit, are you?"

167

"Wait, what?" Shane snapped up his head. "No, I'm saying she deserves more than I've got."

"Nope. You're reducing her to someone who only sees value in dollars, which is unfair. Not to mention inaccurate. I've known Holland for a decade. Before Riley, she always lived a frugal life so she could travel and make jewelry." James laid a hand on Shane's forearm. "Listen, kid. You're kind, smart, and gifted. You look like you belong in a men's cologne commercial, for God's sake. And even though you try to hide it, you have more emotional intelligence in your pinky than most men have in their bodies. Stop reducing yourself and her to a paycheck."

Shane stiffened his spine. He never meant to categorize Holland as someone who could only be happy if he made a certain amount of money. The desire to earn funneled into an overall feeling of wanting to take care of her. "There's another piece to this." Shane twitched his fingers. He stood and snatched a dry paintbrush from his desk to twirl.

James sat back. "Riley."

Shane nodded.

"I'm not gonna lie. It'd be challenging. He's a great kid." James scratched at his chin. "But being in a relationship with someone with a child with exceptional needs adds a layer of complexity."

"Honestly, the diagnosis isn't what I'm worried about." Shane's voice was quieter than he intended. He rapped the paintbrush against his thigh. "My apprehension runs deeper."

James furrowed his brow. "What is it?"

He didn't want to say. Revealing his reasons made everything real, and he wasn't sure if he was ready for real. "If we get together and things don't work out…." His mouth was dry, and he could barely formulate the next sentence. "My heart gets broken twice."

Chapter 20
Today's Special: Glitter Gooseberry Pie with Roasted Nostalgic Nuts

Shane didn't mind picking up the extra catering shift for the high school reunion. The last he heard, Holland would be here tonight, and his stomach coiled in anticipation. Last night, he stared at the cracked ceiling fan above his bed for hours and stewed on his conversation with James. His uncle knew lots of things, but that didn't mean he was an expert on Holland's needs or wants.

The crew—Joey, Tanner, and Kianna—trudged their catering supplies to the door.

Shane pushed a metal cart up the ramp and clamped the brake when he reached the top. "Big night tonight, guys. Need a pep talk?" Shane tugged on his caterer jacket.

Kianna squinted. "I can't tell if you're serious or joking. Since when do you give pep talks?"

Shane shrugged. "I just thought—"

"Dude." Joey readjusted the duffle bag of utensils on his shoulder. "Not sure what's gotten into you. I kind of liked cranky Shane. This new guy has me feeling a little squirrely."

Shane chuckled and grabbed the door handle. "Okay, fine. I'll be sure to drop a few swear words to keep everything in alignment."

A reunion coordinator approached Shane and the team with a clipboard, a checkered tie that looked like it was choking him, and a nervous smile.

"Good, finally you're here." The man frowned.

Shane checked his watch. He and the team were ten minutes early.

"I can't have one more thing go wrong today. Someone spilled a bucket of glitter all over the gym floor. Glitter! Do you have any idea how hard that is to clean? It's like secondhand smoke—it seeps in everywhere. My clothes are going to be sparkling all night. I'll be washing it out of my hair for a month." The coordinator waved for the team to follow him.

Shane tried to keep up with both the coordinator's words and steps.

"The bartender called in sick, and supposedly they'll send a replacement." The man's heeled loafers clicked against the hallway floor. "Heaven forbid anyone would bother to return a call these days. I've got twelve cases of sparkling wine and craft beer..."

As Shane walked through the lobby, he was hit with a wave of nostalgia. This school might not be his, but the building held the same familiarity—the faint scent of gym shoes and socks, and linoleum cleaner on the floor, his voice echoing in the hollow hallways, and sports memorabilia.

A truckload of words flew out of the coordinator's mouth as he escorted Shane and the team to the gym. The man talked...*a lot*...about outlets, fanning out napkins, confirming the gluten-free options, and his memory of senior year homecoming.

Before his ears started bleeding, Shane stopped. "Looks like you have a ton on your hands tonight—no need to worry about us. This team is the best catering crew in the city. We got this, okay?" Best catering crew in the city might be a stretch, as the three crew members were currently giggling at a viral cat video on Kianna's cell phone.

The man exhaled and snapped his gaze toward the corner. He stormed off. "No! No, no, no. The disco ball needs to be at least eight feet high. Come on, people."

Shane swallowed a grin. "Hey, Joey, can you run to the van for the other extension cord? We're farther back than I thought."

"Yep." Joey rolled his cart into position and pressed the lock. "They said the DJ booth was on the north side. Clearly not."

Shane placed food warmers on the table, added chafing containers, and stacked plates. He took a moment to review his surroundings. Everything about the gym was extra—gold and silver streamers and balloons filled every open space like prom, white rice lights strung across the bleachers, and an elephant-sized disco ball dangled in the center.

He mixed the salad with the homemade garlic croutons and Caesar dressing and laid out fruit platters. Music started in the background, and the bass thumped one level too high. Was he already becoming that person, easily irritated by loud music? What's next— yelling at kids to get off his lawn?

As he watched the crowd trickle in, he scanned faces for Holland. His chest sunk lower with each passing minute. He almost texted her earlier to see if she'd come tonight but felt weird about her silence after he turned down her invitation last night. Which he still kicked himself for.

While lining up cups of chocolate and vanilla mousse, body movement caught his eye. The music screeched to a stop. The crowd parted. The air depleted from his lungs. Holland, standing in the room's corner, and she was...*beautiful.* Her long, red hair curled into waves. Through the chaos of the streamers, white linen-clothed tables, and people, he could almost see her captivating green eyes highlighted by the emerald-colored dress. His legs froze along with his gaze.

"Shane. Shane!" Kianna waved her hands in front of his face. "We're running low on noodles. Can you grab more?"

No chance. "Send Joey or Tanner. I'll be back in a minute." Everything his uncle said rushed forward. Maybe he had something to offer. He could make this work. He needed to talk to her and find out how she felt. Friends? More than friends? An annoying coworker she tolerated when her bestie wasn't on shift? Standing a few feet behind her, he paused, and his mind blanked. He should probably attempt to form some sort of coherent thought before approaching. *Or maybe I should stop delaying.* He was about to take one step forward but stopped.

Three blonde women who looked like triplets swooped in next to Holland.

As each woman hugged her, she patted them on the back with a stiff arm.

"Yay! So excited you could make it," one of them said. "We didn't have enough time to chat last week."

Dang. He'd seen Holland fake a smile with a few rowdy customers before, but her face looked like she was chewing on glass shards.

"Did you bring your new man? I'm dying to meet

him," a woman in a purple dress said.

"Oh, um. No. Grrr." Holland tugged on the fabric by her thigh. "He couldn't make it."

The woman pouted. "Oh no. Why not? Did you guys break up?"

He prickled at the over-the-top sympathetic voice. She had the same posh tone as the woman his mom had quarterly brunches with from the country club.

Holland shifted her weight between her feet. "Um…ack. No, not that. He's, um, working and—"

"You can tell us." The woman in blue moved closer. "What happened? I always love listening to juicy gossip."

Blotches on Holland's neck grew.

Would stepping in now be a disaster like when he tried to help with those rude men? The last thing he wanted was a furious Holland throwing spiked pomegranate punch in his face. He studied her face, and she looked genuinely miserable. He shrugged off his caterer jacket and tossed it into the corner. Glancing at his pitifully plain black T-shirt and jeans, he felt his stomach twist at his attire.

Dressy or not, he was going in.

Chapter 21
Today's Special: Disco Ball Delight: Savory Slow
Dancing Followed by Slow Burn S'mores

Why did I even come tonight? The moment
Holland entered the high school gym, the Three Bs
rushed over and cornered her underneath the neon-pink
balloon arch with their graduating year displayed on a
bright, twinkling marquee. After spending time with her
friend Erica, she hoped to see other people she
graduated with. *Nice* people—the ones she occasionally
skipped third period with and ran to the local drive-thru
for chocolate shakes.

"Did you have a big fight?" White Dress asked.

Enough, already. She had dodged question number
twenty in less than two minutes. The stickiness on her
tongue blocked any words from forming. She should
just save face and say he broke up with her. "Actually,
he and I—"

"Hey, babe. Sorry I'm late."

Holland recognized the voice first, and Shane's
citrus scent second. But she didn't recognize the warm
handprint imprinted into her lower back or the shivers it
sent up her spine. Nor did she recognize the lips against
her cheek. There Shane stood with his edgy energy, a
glint in his eye that made her core flip, and a cocky
smirk camouflaging the kindness underneath. She
stood, unblinking.

The women's mouths dropped.

Several moments passed before Holland gathered coherent thoughts. "What…are you doing here?"

A dimple appeared on his cheek. "I thought I just had to help set up tables, but they need me a little longer. I know how important this night is to you, so I'm taking a quick break."

She gulped and leaned into his hand, which *was still there*. "Ah, no worries at all." *What is he doing?* She couldn't keep her thoughts from flailing, but his mannerisms—the relaxed shoulders, the confident, dazzling smile—put her at ease.

"Holland was just talking about you!" White Dress clapped her hands. "I don't think we've had the pleasure of meeting. I'm Brooke—"

"Ladies, if you'll excuse us, I'm whisking Holland away for a minute before I have to check on the food." He flashed them all a grin.

Holland swore the women turned to jelly.

Without waiting for a response, he interlaced his fingers in hers.

Her arm went gummy. "What are you doing?" She followed his lead to the dance floor, and the tingles flashed like fireworks from her palm to her forearm. His hands were warm and slightly rough, showing the effort of his work in the kitchen and his studio. The sensation was almost too much, and if he asked, she probably would've followed him into an abyss.

"Taking my girlfriend to the dance floor during her high school reunion."

A flush heated her face. "I'm not your girlfriend."

He leaned into her ear. "They don't know that."

His warm breath tickled her ear, and she failed to

keep herself steady. She officially could not hold herself up in a normal standing position. Yes, he hugged her at the park, but she was so distraught then she didn't realize his chest was like a brick wall with muscles for days. Her brain slowed and filtered through the firing messages. She felt protected, safe, and supported. And her body warmed.

She swayed to the '90s slow song and moved in synchronicity with his steps. He was smooth as butter on the floor. Was there anything he couldn't do? He was almost laughably perfect. She was wheeled in a circle and now faced the women. She leveled a glare.

They scattered like spilled beads. Who cared if she acted juvenile? Being on the receiving end of jealous stares, instead of handing them out, felt amazing. She cleared her throat and tried *so hard* to ignore the spark that zinged up and down her arm. "You didn't have to do this."

"Ah, I needed a break. And I love this song."

"This song wasn't playing when you arrived." What was happening? Twelve hours ago, she put herself out there and asked him to come over, and he said no. Now, he held her firmly while dancing in the same spot as her senior prom after kissing her cheek like a pro.

He pulled her in a little tighter.

Her gut constricted, and she leaned her head against his chest. The pounding of her heart thudded in her ears. She should pull away. Dancing with him— falling for him—could lead to heartache. But his chest was so warm. And his signature soapy, raindrop scent drifted off him, and she wanted to bottle it and spray it on her pillow tonight. She snuggled in tighter, and his racing pulse thumped against her cheek.

"So, you cook, dance, and rescue women from mortifying conversations with socialites," she said. "You don't have a bat cave or succumb to the powers of kryptonite, do you?"

He chuckled. "Funny. Trust me, you're saving me, as well. I was bored to death serving pasta to your former classmates."

A couple near them who clearly had one too many spiked punches bumped into her and broke the euphoric moment. She looked at Shane, giggled, and resumed a dancing position. A new song started, and she didn't move, terrified if she adjusted her head, the magic would vanish. "Please tell me one mortifying thing about yourself. It'll help me believe you're a mere mortal like me."

"Hmm." His palm pressed on her lower back. "I got food poisoning during my freshman homecoming dance and puked all over my date."

She stepped back with a grin. "No. Really?"

"Sure did." He pulled her back to his chest. "She started bawling. I puked again, and her dad sent my parents a dry-cleaning bill the next day. The chaperones stopped the dance so the janitor could clean the floor, and everyone stared like I ruined their night. No girl would dance with me for a year, so I was stuck hanging by the punch bowl with my buddies until junior year."

"I don't know why, but you made me feel better." She glanced at the team in the corner by the pasta bar. "I didn't know you were catering tonight."

"Yeah, just a small crew. Who I seriously left hanging."

As an '80s slow song wailed in the background,

she pulled her head up, and her face instantly missed the heat of his body. "Do you need to go back?" *Please say no.*

"After this song, I will." He firmed his grip.

I never want this song to end. She returned her head to rest against him and dropped her shoulders. He was like a snug blanket that she wanted to wrap around herself. "Thank you for jumping in with those women and dancing with me. I didn't expect you to do something like this."

"I find everyone is happier when they have low expectations of me."

He said it like a joke, but a touch of sadness funneled through his tone. "Hey!" She chuckled. "I never said I had low expectations."

He didn't respond, but his thumb swiped across her lower back.

She savored the heavenly sensation. The song ended, and she peeled herself away. The void was instant.

He glanced at her.

His lips parted like he wanted to say something. The rise and fall of his chest were more intense than someone with a resting heart rate. *Is he feeling the same as me?*

He inhaled. "Hey, ah, do—"

"What's up, Holland?" her co-worker Tanner asked.

World's. Worst. Timing. "Hey, Tanner."

"Dude, you comin' back yet?" Tanner tossed up his hands. "Joey grabbed the noodles from the van, but we're almost out of drinks."

Shane sighed. "Be right there."

The disappointment dropped like a boulder into her stomach.

Tanner squinted and dashed his gaze between them before his eyebrows shot up. "Wait! Are you two—"

"No." Holland clasped her hands.

"Give me two minutes," Shane said to Tanner.

Ugh. The allure of the moment dissipated as quickly as it arrived.

Shane led her to the side of the gym. "How long are you staying here?"

"Enough to relieve any guilt for my parents taking Riley. And for making the hour I spent on hair and makeup worth it." She flipped her wrist to check her watch. "Which means I can leave here in four minutes."

He looked at Joey.

Joey stared back with his hands in the air.

Shane settled his mouth to her ear. "Can you hang on for fifteen?"

"Why?" She scanned his face. Was this ultra-confident guy blushing?

"Wanna go for a drive?"

"More than just about anything." *Oops.* The words slipped out faster than she intended.

And then, he reached down and kissed her cheek.

I'm officially liquid. Someone, please sponge me from the floor, put me in a bucket, and set me in a room until I recover. Some fourth-world dimension clearly captured her, or she was part of a simulation. No way was this reality.

Fifteen minutes later, Shane rounded the corner with a smile.

She said goodbye to Erica and swallowed hard at the disappointment of him not wrapping her in his arms.

"Ready to get out of here?" he asked.

"You have no idea." Her low heels clicked against the sidewalk and out to the parking lot. The sun had dipped below the horizon, and the warmth of the night air surrounded them as she made her way to his vehicle—which lacked doors.

"I'd open the door for you, but..."

"You have no doors." She bunched her dress in one hand and heaved herself into the vehicle. "Is this thing safe to drive?"

"Safe and legal are two different things." He grinned. "Yes, the vehicle's safe."

The SUV eased from the parking lot.

A moment later, the wind whipped around her free-flowing hair. She gathered it all and gripped it in her fingers. The one time she decided not to bring a ponytail holder, she went into a convertible.

"I have to make a quick stop at a convenience store." He pulled off the road and parked. "Need anything?"

"Nope, I'm good. I'll wait here." After she watched him enter the store, she checked her phone for missed messages. None from her parents, thankfully, but several from Amanda.

—*Hope you're still alive at the reunion. If you see Keelan McDermitt, kick him in the shins for stealing my grape-scented pencil in the ninth grade.*—

—*Do they still have the same disco ball?*—

Holland grinned and typed.

—*Yep. Pretty sure the same DJ, too. Got a heavy dose of bad pop music tonight. Prom all over again, minus the peach vodka and pop. EWWWW.*—

—*I have *got* to tell you all about tonight.*

Freaking out. Sneak preview: slow-danced with Shane. Currently waiting for him in his truck. Off to God knows where. And I think I like it all.—

Her phone rang immediately.

"I have so many questions," Amanda blurted. "Are the muscles real or one of those suits actors wear under a superhero costume? What song was it, and will you be downloading it? And most importantly, where were his hands?"

Holland contained her smile. She looked up and saw Shane heading toward the car. "Sorry, he's coming back. Text later."

"I cannot believe you're leaving me hanging like this!" Amanda said her goodbyes and ended the call.

Shane threw his mystery bags into the trunk and hopped back into the car.

"Where are you taking me?" She tugged the seatbelt tighter.

"You'll see." His grin widened.

Her heart fluttered. "Pretty sure this is how every horror movie starts."

He laughed and accelerated.

The hypnotic humidity swirled with the scent of peonies and evergreens, engulfing her like a therapy blanket. With her hair snugged into a bun, she lazed back in her seat and watched the city zip by. The moon's glow illuminated the darkened sky and picked up a glint in Shane's eyes. Several minutes later, he turned the corner.

She straightened her back and peered out the window. "We're going to the lake?"

"Yes." The gravel crunched beneath his tires, and he shifted into Park. "Is that okay?"

Okay? Spending time at the lake—with him—was everything she could've hoped. *Be cool, be cool.* "Yep."

He grabbed the bags and a blanket from the back and waved toward the beach.

"What's in the bags?"

"A surprise." He winked.

Gah. He needed to stop winking. Every wink gave her a palpitation, and by the end of the night, she might need to check herself into the ER. "Ah, supplies to help you bury the body. Got it."

He chuckled and took a few steps before stopping. "One second." He jogged back to the vehicle, grabbed a sweatshirt, and handed it over. "You looked a little chilly."

I can't even. He was probably just being thoughtful. Like a boy scout. Like a *friend.* But, every step, every motion, every *breath* caused first date flutters and jitters.

Lake Superior sat calm and beautiful, with a whisper of ripples moving in the distance. She kicked off her pumps and padded barefoot on the beach with the sand squishing beneath her feet. The water twinkled with the glow of the full moon. Holland rolled her neck and breathed in the rocky, mineral, freshwater smell, releasing the low-grade headache she carried all night.

Shane snapped the blanket in the air, then spread it over the beach. After crouching, he lined up logs in perfect rows and laid down chocolate, marshmallows, and graham crackers.

She could've watched him do this all night, and it would be the best night she'd had in weeks. "You bought a s'mores kit? And firewood?"

"I mean, we're at the beach, right?" He built a wood pyramid. "I dare you to name anything better than a campfire and s'mores on the beach."

*Nothing. Literally, nothing was bet*ter. Twenty minutes, an entire box of matches depleted, and multiple frustrated laughs later, Holland finally lit the wood on fire.

He high-fived her like she finished the prep work early.

The golden flames highlighted his face. He popped a marshmallow on the end of a stick and roasted it. "Was tonight as awful as you expected?"

"No, I guess not. Only because you stepped in, though." She unwrapped the chocolate pieces and lined them on top of the crackers. "I don't know why being around those women bothers me so much. I never thought I cared what people thought about me, but apparently, I do. Ridiculous, right? I mean, that was ten years ago." Her chest tightened at the admission.

He rotated the marshmallow and held the twig steady above the flame. "I think most people care what others think about them."

She tilted her head. "You don't care what people think about you."

"What?" He flinched. "That's not true." He folded two graham crackers around the marshmallow and tugged. The gooey sugar tail drooped from the stick, and he stuck it into the fire to burn the remnants. "I stew on it more than I should. Especially with my parents."

She accepted the s'more and set it to the side. "Your parents? Aren't they seriously proud of how gifted you are?"

"Thanks. But no." Keeping his gaze on the stick, he worked his jaw in a small circle and focused on the marshmallow. "I'm a huge disappointment. We haven't spoken in months."

Her gut ached from his tone. "Really? Can I ask why?" After several moments of silence, she felt like kicking herself for asking such an invasive question. He was a truly talented artist, smart, kind, and stupidly easy on the eyes. Sure, he had a ferocious, cantankerous shell when she first met him, but that cracked. He was a parental dream—not a disappointment.

"I dropped out of law school." His gaze flickered to her before he returned to the fire.

Several seconds passed before the information settled. "You were in law school?"

"Two semesters shy of graduation."

She flung sand with her toe. "Wow. That's amazing." She'd only met one lawyer in her life—the woman who sat with her at Riley's custody hearing—and thought she was the smartest person she'd ever known.

He checked the top of the marshmallow and returned it to the fire. "Aren't you going to ask me why?"

"Not sure you dropping out of school is any of my business." She twisted off the top of the water bottle. "Besides, I have a pretty good idea why."

He folded his eyebrows. "Think I couldn't handle being a lawyer?"

"I think you would've killed it. I could see you in the courtroom, terrifying the witnesses." She tweaked her lips into a grin. "My guess is that it didn't make you happy."

His chest relaxed.

The flickers of the fire made his cheeks glow.

He locked his gaze with hers before he sloped his head.

A warmth rose on her skin. She wasn't sure if the heat was from the flames or from being next to him. She ached to wrap her arms around him and rest against his chest. She reached for a water bottle and used the opportunity to inch closer.

The sizzle of a burning marshmallow cut through the silence.

"Oh no!" He whipped the twig from the flame and blew, but the crisped marshmallow dropped to the ground.

"Man down!" She giggled. "James will be so disappointed his head chef destroyed a s'more."

"Fail." He dug in the bag for another one.

Once he toasted the new marshmallow to golden perfection, he held out the stick.

She scooped it off with the crackers and handed him one.

"Ready?" He angled the dessert toward his mouth. "You gotta commit to eating the whole thing at once. Don't set it down between bites. Otherwise, they get too messy. This isn't a prom date. I'm putting a ring on it."

She laughed and sunk her teeth into the sticky gooeyness. The melted sugars settled on her tongue, and she sighed at the flavors while ignoring the internal sparks zigzagging from the words *I'm putting a ring on it.* "So good, right?" She swiped a thumb across her lower lip to catch the remnants.

"So good." He clapped off the debris from his

hands and handed her a wet napkin. "I haven't had a proper s'more in so long. Should we add it to the dessert menu?"

"James would love that." She didn't hold back the sarcastic tone. James would freak out with such a messy dessert. The coziness of the fire and the crackling logs eased her into a trance. Soft waves morphed into white noise. Maybe, this summer, Shane, Riley, and she could return for a sandcastle playdate. No news from her parents about Riley was good news. Hopefully, they remembered to use the soft towel she packed for after bath time, not the ones they've had since the '80s...and made him brush his teeth because he was a stickler about having a brush in his mouth...and sang the lyrics to his favorite lullaby when they put him down. *Stop. Just enjoy tonight.* She twisted off the water bottle cap. "Will you tell me how you went from law school to art?"

He mimicked the way she was sitting, crossing his feet at the ankles near the fire. "My grandpa was a lawyer, and my dad's a lawyer. I loved it for a while. The law fascinates me but didn't drive me. I wasn't passionate about it." He picked up a twig, broke it into several pieces, and tossed it onto the logs. "During my undergrad, I told them I wanted to be an art major, but they didn't take my feelings seriously." He shrugged. "Ultimately, I should've pushed harder, but the situation was complicated. The law firm is the family business. I'm an only child, and that dream dies with me."

Oof. A pang pricked her stomach. "Sometimes, I get so wrapped up in my family...drama...I forget others struggle, too. I'm really sorry. That's some heavy stuff to deal with." She stared at the flames. "So, art's what makes you happy?"

A softness overtook his face.

The corner of his eyes crinkled. "Among other things."

The honey tone consumed her. Did he mean her?

"Do you think I'm a quitter?" He fixed his gaze on the fire.

Quitter? A dreamer who paved his path, bucked societal and familial pressure, and did what made him happy? He was a freaking *inspiration*. "You are not a quitter, Shane." She placed a palm on top of his hand. "Sounds to me like you escaped."

Chapter 22
Today's Special: Holy Shitake Mushrooms

Shane navigated his vehicle over several potholes on the way back from Lake Superior. Porch lights and a few barking dogs led the way into Holland's neighborhood. He glanced out of his peripherals and warmed at how cute she looked drowning in his oversized sweatshirt, which she hadn't taken off since they arrived at the beach after the reunion. He had half a mind to tell her to keep the shirt, so he could see her wear it again.

Holland stretched and gripped the rail. "I think this is the latest I've stayed up in years."

"And that was the most marshmallows I've ever had in one sitting." The gurgling in his belly was worth every bite to spend the extra time at the beach. Now, if his car would just stall so he could continue this night, things would be perfect. Tonight was incredible. Watching her smile widen while the fire blazed, and feeling secure enough to share his past, were everything he needed to solidify his feelings. Running away from them worked for a while, but his emotions crashed into him tonight. No doubt existed anymore—he wanted to be more than friends.

The tires crushed the gravel in her driveway. He turned off the car and froze. Maybe if he didn't move, she wouldn't leave, and this night would never end. The porch light beamed behind the hanging flowers, and a small smattering of mosquitoes flew to it. As the sweet scent of ripened strawberries from the garden filled the air, he coiled his stomach. He cleared his throat. "How long have you lived here?"

"Almost four years. I kind of hated it at first, but the place grew on me. Not sharing walls with someone who might be mad when Riley screams is a huge bonus." She tucked a flyaway hair behind her ear. "And we've got a little garden, and I have my flowers."

He glanced at the rows of brightly colored petunias edged along the front of the house. "They're beautiful."

A slow smile spread. "It's all about the presentation."

"Ha. Touché." *Stop delaying.* He needed to tell her this was the best date-non-date he'd had in years, and the second he left, he'd replay every moment.

She sprung from the vehicle and wrapped her purse over a shoulder.

"Here, ah, let me walk you to the door. You know, for safety." *Keep it cool, man. Your nerves are showing.*

"Safety, huh?" She cocked an eyebrow. "Such a gentleman." She sauntered toward the house.

He followed. Maybe she wasn't ready for the night to be over, either. He stayed a step back and toed a pebble on the ground.

She reached the bottom of the porch and twirled her ring. "Besides the distinct misfortune of seeing people I never need to see again, and standing in the same gym I tripped in during the grand march at prom, tonight was perfect." She locked her green-eyed gaze with his. "Honestly, one of the best nights I've had in a long time."

Delicate fingertips pressed into the top of his hand, and the heat seeped up his arm. No other hand had ever left an imprint like that. "I had a great time, too. And we're taking it to the grave that I burnt the marshmallow, and you were the one who got the fire started, right?"

"Of course." She yanked on the zipper of the sweatshirt. "Here, you can take this back."

"That's okay. You can bring it to work." He stuffed his hands into his pocket. He needed to tell her she was amazing, beautiful, funny, and inspiring. *Something.* Let her know how much he admired her for raising her nephew while making everything look easy. Ask about her favorite foods besides chocolate or if she had cousins. *Anything.* He didn't want to leave but should. *Yep,* returning to his place was the smart and responsible thing. He definitely should not do what his body pleaded. She had a child. His actions affected more than the two of them.

Heavy, gradual footsteps thudded against each wooden step. He wasn't imagining anything—her shy smiles, hair tucking, and lip nibbling told him she thought the same. He swallowed. "I guess I'll see you at work this week?"

Color spread across her cheeks. "Yep."

He hated pointless small talk. He wanted to continue their conversation from the beach. Ask her about her dreams, hopes, and past. Did she ever have a dog? Who was her first crush? But nothing came out. His body felt like it carried the weight of a concrete block. He forced himself to take a step back. "Goodnight, Holland."

She dug keys from her bag. "Night, Shane."

Turn around. As he walked, he dragged his feet, and his breath constricted. Everything inside screamed at him to turn around, tell her how he felt, and confirm she felt the same. But this had to be on her terms. He'd grit his teeth and force himself to be patient because she was worth it. He dropped his shoulders and trudged to the car.

"Shane, wait."

The sound of her voice cut through the night air. He burrowed his heels into the ground, and he spun around.

She sprinted to him, her dress flapping in the breeze, and her eyebrows scrunched.

His heart soared directly from his chest into his throat, and he stepped closer.

Standing on her tiptoes, she threw her arms around his neck and pushed her lips onto his.

He wrapped her in his arms and drew her in tighter. The kiss was better than he ever imagined. She tasted like chocolate and marshmallows, and her soft mouth flawlessly aligned with his. He cupped the back of her head, and his body absorbed the moment. Everything was new and different, yet perfectly natural all at once. All nerves, all hesitation, vanished. *She feels the same way I do.* No more daydreams, no more worries—this was real.

Several moments later, she pulled back and looked with wide eyes. "Oh my God, I just did that! I can't believe I just kissed you."

Hurried words flew from her mouth, and her cheeks flushed with reds and pinks. She spun to the house, turned back with a beaming smile, and cupped his face in her palms.

Her feet shifted like she was restraining herself from dancing.

Energy radiated from her, and she lowered her arms. "Gah! You're amazing. Tonight was amazing. I'm leaving now 'cause I'm dying, and I don't know what to say, and I always know what to say. You officially have me tongue-tied."

Her cheeks ballooned into a serious shade of pink.

The record books could hold her reaction as the most adorable things he'd witnessed in his lifetime.

"Oh no, tongue-tied...I didn't mean...you know what I mean! Um, goodnight." Without another word, she ran into the house.

He stood smiling for an extraordinarily long time. This just changed everything.

****

Holland leaned against the front door and savored the lingering sensation of Shane's mouth against hers until the sound of tires rolling out of her driveway faded. She touched her pulsing lips. What now? Play it cool? What did this mean? She was fairly confident the way he acted meant *something* with how his hands held her and feeling the strength in his fingers leaving a trail of warmth up her back. The way he kissed her—both firm and soft.

She pushed herself off the wall and went into the bathroom to wash the evening off her face. Worried the lust zings would rinse away, she debated brushing her teeth. After snugging on her PJs, she launched onto her bed and squealed. As she tapped her fingers against her belly, she replayed every moment. She rolled over and grabbed her phone.

Twelve thirty a.m. Too late to text. Too late for him to text. She lingered her thumbs over the screen. A message popped up, and her heart thudded.

—*Who do you call when you hurt your foot while driving?*—

—*Who?*—

—*The Toe Company.*—

—*That's a perfectly awful dad joke. Looks like I have competition. I give it seven out of ten.*—

Shane sent a clapping emoji, along with more texts.

—*You're being generous. In other news, I reviewed all the evidence from the evening, and the jury agreed. This was the best night I've had in a really long time. What time are you picking up Riley tomorrow?*—

—*3:00 p.m.*—

—*Can I take you for breakfast?*—

—*Only if I can take you for lunch.*—

—*Deal!*—

Chapter 23
Today's Special: Blast-from-the-Past Pasta Salad

A date. A real, honest-to-goodness date, and Shane's stomach flipped as he lay in bed and replayed every moment from the previous night. Any hesitation he had Holland didn't feel the same vanished the second her lips touched his last night. He planted his feet firmly on the ground to avoid sprinting to the shower. The streaming water felt warmer on his skin this morning, the spring-meadow soap smelled a touch crisper, and the sun peeking through the frosted glass window looked a little brighter.

James was right—Holland seemed to value emotional support over everything else. After shagging a towel through his hair, he stared at his closet for an eternity. Button-down? T-shirt? Jeans? Slacks? He pulled down and rehung multiple shirts before he shook his head. *Come on—this was Holland*—his friend, his coworker, his...he coughed and reached for a button-down.

His phone flashed Holland's name, and his energy spiked.

—My ex-boyfriend was lactose intolerant. I broke up with him because he couldn't stomach my cheesy jokes.—

Even with subpar jokes, she was beyond adorable.

—Five out of ten. Is this how our date will be?

—So, it is a date? *Neatly folding my sweats back into my drawer and pulling out a dress instead*.—

—After the bag of marshmallows from last night, I might join you with the sweats. P.S. You could wear a poncho and still be beautiful.—

Too much? Too soon? He needed to attempt to play it cool for a little longer.

—Hold, please. Need to grab a fan for my face.—

Shane paced his loft. He tugged the corner of his comforter to remove all wrinkles, refolded the towel in his bathroom, and organized the mugs on his kitchen counter. The date countdown clock's minutes were stuck. He needed to go for a drive. He shoved his wallet into his back pocket and grabbed his keys.

A loud knock rapped on the door.

Isn't James at work? He opened it and flinched before his core went cold.

"Hello, Shane."

His brain moved in slow motion. All words were lost, and his mouth turned arid. He blinked, and his breath trapped inside his ribcage. "Cherise. What are you doing here?"

"Long time, huh? Can I come in?" A deep, brown-eyed gaze locked with his. With stiffened shoulders and no smile, she stood, waiting. "We need to talk."

With what little mind-body connection he had left, he stepped back and held the door open. Ten months had passed since he packed his belongings and moved out of their apartment. And here she was, sitting on his tiny couch, in a different city, with an unreadable expression. Nausea bubbled inside of him, burning his chest. He pulled a chair opposite her and tried to inhale more than a shallow breath.

Holding her chin high, she stepped into the apartment. "You look good."

He dropped his mouth.

She rolled her eyes and flipped a lock of dark brown hair over her shoulder. "Don't look at me like that. I didn't mean it that way. You look healthy. Happy. The bags under your eyes are gone. Your color's better. Whatever's happening in Duluth is working."

Surely, she didn't come here to chitchat or comment on his mental health. So, maybe avoiding her calls these last few months was not the best move, but having her in his space depleted the oxygen from the room. The ceiling fan must be malfunctioning with how quickly his loft became sticky. "How did you know where I lived?"

"Your mom told me you were living with James."

Her voice was courtroom ready—steady and without emotion. He didn't respond. Although his mother and Cherise had been close for a decade, their ongoing relationship weaved a sliver of betrayal through him. The beginning sweat beads brewed beneath the surface. He hopped up to flip the standing fan on and paced. She deserved a proper apology for how things ended, but he couldn't bring himself to do it. He pulled in a deep breath. *Let's get this over with.* "Hey, what happened with us…I'm really sorry. I handled our breakup so badly. The way I left wasn't fair to you."

She wrapped her arms around her designer bag and swiped her thumbs across the fabric. "That was a really tough day."

Here it comes. His heart stopped beating.

She sighed. "But I'm the one who should apologize."

What?

She looked out the window and tugged on the corner of her purse. "Now that I've gotten clarity, I'm mortified at what I did."

No way did he hear her right. "What do you mean, what you did?" He squinted like the action would help clarify what she meant. "I'm the one who ended our relationship."

She expelled a drawn-out exhale and shifted in her seat. "For so long, I tried to mold you into what I needed and didn't stop to think of what you wanted."

Huh? He and Cherise had been together since high school, and for years, he considered her his best friend. And, even though the last several years of their relationship felt more like a business partnership, often filled with severe tension mixed with soul-crushing complacency, he never blamed her. But molding him? He leaned back against the kitchen counter and tapped his fingers against the edge. "I don't understand."

"You know how goal oriented I am, right? With school, with life…." She swirled her hand in the air.

He grinned. "Especially when you trained to qualify for a marathon."

"Exactly!" She smacked a hand on her thigh. "I made you run with me every morning, and you hate running."

He stopped drumming his fingers against the ceramic. "Exercise was good for me."

She clasped and unclasped the purse buckle. "I spent years pushing my agenda onto you. I knew you didn't want to go to law school." She inhaled an uneven breath. "You becoming a lawyer was my dream. And your parents' dream. They expressed concern, and I assured them you wanted to practice law."

His thoughts spun. His parents had forced law school down his throat since kindergarten. He had withdrawn over the last few years, but they never seemed worried about his mental health. The only message forced on him was he needed to pass the bar. He lowered himself to a chair. "What do you mean, *expressed concern*?"

"Your mom told me multiple times you seemed unhappy, but I convinced her you were fine." She bit the corner of her lip. "I told her you were just stressed—because doing so met *my* needs. *My* vision. Not yours."

Her usual self-assured voice wavered.

"Shane, I'm so sorry." She looked at her hands.

He heard the words, but his brain couldn't absorb the information. They talked about him? His mom was worried? Why didn't they say anything? "I stopped speaking to my parents months ago."

"I'm really sorry to hear that." Her face fell. "Had I known, I would've told you this sooner."

He trapped his bottom lip between his teeth and glanced at his watch. "They still reacted horribly." But, her words provided a glimmer of hope the relationship with his parents was not irrevocably damaged.

"One more thing." She stopped fidgeting on the couch and straightened her back. "We have to talk about what happened the day you moved out."

He shook his head. That day rocked him for weeks, sending him into a questioning tornado where he evaluated every decision he'd ever made. No reason to relive it now. "We don't need to do that."

"Yes, we do. At least, I do." She leveled her stare. "I panicked...I wasn't thinking straight. To lie and say we could have kids once we were married was beyond emotionally manipulative."

She said it. He always wanted kids. But Cherise held a steadfast conviction she didn't want to have children. He spent months...*years*...talking about it, hoping she'd change her mind and saying anything he could think of to prove they should have a family. Sometimes, he'd take a scenic route home to drive by a park and point out the families playing. He begged her to reconsider and told her his fatherhood dreams. And the day he proposed—besides knowing they weren't meant to be—part of the trepidation was he gave up his dream of having a family.

But, when he walked out of the door the final time, he almost froze, her words rattled him to the core.

She had grabbed onto his arm and told him she changed her mind and wanted children.

He questioned his reality and whether he had made the right decision. And her declaration compounded the guilt of leaving tenfold since she finally agreed to what he wanted. "Cherise..."

"I'm serious, Shane. My plan never consisted of any family besides me and you. I've proudly never wanted children. But I knew you did, and I was terrified of being alone." She pulled her lips into a hard, straight line. "After all those years, I panicked. I didn't want to lose you, so I lied. I planned to tell you after our wedding I changed my mind again and didn't want kids."

As he leaned back, he heard the chair creak. He

struggled to decipher the conflicting heaviness and lightness in his chest. For nearly a year, he beat himself up for leaving her crying on the floor. He berated himself for his unfairness toward her after she told him what he'd waited so long to hear. He exhaled a trapped breath and rechecked his watch. "Why are you here? Just to tell me this?"

"I've been calling to let you know I'm getting married."

She looked like she swallowed a golf ball. A spiderweb of relief spread through his body. "You're getting married?"

"I am. He's good to me, and we have a ton of similar goals. And I'm happy. I didn't want you to hear it from someone else." Her eyes brimmed with tears, and she flicked at her cheek with a thumb. "Sorry, I'm more emotional than I thought I'd be. I guess I wanted to start my new life by closing this chapter. I've hung on to so much guilt about everything that happened with us."

"You've been hanging on to guilt?" *Ironic.* He'd been trapped under a boulder of guilt and only recently crawled out. "So have I. It's inhibited me from moving forward as much as I want."

"Well, you need to forgive yourself." She stiffened. "I was equally part of the failed relationship. And let's take a moment and be thankful it *did* fail. I thrive in chaos. You never have. You're a dreamer, and that's something really special about you. I never gave you credit for your talent or passion. I didn't support it because it didn't align with my goals. Still doesn't."

Her voice turned matter-of-fact.

She shrugged. "The law, billable hours, making

partner—that's what drives me," she continued. "I was desperate for it to drive you, but it never did. No doubt in my mind, had we gotten married, we would've been miserable and divorced within five years."

The words unleashed the tension in his core he held like a bulldog.

She looked at her watch. "I should go. My fiancé dropped me off and is coming back to get me." She reached the door and paused. "Take care of yourself, Blackwood."

"You, too." After all this time, he was free. And now, he could focus on what was important—making things work with Holland.

Chapter 24

Today's Special: Potato Pancakes and First Date Scrambles

Here he comes. Shane's vehicle pulled into Holland's driveway, and her pulse skyrocketed. Yes, she kissed him last night. *Swoon.* And she wanted to do it again. But the embrace was an impulse decision fueled by homemade s'mores and campfire intoxication. Nine thirty a.m. on a Sunday meant no cover of the dark sky existed to hide her flushed face. The rules had changed. She leaned against the doorframe and refrained from jumping into his arms.

He trotted with a brilliant smile, holding a bouquet of sunflowers. "Morning, sunshine."

Her heart needed to stop jackhammering against her chest before she passed out. She wrapped a hand around the stems. "How did you know sunflowers are my favorite?"

"Lucky guess?" He pointed at the sunflower blanket and pillow on her couch.

"That's fair." She grinned and led him to the kitchen. "I'm gonna put these in water, and then we can head out." Why were her hands trembling? She'd known Shane for months. She texted him nightly. On the days she worked without Amanda, she and Shane spent every break together. And now, one, single kiss pushed her into a world of butterflies and nerves. She toed off her shoes. The wooden step stool screeched against the linoleum floor, and she moved to climb on it.

"What are you doing?" he asked with narrowed eyes.

"I can't reach the top shelf."

"I'm literally standing right here." He chuckled and shook his head. "You can just ask me to grab it."

"Oh!" She giggled. "Okay, thanks."

He pulled the vase down and handed it over.

She filled the container with water, fanned out the flowers, and felt fingertips rest on her waist. A soft gasp escaped. She placed a palm on the counter and savored the fire spreading through her belly. *Oh my.* Biting her lip, she turned to face him, and her stomach flipped. *Go for it again or wait?* "I, ah…"

He swiped his thumbs across her cheeks multiple times.

The heat from his palm sent a wave of shivers through her, and she leaned back into the counter for support.

His dimples appeared. "I had the best time last night."

Hearing the quiet, silky tone in his voice, she couldn't stop her knees from quivering. The night *was* perfect. But the evening was more than that. A barrier had broken. The gigantic leap from friends to something else occurred—something scary, wonderful, new, and exciting. Logic and butterflies competed. The butterflies gained steam, and she verged on imploding. "Sure was."

Eye contact was nearly impossible. If she looked at him too long, she'd reveal every emotion for him to read. She peeled herself from the counter. As she moved closer, she knew exactly what this moment meant. She could write last night's kiss off as a one-time fluke. If it happened again, she couldn't hold back. Every buried feeling would boil over. Giving up control and depending on someone made her skin prickle, but Shane was safe. And she was ready. She leaned in.

He cupped her face with both hands and pushed his lips against hers.

All leg support vanished. Her pulse quickened, and she sank into the kiss.

Moving back, he flicked his gaze between her eyes.

"So...that's how it'll be now?" She lifted an eyebrow.

His face filled with color. "Oh no, I should've asked first. Sorry, I got swept up—"

"Permission eternally granted." She sank against his chest. Was this all real? It seemed so fast, but she also felt like she'd known him forever. She melted into the embrace of his strong, beautiful arms, his gentle fingers pressing against her back. *Perfection.*

A low, bellowing rumble filled the kitchen.

His eyes widened. "Was that your stomach?"

Heat flushed her cheeks at the decibel of her empty stomach's growl. "I'm seriously so hungry."

He chuckled and waved her toward the door. "Come on. Let's get some breakfast."

She snatched her shoes from the ground and skipped out of the room. When she felt his hand grasp hers, she smiled. A day full of firsts—the first time he kissed her, the first time holding hands in her house, the first time feeling...*this.* She'd never forget today, and it only just started.

****

The server set a heaping plate of steamy eggs and fried potatoes on the table at The Edge—a family-owned restaurant downtown that had the largest portions of hash browns Holland had seen to date. She shifted on the wooden chair, which was not nearly as comfortable as Salt & Sugar's chairs, and dove in to quiet the roars in her belly. "This is so good," she said between savory bites, the creamy eggs practically melting on her tongue. "Pinkie swear we won't tell James how good this place is."

"Deal." Shane dashed salt into his hand and sprinkled it on top of his omelet. "Let's plan a break-in and steal the potato pancake recipe. They're phenomenal."

"I'm in." She nodded and sipped her orange juice.

"So." He cleared his throat. "I had an interesting morning."

The hesitation in his voice gave her pause. "Oh, yeah?" She lowered her fork. "Do tell."

He spread a generous layer of butter onto the warm, freshly toasted bread. "My ex stopped by to chat."

The sting to her ego was immediate. "Really? That's random. Right?" Attempting a light and neutral voice went down in a fiery blaze. Was it random? Had she popped over before? Their first actual date and he brought up an ex—not a good omen. Her mouth turned dry, and she slammed her juice.

"So random." He scooped a healthy spoonful of blackberry jam onto the toast. "When I saw her standing there, I swear I almost fell over."

And? "I bet." She bit into the pancake. "Was

everything okay?"

His smile widened. "More than okay. She's getting married and wanted to tell me in person." He relaxed his shoulders and added a pinch more pepper to his eggs.

An ex was getting married. The news was big, but he rattled it off with the same enthusiasm as a weather forecast. She felt her throat tighten, and she gulped down water to calm the sensation. "Wow. How do you feel about that?"

He set down his fork. "Relieved. I'm really happy for her. I've been carrying around weight about the whole situation, and it disappeared."

Sigh. She released the tension in her stomach, and the pancakes reverted to being delicious.

"Enough about her. I want to spend the rest of this day talking about you." He sipped his coffee with a grin. "And planning our recipe heist, of course."

Having alone time with him was a rare treat since she had a babysitter, and she soaked in the tingles every time he extended his hand over his plate to touch hers.

An hour later, the server dropped off the check.

Shane picked it up.

"Split the bill?" She reached for her purse.

"Seriously?" He snapped up his head. "No chance." He laid his card on the table and leaned back on the chair.

The server cashed him out.

She walked to the exit and felt his fingertip graze her lower back. *Swoon times infinity.* Outside on the sidewalk, she gravitated toward him like she was magnetically attracted and indulged in the sensation of his thumb swiping against the top of her knuckles. "Can we take a walk on the trail for a bit?" She was thankful for the rare cloud cover on this late summer day. "I need the contents of my breakfast to settle. Or, we might have a situation like your freshman homecoming dance."

"Hey!" He laughed. "I told you that story in a moment of weakness, and it was never to be talked about again."

She giggled and followed his lead to the end of the sidewalk. A sweetened pastry scent filled the surrounding air near a bakery. After crossing the street, she looped her arm around his while chirping birds and laughing children rang in the background. She matched his footsteps and moved slowly, but deliberately, and soaked in every sensation—the meadowy smell of freshly cut grass, how naturally her body settled into his while strolling, and the soft crunch of scattered twigs beneath her feet.

"Have you talked to Riley today?" He tugged her arm closer to his side.

"No. I didn't want to interrupt his routine." She had to restrain herself from contacting her parents for a status update. "I hope he did okay. My parents aren't always the best caretakers."

His steps slowed. "What do you mean?"

Where did she begin? As a teen, having a mom who called her in sick at school so she could eat ice cream and watch soap operas was fun. Not fun was those same parents missing her high school graduation because they found a once-in-a-lifetime deal to go to Italy. "When they had grandkids, they wanted the relationship with their grandchildren to be like how they raised us—like free-range chickens." A dad with a stroller headed toward her, and she slid over for him to pass. "Accepting Riley's autism took them years. My mom kept saying, *it's a phase. He'll grow out of it.* Her reaction really upset me—like she denied his truth. And, because she refused to accept he was autistic, she also refused to follow the therapist's recommendations. When I'd drop him off, she'd say, *he'll be fine.* But when I picked him up, he'd be in the middle of a meltdown or in the corner crying."

Shane kicked a small rock out of the way. "Can I ask how you ended up with custody?"

She closed her eyes and remembered a knock on the door and her confusion at seeing a silent, disheveled two-year-old holding a ratty teddy bear. "Two police officers and a social worker showed up at my apartment. The social worker pulled me aside and whispered my sister essentially didn't want to be a mom anymore and named me next of kin. Until that point, I'd never even babysat a kid. I had no idea what to do."

"That had to have been so scary." His arm stiffened. "What did you do?"

"I was in shock, honestly. I threw on cartoons and grabbed a blanket, and he lay with me on the couch until he fell asleep."

"They dropped him off? Just like that?" He froze and then continued walking. "I guess that shouldn't surprise me. I studied family law, but I would think the social worker should've offered more services."

That night was tough. Some nights since then were even tougher. But she wouldn't change anything. "I know. But they're so strapped. They gave me a few brochures, did a quick consented safety search of my place, left some emergency numbers, and said they'd be back in a week to check on us." She continued strolling the path.

"Let's grab that seat over there." He pointed at the black iron bench facing a multi-colored rose garden. He dropped onto the seat and rested an arm across the top.

She snuggled in. *Snuggled in—with Shane.*

"Did you call your sister?" he asked.

She looked across the park—kids running, balls flying, and dogs pulling on leashes. She'd have to bring Riley here sometime. "After Riley fell asleep, I freaked out and called my parents. They were traveling overseas and weren't returning for a few weeks, so they couldn't do much. But, I got Layla's number."

He shifted on the seat. "You didn't have your sister's number?"

"I didn't even know she had a kid!" She chuckled, even though being kept in the dark wasn't funny. She and her sister were never close, but the hurt cut deep when she found out Layla had a child and didn't tell her. "We hadn't spoken in three years."

He brushed his flattened palm up and down her arm. "Really? Did you guys have a falling out or something?"

Where did she begin? A lifetime of push and pull, arguments, and a growing resentment burrowed deep. "The story's hard to describe. Layla's sort of self-centered, I guess. She and my parents fought all the time. She left the house at nineteen and never returned. From what I understand, she traveled around the country with various boyfriends. Soon, one year turned into two, then turned into five. She never reached out, so I didn't, either."

He released a low breath. "That's tough. I don't have siblings, but I think not talking to them would be hard." He rubbed a thumb on her shoulder. "But you called after the officers dropped off Riley?"

She nodded. "I left like twenty very loud, tense, swear-filled voicemails. Thinking about it now, I'm super embarrassed. I screamed I wasn't a babysitter, and she needed to pick up her kid." Flames shot to her face, reliving the words she once used to describe the human she loved most. "Do you think I'm awful?"

A soccer ball rolled up to his leg, and he kicked it back to the field. "Are you kidding? Not at all. I don't know what I would've done in that situation, but I'm pretty confident I wouldn't have been nearly as nice."

Holland let her thoughts drift back to that first year. She had no idea about using timers, interval play, or behavior therapy. Every day she scrambled, choked on tears, and failed to catch full breaths. But then, days passed without snotty sobs. Laughter, hugs, and high-fives replaced knots in her stomach. "After a couple of weeks, my anger at Layla for not coming to get Riley transformed into the fear she *would* come back. I didn't want him to leave. And then it morphed into gratitude he was with me." The kids screaming and pumping their legs on the swing set caught her attention. Her parents said they'd bring Riley to a park yesterday. Hopefully, they followed through, especially since Riley overheard. "A year later, I filed paperwork to become his permanent guardian."

The sun peeked through the clouds. Shane lifted himself off the bench. "Let's go under the tree. Your skin is too pale to see the sun."

"Hey!" She nudged him and stood. "You're not

wrong."

He interlaced his fingers with hers and led the way to the opposite side of the park.

From here on out, she never wanted to walk any other way.

"So, did Layla get visitation rights?"

"Technically, yes." She followed him down the path. "Since she didn't appear for court, the judgment defaulted in my favor. They added an option for visitation to the paperwork. At some point, I need to revise it to rescind her rights, but spending all that time and money when she hasn't even called seems pointless."

His lips dipped into a frown. "Poor kid. Was he devastated his mom left?"

Situations like abandonment are when autism is a gift. "He just sort of...adjusted. I'm not sure he was traumatized by her absence." After finding a gazebo with a bench, she resumed folding herself against him and melted into the embrace. She hadn't talked about this for years. A warmth filled her with his genuine curiosity.

He lightly drummed his fingers on her arm. "When did you know he was autistic?"

"Not for almost two years." She watched as several butterflies traveled from flower to flower. "We got kicked out of five or six different daycares, because they couldn't control him, and I swear I almost had a breakdown. The pressure was so intense. Finally, one provider recommended I get him tested."

Several seconds passed. "I'm picturing how I'd handle this situation. I probably would've withdrawn from everyone. You two persevering through everything is incredible." He shifted and then pulled her back. "Can I ask how you felt when you found out he was autistic?"

She thought about the emotions she had when she first heard the diagnosis. "I was relieved. I thought I just sucked at being a parent. He wasn't even close to being potty trained by age five, couldn't brush his teeth, and hardly ever spoke." She inhaled a heavy breath. "I don't know if that sounds awful or not, but for the first time in a year, I had hope once I knew he had ASD."

"You're pretty amazing. You know that?" He kissed the top of her head.

She wanted to pinch herself. Was being with Shane too good to be true?

Chapter 25
Today's Special: Baking in Good Feelings then Glutened in the Gut

Shane grabbed a bucket of cucumbers off the shelf in the restaurant cooler and fixed the sticker on the plastic wrap. Yesterday hit the official month since the night of the reunion, yet his heart still flew into overdrive with the thought of Holland. No doubt about it—he had fallen. Hard. Under the cover of the fridge to hide his goofy smile, he pulled out his phone and texted Holland.

—*What are you doing tonight?*—

—*Eating a pint of ice cream and pinpointing the exact moment where things went wrong in the tenth grade when I thought bangs were a good idea. You?*—

—*Hoping to come over and see the little man.*—

—*Ahem.*—

He smiled at her response and sent the next message.

—*And you, too, of course.*—

—*Yay! I'll throw in extra nuggets.*—

—*How about I bring Chinese takeout for you and me?*—

—*You're kinda the best.*—

—*True story.*—

An hour later, Shane checked his watch for the millionth time in less than ten minutes. "Will you toss me that towel?" he asked the line cook. He flung the towel over his shoulder and moved into the refrigerator to rotate the stock. Spasms shot through his legs, and he bounced on his feet.

This past week, he saw Holland every day at work and called her each night, but four days had passed since he spent time with her outside of the restaurant.

Holland said Riley had a tough time with a recent change in medication.

He respected her need for no visitors. But not seeing her was brutal. The only saving grace was he channeled his energy to the studio and reframed several pieces, installed shelves, and ordered a digital payment system.

Everything in his life aligned for the first time—his heart, shop, and passion. A perfect trifecta. A few nights ago, he ran to the store for cupcake ingredients. The previous baking session ended with most sprinkles scattered on the floor after Riley used extra flair in decorating.

This time, he was prepared. After visiting three stores, he found the ultimate item—train cupcake toppers. No doubt, Riley would love them.

He swung open the refrigerator door, simultaneously getting hit in the face with steamy kitchen air and Amanda's booming voice.

"Ladies and gentlemen. May I have your attention, please?" Amanda cupped her mouth. "Mr. Shane Blackwood was spotted smiling during his entire shift. Yes, friends, you heard that right. Smiling. Critics are calling it the breakout smile of the year. Is this an anomaly? An apparition? Only time will tell. Stay tuned while I uncover the mystery of the stolen frown."

With a grin, he shook his head. "I see why you and Holland make such great friends."

"Truer words have never been spoken." She leaned against the wall and sipped on lemonade. "My girl gettin' to you?"

She has no idea. "A gentleman never tells."

"I'll remember that the next time I see one." She grabbed the tray from the shelf and loaded it with ice water. "You just keep making her happy, and you and I have no problems."

She said the words while smiling, but the message was loud and clear. Shane tossed the paper towel into the garbage and searched for James. After failing to locate him in his office or the front of the café, he texted him.

—*Where you at?*—

—*My wit's end.*—

—*Ha. You kill me. I need a quick chat before I leave.*—

—*Outside freezer, double checking the inventory.*—

When Shane stepped outside, warm air rushed him. He trotted over to James. "Hey, we need to change the menu for Friday. It shouldn't be a big deal, but there aren't enough Kalamata olives and capers for *puttanesca*. But we have an abundance of Parmesan and Pecorino, so we'll do *Cacio e Pepe* instead. Can you update the website?"

"Yep." James held the clipboard over his head to shield the sun. "You headed over to Holland's?"

He fought to keep a blank expression for his nosy uncle.

"I'd ask how things are, but the perma-smile tells me all I need to know." James smiled. "You two playing it safe?"

"You're not seriously giving me the birds-and-bees talk, right?" Shane didn't need to tell James this, but he and Holland moved quickly, emotionally. But physically, most everything else was off-limits. He wanted to build a foundation before potentially complicating their relationship. As *extraordinarily* difficult as that was. "You're killing me, man."

James laughed and slapped him on the chest. "Okay, okay, I'm the worst. I feel like a—"

"Overbearing mom? You are." Shane cross-checked the inventory list, then sprinted to his car. He could not waste any more time.

****

Holland rinsed soapy water from the last dinner plate. She grabbed a spray bottle and scurried around the room, wiping all the food spills.

Shane's signature five-tap knock rapped on the door.

"Come in!" Her heart raced as quickly as her feet to hug him.

Riley's bare feet pattered down the hall. "One, two, three, eyes on me." He nudged Holland out of the way and threw his arms around Shane.

"Hey, Buddy! So happy to see you." Shane squeezed him and moved the grocery bag to his other hand. "Hey, beautiful," he whispered above Riley's head.

Heat swooshed across her face—*as usual.* She reached over Riley to grab Shane for a quick kiss.

A squished Riley giggled and poked his fingers into her ribs.

"Okay, okay." Holland laughed and stepped to the

side.

"Riley, I brought a surprise." Shane handed Riley the grocery bag.

Riley dug in and held up his loot. "Trains? I love trains so much!"

"I know. Me, too." Shane moved to the kitchen with Riley and Holland at his side and lined the ingredients on the counter. "All right, let's get our chefs' hats and aprons." He wrapped an apron around Riley first, then her.

For years, she had lived a rule-less lifestyle—traveled, ate, and watched what she wanted. So many times, she thought of routines as crushing, whether they crushed her creativity or killed her happy buzz. Since Riley, she discovered the joy in routine. Catapulted to the top of her list—Tuesday Baking Night.

"Ready for this?" Shane tousled Riley's hair. "First, we crack the eggs. Then, we mix the ingredients, then bake the muffins. In the end, we will put the trains on top of the cupcake."

Riley gripped an egg in his palm. "Then one, two, three, cheese."

"Yep," Shane said. "Then we can take a picture."

Holland's heart was normally full, but when Shane, Riley, and she were together, it busted at the seams. Nothing else brought her as much happiness as Riley and Shane baking with matching outfits. And watching her boyfriend in a chef's hat as his forearm muscles flexed while he mixed batter...*uff.*

"You sure you don't want to try this time?" Shane rested a hand on her hip and reached for the spatula.

She was pretty sure he used any excuse for physical contact. And she soaked the moments in.

"Nope. I'm sticking to my no-baking rule. For everyone's safety." Besides, she loved the two boys in her life had built a special bond.

"Okay." He kissed her forehead and turned back to monitor the egg-cracking situation. "Great job, Riley! One more egg, then we'll do more ingredients."

Riley cracked the last one, and all the shells splintered into the bowl. "Oh no! The shells."

"It's okay. Let's scoop them out like we're fishing." Shane puckered his mouth, flicked his cheek, and released an air bubble sound like an aquarium.

Riley laughed and tried to mimic the gesture.

She would never, ever get sick of watching those two interact. "Haven't heard that before. Impressive." She moved to preheat the oven.

After mixing all the ingredients, Shane monitored Riley as he set the train toppers across the counter in a perfect line.

She reached into the fridge for lemonade and then glanced at her two boys bonding over cupcakes and giggling over goofy sounds. The kitchen was alive with laughter and the sweet smell of melting chocolate. A beautiful magenta-golden hue spread throughout the kitchen with the evening sun—a perfect moment in a month of perfect moments.

Ding-dong. Her head jolted. "Weird. I'm not expecting any deliveries."

Shane set down a cupcake topper. "You want me to answer it?"

She shot him *the look.*

He threw up his hands. "Sorry, sorry. My girlfriend is a strong, independent woman who doesn't need things like that. Pretty sure I quoted you correctly from our last fight, right?"

"We don't fight. Yet." After she removed her chef's hat and wiped her hands across the apron, she looked through the peephole. Her brain took several long seconds to register who stood on the patio. And when she did, the recollection violently stripped away the oxygen from her lungs. *This can't be happening.*

She cracked open the door. Standing like a statue staring back was a near mirror image—same red hair, green eyes, and curvy body frame. "Layla," Holland whispered and braced herself against the doorframe. "What are you doing here?" Her sister stood with an unreadable expression while death-gripping her purse strap.

"Hey, sis. Long time." A faint smile appeared before her jaw went rigid, and she dropped her arms. "I came for Riley."

Chapter 26
Today's Special: Boiling Sister Stew and Shocked Side Salad

Holland stared at her sister standing on the porch, and her heartbeat screamed in her ears. One minute prior, she was enjoying Baking Night. And now, she was faced with her living nightmare. She stepped outside and shut the door. "Five years, Layla." She slammed her arms across her chest and kept her voice low, so it didn't travel to the cracked-open kitchen window. "You haven't seen Riley in over five years."

Layla dropped one foot back on the porch but maintained braced shoulders. "I know. And I have a million things to apologize for. I'm sure this might be upsetting for you or Riley, but—"

"Upsetting? Are you actually serious?" She clenched her teeth. "You don't get to do this. You are not allowed to act like you can even grasp Riley's emotions." The ball of rage inside her grew at a feverish rate. She'd thought about this moment after winning custody. An entire monologue was planned if Layla ever showed up. But now, Holland's mind blanked, and all she saw was red.

Layla's chest rose and lowered. "Can you hear me out for a minute?"

Her tone bordered on a fine balance of soft and defensive, but she held her body steady. "No. There's nothing to say." Holland vigorously twirled her comfort ring. "How dare you show up! Not even a phone call?"

"Would you have answered?"

"No."

Layla's green eyes narrowed at Holland. "I know I have a lot to explain." She dropped a hand from her purse and wrung her fingers. "I was so stressed out, and Riley was such a difficult baby. He cried all the time and was impossible to console. Nothing I did helped. I was on my own, dealing with a plethora of issues, and…I couldn't raise him anymore. That sounds awful. I know it does. But I mentally struggled and didn't know who to turn to. I'm so ashamed of my behavior."

Fire consumed Holland's insides. Her sister couldn't possibly be serious. Riley cried all the time? Kids cry! "Are you trying to make me feel bad? You left him! This incredible, sweet boy. You just left, Layla—threw him to the side like trash. Didn't even bother to call once to see if he was okay."

Layla winced. "People give up their children all the time. Most consider it an act of love—"

"Unbelievable." The rage boiled over. Holland closed the gap. "A mother who gives up her babies for adoption is *not* what you did. You abandoned him. He deserves so much more."

Layla tiptoed back and leaned onto the railing. "I know it seems like that from your perspective, but I didn't leave him on the side of the road or anything. Mom gave me your address, and I told the social worker where to find you. I knew you'd be better than me. And I definitely knew you'd be better than Mom and Dad."

"I was twenty-two! I didn't know how to raise a

child." She grabbed Layla by the arm and the wooden planks creaked beneath her feet. Holland pushed Layla farther down the porch. "You didn't send any clothes. You didn't leave a note about what he eats, his favorite song, if he had allergies, or what diapers to buy. Nothing, Layla. You left him, a disgusting teddy bear, and the clothes on his body. Who does that?"

"I was in crisis..." Layla's shoulders slumped, and she pressed her thumbs against her forehead. She focused on her feet for several moments before meeting Holland's glare. "Does he still like *Twinkle, Twinkle Little Star?*"

How dare she pretend like she cares or pretend like she knew what Riley might like! Riley was in diapers, not talking, and drinking from a sippy cup the last Layla saw him. And now he makes cupcakes and jewelry, goes to school, and zips his coat, *and she knows nothing!* "You don't get to know. You haven't earned the right to know anything."

Layla sighed. "Holland, I'm his mom."

Those words were a knife that stabbed Holland in the stomach. Of course, Layla was Riley's mom. But for the last five years, Holland was his mom. She couldn't stop her chin from trembling. Thoughts of clawing at Layla combined with images of police officers dragging away a screaming Riley. Acid rolled in her belly and shot fire through her chest. "You had a social worker drop him off and never once checked on him," she said through gritted teeth. "A mom? You've got some nerve to call yourself that. You are *nothing* to him. Do you hear me? He doesn't even know you exist."

All the color drained from Layla's face, and her

mouth screwed tightly. Several heavy moments passed before she took a sharp inhale. "Listen, I understand how you need to use me as a punching bag right now. I get—"

The sound of footsteps and a door opening made Holland snap up her head.

"Mimi! Where are you?" Riley's voice called from the other room.

She sprinted to the door to block his view but wasn't quick enough. She barred him with an arm from going farther and tugged him into her side.

"One, two, three eyes on me." He peered at Layla.

She sucked in a short, quivering breath. "Oh my God." She flew her right hand to her heart and lowered her body. "He's so beautiful."

Tiny fingers dug into Holland's side.

"Riley!" Shane called from several feet away. Reaching the doorway, he locked a narrowed gaze on Holland before shifting to Layla. "Is everything okay here?"

Holland tightened her jaw. "Get him inside."

Shane tugged on Riley's hand. "Come on, Buddy. Let's watch the timer. The cupcakes are almost done."

The latch to the door clicked, and Holland reeled toward Layla. As the heat in her body transformed into iciness, she shot Layla with a lethal venom-dagger look.

Layla's sandaled feet fumbled a step back, and she put up her hands. "I don't want any trouble. Truly."

No trouble? She must be joking. What did she expect would happen showing up unannounced? The only thing Layla would get was trouble. "Get off my property. You're trespassing, and I'll call the police."

Layla lifted a brow. "You wouldn't."

"Do you really want to try me?" Holland leveled her stare. "Listen to me, Layla." She dropped her voice to a steely, cool tone to articulate each word.

Listening to others was never Layla's strong suit. This time, she'd hear every word. "I will do anything to protect him—literally anything. And that includes letting him see you."

Layla dropped her mouth. "This isn't over, Holland. No matter what you think, I deserve to see my son. You'll be hearing from my lawyer." She bolted down the stairs.

With her chin trembling, Holland stood frozen.

Layla climbed into her car and peeled out of the cul-de-sac.

The moment her sister was gone, Holland dropped to her knees, stuffed the apron into her mouth to muffle her sound, and screamed.

Chapter 27
Today's Special: Molten Lava Mama-Bear Cake

Holland didn't have the luxury of tears right now, as Layla's interruption on her doorstep a few minutes ago would already throw Riley off his baking routine. She knelt on the porch and fisted the corner of her apron until her knuckles turned white. Her mind flashed, her body shook, and pounding sounded in her ears. A fierce churning in her gut kicked unlike anything she'd ever experienced. She peeled herself off the porch floor. *Layla will not take Riley.*

What was Riley thinking? Was he confused? She never spoke about Layla. Riley might or might not grasp the situation, and she never wanted to put herself in a position to explain why his mother wasn't around. She pulled in a deep breath and exhaled slowly through her nose, as she borrowed the calming technique Amy taught them during therapy. After repeating the pattern four times, she lifted her chin and returned inside the house. "Mmmm. Smells good." She choked out the words.

Shane rested his hands on her shoulders. "Are you okay?"

No. She nodded, but if she answered aloud, the tear dam would break.

His eyes furrowed. "Was that…"

"Yes," she muttered, then stepped over to Riley.

"Did you start frosting without me? Silly."

Riley held up his chocolate-covered fists. "Monster hands."

Autism was a godsend. Riley seemed unfazed by the interaction. Since Layla wasn't carrying any packages or candy, Riley probably lost interest. *Hopefully.*

Riley pushed a finger into his mouth and licked. "Yummy!" He twinkled his fingers in front of Holland's face. "Mimi, try. Yummy."

"Ew! I don't want to lick your fingers. What if I chew them off...num, num, num?" She used all her effort to force out a chuckle, but her voice broke. She was broken. *Layla could take Riley away.* Everything in her body told her to pack him up and run—shove his purple blanket, nighttime book, and favorite bathrobe into a duffle bag and drive. Or fight. Or cry. Or...something. Riley held her entire heart in his sticky, glazed fingers. If Layla was serious and contacted a lawyer, then Holland's world would crumble.

Her lips trembled, and she kissed the top of his head. "Mimi has to use the bathroom. Be right back." She covered her mouth and speed-walked down the hall. The second after she shut the door, she slid down the wall. She buried her head in a towel and bawled a silent cry. Her stomach twisted so tightly she got sick.

Hands slapped on the door. "Mimi! Train's ready."

"Just a minute, Bubby." After heaving herself up, she splashed cold water on her face and looked at her red eyes and cheeks in the mirror. She prayed Riley would be so focused on the cupcakes he wouldn't notice the change in her appearance. Her limbs felt like they weighed a million pounds. She dragged herself down the hall and batted her tears back.

Shane set the frosting knife into the sink, and his face dropped.

She shook her head and pleaded with her eyes not to say anything.

His eyebrows bunched together, then he nodded.

"Ready? One, two, three. Cheers!" She touched each cupcake and took a bite. Her mouth was dry and felt uncooperative, and she could barely choke down the dessert. Twenty minutes later, she put on Riley's favorite train video channel and motioned Shane toward the living room.

"Are you okay?" He pulled her in for a hug and stroked her hair.

For the first time, she wasn't calmed by his touch.

"What did she want?"

"She wants Riley." Her breath caught in her throat again, and she gnawed on the inside of her cheek. "She said she got a lawyer. I don't know if she's just threatening me or if she's coming back with the police. If she challenges my legal guardianship, we'll end up in court, and I can't afford a lawyer."

He stepped back and gripped her hands. "She has no legal right to come here with the police and take Riley away. There've been no complaints. Even if she called the police, they'd have to see he was in imminent danger, which he's obviously not."

The thought of losing Riley nearly made her crumble. She peeked at him, and her stomach turned.

He kicked his legs under the table while his gaze remained unblinking at the images on his screen.

"But she said she's coming back! What am I going to do?" The walls closed in. Not enough air existed in the room. She yanked off the apron and tried to capture a proper lungful of oxygen. Her body trembled, and she slumped down on the edge of the couch.

Shane sat and massaged her neck. "We'll figure this out. Walk me through what she said."

A million thoughts collided at once. The image of their conversation was fuzzy, even though it just happened. But Layla's intention was clear—she wanted Riley. "I need to find out if my mom knows about Layla coming here. Can you watch Riley?" She didn't wait for a response and grabbed the phone from the side table. She jogged down the hall to her bedroom, dialed, and paced. *Come on, come on. Pick up!* On the fifth ring, the call was answered. "Layla came here tonight." She kept her voice an octave below yelling and moved to the bedroom corner to prevent Riley overhearing their conversation. "Did you know about this?"

"Layla? She's in town?" Gina screeched. "Oh, Honey, we haven't seen her for so many years! I've been praying for her to return. How is she? Was she healthy? Did she look okay? Is she coming to see Dad and me?"

Her mother took the knife Layla stabbed her with and twisted it. "Are you freaking kidding me? She wants to see Riley."

"That's wonderful!"

"Am I living in some sort of alternative universe right now?" Holland ground her knuckles into the wall. "None of this is wonderful. You don't understand how terrible this is?"

"Terrible?"

Gina sounded genuinely shocked.

"Holland, this is *incredible.* When we spoke last

week, she asked for your address but didn't mention coming here. How long will she be in town? I can't wait to see her!"

"You told her where we live?" Holland pushed her palm into her temple.

"Well, Honey…I mean, I didn't know if she wanted to send you a card, or—"

"Are you serious?" Heat rose in her chest. "Do you have any idea how much this will negatively affect Riley?" Holland removed the phone from her ear and inhaled a fiery breath. Her mother's perpetual cluelessness reached a heightened level. "Layla coming here was *terrible,* awful, horrible, vile, what other freaking words can I—"

"Michael!" Gina shouted at Holland's father. "Layla went to Holland's tonight."

"What? Is she okay?" The rest of Dad's words were muffled, but his elation was profound.

Unbelievable. "What's wrong with you all? How are neither of you asking how Riley is? Or me, for that matter?"

Gina sighed. "This is just such a shock. What did she say?"

I'm living in a twilight zone. Holland balled the corner of her bedspread into her fists. "Do you understand how devastating this is? She's a *stranger.*"

"Riley doesn't have issues with strangers."

"That's not the point! *I* have issues with strangers. I have no idea if she is unstable or dangerous. If she's on drugs…" Even though Layla's clear eyes and speech indicated she was sober. *But still!*

Gina continued talking to Michael and ignored Holland's pleas for understanding.

The familiar, sickening sensation of being left on an island unprotected and unsupported seeped in. She'd dealt with this feeling over the years, pushed it under the rug, and buried it deep because what other option did she have? But now Riley was in the picture and everything changed.

She ended the call, flung the cell onto her bed, and wondered if her mother noticed the dead end on the other line. Trudging down the hall, she dragged her feet on the carpet. She returned to the kitchen.

Wooden trains lined the space between Shane and Riley. After Shane glanced up, he stood and opened his arms.

She collapsed against his chest. "This can't be happening." When she felt Riley nudge himself in between their embrace, she couldn't stop the tears from brimming again. She hugged him and kissed the top of his head.

He ran back to the trains.

He was her everything. And Layla threatened to take him away. How dare she show up like this—no phone call, no email, and with complete disregard for anyone but herself? Ten years had passed since Holland last spoke to her, but some things never changed. Layla was still the same selfish jerk she was as a teenager.

"Tonight, let's just follow the routine," Shane whispered and rubbed her neck. "We'll do the dishes as usual. I'll leave when you do bath and bedtime. And when he's asleep, call me, and I'll come back."

She nodded and swiped her thumbs under her eyes.

"We'll figure this out together." His chest tightened against her cheek. "I think I can help."

She hoped so. At this point, she had no more

options.

****

Seated in his vehicle a block from Holland's, Shane stared at his phone for almost an hour. He knew what to do, but every time he picked up the cell to make the call, he froze.

He tossed the phone onto the passenger side and rested his head on the seat. Chirping crickets surrounded him, providing a blanket of white noise to counteract the thoughts about the disastrous event when he last spoke to his dad—slammed doors, raised voices, and Shane throwing an adult tantrum. An equal number of words were left unsaid as regretful words hurled.

But now, the situation changed. Tonight, the look on Holland's face crushed him. Her shaky voice and frantic twirling of her favorite ring gutted him to his core. He could help—at least *try* to help. No longer was avoidance about him and his ego. The people he cared about needed him. *Be a man, face your fears, and swallow your pride.* He twitched his fingers, and acid crept into his throat. He exhaled a shaky breath and dialed.

On the second ring, the call was answered.

"Dad?" He cleared his sticky throat. "I need your help."

Only a second passed. "Whatever you need, I'm here."

Chapter 28
Today's Special: Charcuterie Board of Emotions

After Layla's surprise visit yesterday, Holland battled with blankets all night. But, she refused to allow lack of sleep to impact today's fight. Armed with a Saint Bernard-sized mug holding enough caffeine for a hundred troops and a binder loaded with written ammunition, she left the house, determined to stop Layla from taking Riley. Holland walked Riley to his classroom and gave him a long, drawn-out hug. She rocked him, squeezed, and planted kisses on his head.

He finally tapped out. "Mimi, school."

She bolted out of the classroom to the parking lot to meet Shane. She jumped into the vehicle and plunked her mug into the console.

"It'll take about two hours to get to Edina." He pulled into the road and crossed lanes. "We need to pick up Riley by three, right?"

"No, my parents are picking him up." She exhaled a heavy breath.

He lifted an eyebrow. "Really? That's a new development."

All of this was a new development. Last night, after she put Riley to bed, Holland spent hours sifting through her original court documentation with Shane by her side. Her head swirled like a lightning-speed carnival carousel, and the complex words overwhelmed her.

Shane had explained the different terms like de facto, guardian *ad litem*, and *in forma pauperis*.

The words were all Greek...rather Latin...and she tripped on the terminology. All she knew was the judge gave her custody of Riley, and Layla didn't have the decency to show up and fight for her child.

Once Holland was alone, she called Amanda for moral support.

She offered to bring "wine, chocolate, or nunchakus."

Afterward, Holland called her parents. She still fumed at their complete lack of empathy but didn't have the luxury of holding a grudge. She told them she had an appointment and asked them to pick up Riley.

And then, she turned on lioness mode—bulleted lists created, files gathered, and calls made. She didn't care what she had to do—including spending as much time with Shane's estranged dad, who graciously offered to help for free.

The vehicle thumped over a large bump on the road, and Holland's mind snapped back to present mode. She slapped her palm against her forehead. "I'm meeting your parents."

"Yeah?" Shane moved to the highway entrance ramp and accelerated.

"Shane!" She gripped his arm and looked down. "I'm wearing leggings. I took like a three-minute shower."

A slow grin appeared. "You look beautiful. And they won't care."

Her heart thumped wildly in her chest. "And...*I'm meeting your parents*."

"Repeating the words will not change the reality." He kissed her hand.

With the whirlwind of the last twelve hours, the gravity of the situation didn't occur until now. But her desperation to keep custody of Riley outweighed the typical nerves. "Is this too fast? We've only been dating for like a month."

"Not too fast for me." He peeked out of his peripherals. "You know I'm all-in, right? I knew I'd bring you home soon to meet the family."

For the first time since her living nightmare began, she softened. Instead of battling demons solo, she had a partner. Shane's tremendous act of love by calling his father wasn't lost on her. Burnt orange leaves on the trees whipped by outside the window. She replayed the questions for Shane's dad. Did the judgment still hold? Wasn't there some statute of limitation? Should she file a restraining order? She needed to hear she had some control. "Are you nervous about seeing your parents again?"

He shrugged. "Yeah, a little. My dad and I only talked for a few minutes. Pretty sure I'll need to address what went down. Even though I secretly hope we get there and pretend nothing happened."

Attempting to give him a fraction of the comfort he'd provided the last eighteen hours, she reached for his knee. "I know seeing your parents is tough, but you can do this." A meet-the-parents moment hadn't happened since high school, but she always assumed she'd be more nervous. But she was laser-focused—Riley first, everything else second.

****

Shane turned down the road to the familiar

neighborhood and tensed his leg muscles. Maybe a call saying Layla changed her mind would save them—a Hail Mary pass to buy him a few more weeks to prepare for seeing his parents. He eased up on the gas pedal and cracked the window. The perfectly manicured lawns with straight-edged bushes set against the multi-level, three-car-garage homes used to provide him with comfort. Now, his stomach was sour, and the looming sense of an impending difficult conversation lingered like a cloud. He rolled into the driveway and turned off the engine.

Holland's eyes grew wide. "Oh my…this is your house?"

"No." He swallowed. "This is my parents' house."

"You're talking like a lawyer." She stuffed the folder from her lap into her bag. "This was the house you grew up in?"

He nodded.

She dipped her head. "It's…huge."

After forcing his legs to move, he finally exited the car. He glanced at the Colonial-style, six-bedroom brick home and said nothing. His parents had done well for themselves, but life was so much more than square footage. His chest tightened. He exhaled an aggressive breath, swiped his damp hands on his jeans, then reached for Holland's hand.

Her creased forehead showed she was just as nervous.

As he gripped her hand, he took the lead in walking to the door. Although his father was pleasant on the phone yesterday and canceled all his client appointments today, Shane had no idea what laid behind the mahogany double doors. He lifted the antique chrome knocker, and the door burst open. His mom grabbed him like he had arrived home from deployment.

"Shane! Oh, my sweet boy! Let me look at you."

Maggie Blackwood was sharply dressed as usual, with black slacks, a crisp button-down blouse, and her gray bob set like she stepped out of the salon. All five feet of her reached up and held him by the shoulders. "You look so rested. Your color!" She hugged him again. "I've missed you."

Test one—passed. No mention of fights or law school, for this moment anyway. Shane cleared his throat and accepted he'd always be her baby. "Mom, Holland. Holland, my mom."

"Hi, Mrs. Blackwood." Holland extended a hand.

In true form, his mother ignored the handshake and seized Holland for an embrace. Shane said a silent prayer of thanks to the Intimacy Gods that his mom didn't clutch Holland's face and maintained a proper, first-time-meeting-someone distance.

"Please call me Maggie. I'm so happy to meet you."

Leather-loafered footsteps approached the door, and Shane's heartbeat paused. His father, Ken, reached out for a handshake. Shane accepted the greeting.

Ken pulled him in for a half hug and a firm pat on the back. "Shane."

"Dad." And that would be the extent of their talk. *For now.*

After introductions, Ken shifted toward Holland. He pointed at the manila folder in the bag clutched against her chest. "Is that the paperwork from the proceedings?"

Holland nodded.

Maggie's signature single clap echoed against the walls. "I'm just about to pull peanut butter bars out of the oven, and I made those pinwheels you like, Shane. I'll bring in fruit and drinks. Holland, dear, do you drink coffee?"

"Probably too much." Holland grinned

Maggie leaned toward her. "My kind of girl."

Ken stepped back and waved an arm to escort her into the home. "Let's go into my study." He walked a few feet before he tilted his head. "Shane, you're welcome to join."

Gee, thanks. Shane withheld his frown and nodded instead. Time to push any harsh feelings to the side and accept his dad was doing them a massive favor. Holland might have been nervous, but she walked with her head high and followed his father to the study.

"Shane." Maggie laid a gentle hand on Shane's forearm. "Why don't you be a doll and help me in the kitchen?"

And, here it is. He trailed his mother down the foyer, feeling like a twelve-year-old on the way to detention. Being back at home was surreal. The house felt the same—a little cold, dark, and clean. But it also had the faint scent of fall-inspired candles, family photos lined multiple walls, and a bookshelf filled with old soccer and peewee football championships remained untouched.

Maggie grabbed mitts from the drawer and moved to the stainless-steel double oven. She pulled out the bars and set them on the potholders on the granite countertop.

He reached for a glass from the floating shelf and

filled it with lemon-infused water from a crystal pitcher.

"Could you grab the platter from the top shelf?" Maggie jutted her chin toward the wall.

The smell of chocolate, corn syrup, and peanut butter permeated the room, and if his stomach weren't so wound up, he would've appreciated the dessert. He grabbed the platter and set it on the counter. "Mom."

She kept her back to him and poured coffee into the silver carafe. "What does that sweet girl take with her coffee? Milk, sugar?"

He stepped closer. "Mom."

"I'll bring both." She opened a cabinet and pulled out a glass sugar container. "Grab oat milk for your dad and the whole milk for me."

Tightness cramped his chest. She needed to stop avoiding him. "Mom."

"I'm bringing crackers, too. Does she like crackers? Maybe cheese?" She scurried to the fridge. "I only have brie and gruyere, but that should do." She organized the food like a pro, and when one broke on the platter, she swore.

He touched her forearm. "Mom."

She set down the cracker and laid her palms flat against the counter. "I know, Shane." She took a breath. Her thin shoulders showed a whisper of a quiver before she faced him. "I'm so very sorry."

"No, *I'm* sorry." He stared at his clasped hands. "I should've never handled it the way I did."

She shook her head. "I'm your mother. My job is to support and listen. And you *told* us. A thousand times over."

The guilt in her voice shattered him. "Don't blame

yourself. I'm a grown adult. I should've properly talked to you, not filled you with years of innuendos." He dropped his shoulders. "This was Dad's dream, and I let him down. He was so angry that day, and I didn't know what to do."

"He *was* angry. But, honey, he should've never called the law school dean. We were both in panic mode. In a completely misguided way of supporting you, we thought contacting the school would protect you. When you didn't respond to my message, I felt horrible."

Shane took a sip of water, and let his gaze wander to the window. "Why didn't you two reach out?"

She returned to arranging the cheese slices. "We wanted to give you space."

Now that her pained expression faced away, he relaxed his chest. For months, he pictured this conversation, and various scenarios had played out. Some with him storming off while vowing never to speak to his parents. Some of them hugging it out, exchanging words of forgiveness. None of them ever consisted of Holland being in one room with his dad while he and his mom built a flawless charcuterie platter. He snipped grapes from the vine and added them to the corner by the brie.

"Your father's been stressed for years." Maggie's words interrupted the silence. "He hides his anxiety well, just like my dad. But I saw it in him, Shane. He's *buried* with work. He never relaxes. Life just flies by, and he doesn't stop to appreciate it. I think part of him was jealous you stepped away from that madness."

The words trickled in like a relief I.V. Months of stress, and the shame of letting down his parents, slowly evaporated. He wrapped an arm around her shoulder. "We good?"

"We're always good." She placed a hand on his arm and reached for a knife. "This girl, Holland. She's lovely."

You have no idea. He gathered the snipped grape vines and tossed them into the trash. "She is."

She scrunched her eyebrows and cut the chocolate bars. "Your father immediately went into lawyer-client privilege mode and refused to tell me anything. But she's clearly in some sort of trouble. Can you tell me what's going on?"

To check if Holland was there, he looked behind his shoulder, and contemplated how much he should share. Until he got her permission, he'd keep it vague. "She's been raising her nephew for the last five years. And last night, her sister—the birth mom—showed up to see him."

Maggie set the knife on the edge of the pan. The soft wrinkles around the corner of her gray-blue eyes deepened. "Oh, dear. What a tough situation. Is she unstable?"

He picked up the knife and cut the bars into squares. "I don't think so. Holland doesn't even know why she left."

"Custody hearings are difficult for a non-birth parent. Maybe Holland should let her sister see the boy." She reached for the spatula and scooped the dessert onto the platter. "Might be hard on a child, so I can understand the hesitation."

"I don't think his emotions are what she's worried about."

Maggie tilted her head.

He arranged the chocolate pieces on the platter. "He's autistic. So, he might not grasp the emotionality of the situation. I think she's more concerned about his safety."

"He's autistic?" She set down the spatula and studied Shane's face. "That certainly complicates things, I imagine. Her apprehension is understandable. Sending your child with someone you don't trust would be heartbreaking."

The empathetic tone in his mother's voice shined a spotlight on Holland's plight. *Of course,* it'd be heartbreaking. But hearing those words from another mother drove home the point. "For sure. But Riley's autism means he has needs above and beyond most kids. He sticks to a serious routine. Otherwise, everything blows up. He might throw a tantrum, have a meltdown, or run off because he's overloaded. Adults have to be hyper-vigilant to keep him safe."

"You seem to know a lot about caring for a child with autism." She paused for several moments and grabbed a towel to wipe off the chocolate drips that fell on the counter. "You must really care for him...and her."

He felt his heart soften. "I do."

She took a long pause and began cutting lemon slices. "But don't you think a child having contact with their parent is the best option in the long run?"

"I don't know, is it?" His tone was more defensive than he hoped. His mother was trying not to antagonize him, but he cared about Riley more than any other child.

If Holland didn't trust Layla, then neither did he. He hung the dishtowel on the oven handle and leaned against the counter. "I'm not a parent. But being with Holland and Riley, I'm getting a taste of what it might be like."

Only Holland knew what was best for Riley.

Shane's job was to back up her decisions.

Maggie squeezed him on the shoulder. She looked at the platter and dusted off the tiniest cracker crumbs in the corner.

The plate looked like it belonged on the cover of an international food magazine. How did it only sink in now where he inherited his kitchen bullheadedness? "I don't think Layla will give up. I'd move heaven and earth if I couldn't see my kid. But Holland won't give up, either." He sighed and crossed his arms. "She's been Riley's mom longer than Layla ever was, and she'll fiercely protect him from someone she sees as unfit. I don't know what the best course is."

"Well, thankfully, you're her boyfriend, not her lawyer. Which means you get to support her and not determine the course of action." She lifted the plate. "But I can tell you, as a mom, I don't think I'd ever stop trying."

His mom just articulated his fear. No way would Holland give up, no matter the consequences.

"Grab that tray with the coffee and mugs, please." She nodded her head to the corner. "And Shane?"

He picked up the platter and an extra set of napkins. "Yeah?"

"I'm really proud of you."

The words warmed him, and he allowed himself to enjoy the moment. But as he and his mom walked the food to the study, he couldn't stop his stomach from twisting. If his father couldn't help Holland, then she might lose Riley forever.

Chapter 29
Today's Special: Reconciliation Risotto with Apprehension Aioli

Shane piled scattered forks and spoons on top of the plates on the cherrywood side table in his father's den. Remnants of the cracker and cheese platter from earlier strewed across the desk, and he wiped them with a towel. An embarrassing yawn escaped, and he peeked to check if Holland noticed. He shouldn't be this tired. Holland had been the one to sit in his father's stuffy office for hours, sifting through paperwork while he and his mom strolled through the neighborhood.

"Are you sure you can't stay for dinner?" Maggie asked Holland as she gathered empty glasses.

"I appreciate the offer and would love to take a rain check." Holland tapped the stack of papers on the desk to straighten and put them in the folder. "I need to be home in time for bath and bedtime, or Riley will have a tough time." Exhaling a heavy breath, she stretched her arms above her head and cracked her neck.

She flexed her fingers, which were probably cramped from taking six hours' worth of notes.

"Shane, a word?" Ken pointed toward the door.

Shane could be fifty and still get intimated by his tone. "Sure." He kissed Holland on the cheek. "I'll be back in a few." He followed his father and walked through the French doors to the patio. The sun peeked through the trees surrounding the lush greens of hole number nineteen—the most coveted spot at Whistling Pines.

Ken gripped the railing and stayed silent.

He fell into his usual mode of operation—initiating a verbal game of chicken. He'd be hell-bent on not talking first, no doubt.

"Seems like it stays warmer longer every year."

Ken surprisingly broke the silence. *Interesting...*

"Not that I'm complaining," he continued. "But we're almost in October, and the trees only started changing this week."

Shane cleared his throat. "Thanks for helping Holland. I really owe you." No time like the present to dive headfirst into an awkward conversation. Ken swooshed it away like he was batting at a fly.

"She loves that little boy and clearly wants what she thinks is best. There doesn't seem to be any ill will as I've seen with other cases. She's not withholding Riley from her sister as a means of punishment or control."

His father's kind tone dulled his nerves. "She'd never do that."

"Happens more than you think. With both parents." Ken straightened and fixed his gaze on the greens. "I tried to prep her, but I'm not sure she's fully grasping the likely outcome. You advanced far enough in your education to know how the courts will rule. Unless we can prove Layla was negligent, abusive, or an active drug addict, the court will allow access to Riley."

Hearing his dad confirm his suspicions made Shane stiffen his back. Last night, he'd stayed up until two a.m. researching custody cases, and ninety-nine percent of the verdicts ruled in favor of parental visitation. But he maintained hope his father knew of a magic loophole. He tapped his finger against the wicker chair and watched a golf cart drive to the next hole. "Holland never terminated Layla's rights." If he could go back in time and tell her to do it differently, he would. If Layla had her rights terminated, then Holland could've adopted Riley and avoided this turmoil.

"She made the right decision at the time." Ken pulled out a handkerchief and wiped his nose. "You must've learned how difficult ending parental rights is once they've been established, even if both parties are willing."

Shane's pulse increased. "Yeah, but now—"

"Now, she'll need to accept Layla will have some rights to Riley. Most likely, Layla prepped for quite some time for her surprise visit yesterday." Ken leaned a hip against the railing. "She probably has steady employment, permanent housing, and a bank account. My guess is she's actively making reparations for owed child support."

Child support. Maybe one positive would come out of this mess. "I didn't even think of the money."

Ken nodded. "Well, if Holland gets an unexpected check, you'll know the process started."

Shane inhaled a constricted breath.

Holland never actively spoke about finances or lack thereof. But when her car broke down last month, worry filled her face. And last week, before she left to buy Riley shoes, she first checked her online bank account. Anyone could deduce money was tight.

"If Layla's lawyer is worth their weight, they'll already have submitted alcohol and drug test results."

Ken watched a few putters cross the greens. "Not a smart move to show up at Holland's house, but unless she does it a few more times, the judge will sweep that under the rug."

A tugging began in his lower stomach. "So, what are we looking at here?"

"We're looking at a real possibility Holland will lose some rights." Ken exhaled. "The system's not always fair or perfect. But the courts will always rule in favor of the birth parents."

None of this was news. For years, he was on the other side, reading court cases and verdicts—words on a page, lectures in an auditorium. He was detached and unaffected. The law was one-dimensional. Having those same codes and legislation affect someone he deeply cared about gutted him. "What happens next?"

Ken exhaled and faced Shane. "If Holland fights, as does Layla, we're talking months, maybe years, of an emotionally draining court battle. I'm doing this pro bono, but that doesn't mean other expenses won't exist—filing fees, court fees, time off work. Layla's lawyer will call Holland's character into question. The courts will force her parents to testify against one of their daughters. The routine she spoke about with Riley will be severely interrupted."

Holland could master-juggle anything lobbed her way. She was the strongest, most dedicated person he knew. But everything his dad said sounded awful. Shane scratched the top of his arm and stared at the golf course. "What can I do?"

His father laid a firm hand on Shane's shoulder. "Talk to Holland. Help convince her to at least hear Layla out. Maybe they can come to an agreement."

Clearly, his father had never run into the brick wall of Holland's stubbornness. "Getting Holland to agree is gonna be tough." Shane wrung his hands. "Layla's messing with her kid."

"But Riley's *not* her child, no matter how much she loves him." Ken leaned toward him, taking a pause. "She's a wonderful young woman—smart, diligent, respectful. She must've taken twenty pages of notes today. Clear as day, she wants what's best for the boy."

"We both want what's best for him." His voice cracked. Hopefully, his father didn't notice. Shane's relationship with Holland and Riley was delicate, even borderline sacred. And he and his father had not healed enough to discuss his relationship.

Ken twisted the dial on his watch. "The fact you contacted me indicates you two are pretty serious?"

Shane didn't respond but was sure his face gave his father the answer. *No more avoidance. Have the talk.* His pulse pounded in his ears. "I'm so sorry, Dad, for what happened with us. I should've talked to you like a man, not stomped out like a toddler."

Ken's stiff shoulders softened. "And I should have respected you like a man and not treated you like a child incapable of making his own decisions."

Fragmented thoughts spun. *Dad just apologized.* The tension in his shoulders began to melt. Ken stood still for so long, taking in large pulls of air, that Shane almost asked him if he was okay.

"When I was younger, my dad wanted me to play football."

Football? Shane's head tilted. What did a sport have to do with anything?

"And I didn't want to play," Ken continued after

several long beats. "But he insisted, and I became deeply resentful. Every lap, every game, and every practice, I cursed him." He stared at the golf course. "I promised myself I'd never do that to my child. And here, I did the *same*. Even worse, if I'm being honest." He folded his arms in front of his chest. "You were so darn independent...and talented. When you'd paint, you'd close yourself off for hours. I don't have a lick of artistic talent. I worried I'd lose you if you didn't need me anymore. But, if you became a lawyer and worked at the firm, I could keep you close. I forced you to be in my dream, not support yours."

The words blew Shane away and explained so much about his childhood. His brain worked overtime to commit this conversation to memory. He needed time to process. The guilt of ignoring his parents for months mixed with relief, and he couldn't slow the messages. But one thing was certain—right now was the closest he felt to his dad in a decade.

Ken checked his watch. "Time to head out and pick up the little guy, huh?"

Shoot. Shane had more things to say but couldn't form anything coherent.

Ken took a sharp inhale. "Being with a woman who has a kid with that level of needs might be quite a challenge."

The potential adversity didn't matter. Holland and Riley were quickly becoming his family. "They're both worth it," Shane said softly. "I've never been happier in my life."

Ken slapped him on the shoulder and strolled back into the house.

When Shane stormed out of here months ago, he

envisioned reconnecting with his parents differently. And he owed it to Holland and Riley, who were cosmically attached to love and touched lives wherever they went. His heart warmed every day having them in his life. But today, his gratitude cup overflowed.

Now, he had to convince his girlfriend the best thing was to hear Layla out. She was strong-willed and stubborn. But he'd never witnessed her level of inflexibility as he did last night.

She wouldn't even entertain a *hint* of a possible sit-down with Layla.

But he agreed with his dad. The best option was to come to an agreement outside of court.

He had his work cut out.

Chapter 30
Today's Special: Brain Fog Filet Marinated in Disappointment

Holland rested her right elbow on the window ledge in Shane's car. The lines on the highway blurred on her way home from his parents' house after spending the day talking about her legal options. He chatted from the driver's seat, but her pinball-machine thoughts muffled his words. Affidavits, documentation, notarization, and a gazillion other things she needed to review tonight swirled in her mind. She dug in her bag for a pencil, then flipped open the notebook. After scribbling five more pages, she stopped when she felt a hand tap her leg.

He moved a hand onto her notebook while keeping his other on the steering wheel. "Want to take a break? My dad dropped a ton of information on you today."

Nope. "Yeah, I probably should." She massaged her aching fingers.

"How are you feeling?" He rolled up the cracked window. "These last twenty-four hours must be brutal."

She shifted positions and rested her head on his shoulder. "They were." She didn't want to talk. Dissecting everything Shane's dad told her was the top priority. A long custody battle loomed on the dark horizon, and her stomach was sour. "Hey, today was huge for you, too." The notebook on her lap felt like it was taunting her, and she clicked her pencil against the cover. Of course, Shane's feelings were important. But right now, she was in crisis mode. The minutes spent talking about anything but Riley distracted her from her fight. "How was seeing your parents?"

"Amazing. By the end of the day, I felt like nothing had happened." He flipped on the blinker and checked the blind spot to go to the fast lane. "They both really liked you."

"What a bizarre first impression for your parents meeting your new girlfriend." She reached for the water bottle on the floor. With the chaos and nerves of the day, she barely registered she was with Shane's dad for hours. Ken was so kind—much different from the cold, distant, and agenda-pushing man she'd formed in her mind. "They're really nice people."

"They are." He adjusted the seatbelt away from his chest and cleared his throat. "So, my dad told you about the options for court? And possibly doing mediation and guardian *ad litem*?"

"He did." She stiffened her back. "And I appreciated him taking the time to explain it all. But it doesn't matter. I'm not doing it. I'll fight Layla to the end."

He breathed in through his nose. "I really think you should consider—"

"I'm not backing down. Riley deserves someone in his corner, protecting him. I refuse to give up on him the way my sister did." No matter how much sitting before a judge and pleading her case intimidated her.

He pulled his lips between his teeth. "Understood."

What would having truly reliable parents be like? To have a coach in the corner handing her a mouth guard and lacing her gloves as she braced to take on the world. Until Shane burst into her life, she flew solo.

Protecting Riley would always come first. He'd never have to wonder if he was part of a team.

Layla was a ferocious, fight-to-the-death kind of person. She always won their sibling rivalry fights, wearing down Holland until she broke.

But Layla had never witnessed Mama-Bear Holland. She would do *anything* for Riley—including keeping his unstable, irresponsible, probably dangerous mother away.

****

"Bubby!" Holland bolted into her parents' three-bedroom rambler and squeezed Riley tight against her chest. Often, she welcomed a brief break from Riley. In the past, spending the afternoon in Minneapolis while her parents watched him would've been a treat. But today, she nearly collapsed with relief to have him in her arms. "How was school?"

He buried his head in her stomach. "Ms. Amy said I did so good."

"I'm so proud of you!" She kissed him multiple times on the top of his head. "Did Grandma feed you chicken nuggets and peas for dinner?"

"Yep! And a cookie for dessert."

She glanced at her mom, who was supposed to hold off giving the cookie to Riley until their car ride home.

Gina shrugged and poured herself a nightcap.

"I'll set the timer for ten minutes." Holland pulled out her phone and started the clock. "Go say goodbye to Grandpa and get your backpack."

Riley's footsteps thumped down the hall, along

with rhythmic clapping sounds.

Holland waited until he rounded the corner. "Thanks for watching him."

"You never told me where you went today. You and Shane have a date?" Gina wiggled her eyebrows.

She braced her shoulders. "I went to see a lawyer."

Gina's face fell. She set the glass of brandy on the counter. "Honey, no. For Layla?"

"For Riley." The firmness in her voice was intended, and she leveled a stare. "I needed to see what my options were. If Layla comes for Riley, then I'll be ready."

Gina put a palm against her heart. "Holly…"

"Don't." Why does she always take Layla's side? In her mother's eyes, Layla could do nothing wrong. When Holland and Layla fought as kids, Holland was either sent to her room or she lost dessert. Layla was born with a permanent get-out-of-jail-free card, and the difference in punishments was freaking unfair.

Gina slid into a chair and dropped her head into her hands. She took several shaky breaths. "Layla called us tonight."

Holland's breath constricted. "And?"

"She didn't know Riley was here. I told her, and she asked me to put him on the phone."

Holland's gut coiled. "What the…you didn't, right? Tell me you didn't."

"What was I supposed to say, Holland?" Gina's head snapped up. "She's his mother."

"Layla forfeited that right a long time ago." She bit her lip to refrain from screaming obscenities. How does her mother not see her side? All of this was basic child-rearing. You leave the child, you lose the child—done and done.

Gina grabbed a fidget toy from the table and clicked her fingernails against the plastic. "Well, you'll be happy to know Riley refused to get on the call, so she didn't talk to him."

Thank God. "Please tell me she didn't come over to see him."

"No, she didn't." She laid the toy on the table. "But we talked for quite a while. She's been working hard on herself. She got a job, started taking night classes—"

"Oh, how nice to be able to do that." A sting flew through her veins. When she got custody of Riley, she had her college dreams shattered. Work, therapy, and bills pushed her to max capacity, leaving no room for academics. The comment hung in the air, and she tried to suck it back. She crossed her fingers the universe wouldn't punish her by thinking she complained about the gift of custody. "Well, I hoped you told her to stay away." *No chance she did.*

Gina retrieved her glass and sat again. "I told her she should probably call you before she stopped by the next time."

The next time? Holland's cheeks burned. The next time Holland would slap her with a restraining order.

"And I told her how you like having a routine for Riley."

"He *needs* a routine. I don't do it because I *like* it." Holland's muscles tightened. Her mother would never understand Riley's needs. No amount of videos or articles or partially attended quarterly therapy sessions would ever cram the necessity of Riley's lifestyle into her mom's head. Why does she even bother? Holland spun on her heels and left the room before too many choice words escaped. She stomped through the house and shoved Riley's scattered toys into her purse.

Gina's hurried footsteps sounded behind Holland.

"You and Layla need to talk sit down and talk. Maybe she'll open up about her struggles—"

"I *cannot* believe you are defending her." She slammed Riley's stuffed caterpillar into her tote and clenched her jaw. "Don't you think Riley deserves better? Do you even care? He's your grandson!"

Gina pressed her hands into Holland's forearm. "And you're my daughter. And so is Layla."

Did her mom have any recollection of what a horrible caretaker Layla was? How do any of them think Layla can even keep Riley safe?

When Layla babysat her as a child, she'd shove a television remote and bag of chips in Holland's hand and bolt out of the house to chase boys. Holland flashed to when she was in high school. Layla left for good like Holland was an afterthought.

She'd never allow Riley to be an afterthought. *Never.*

"Listen, Holly." Gina tugged on her nightgown. "If Riley did something irresponsible, wouldn't you hear him out?"

Holland narrowed her eyes and seethed. "Abandoning your child for five years is not irresponsible. I'm not—" The sound of the timer cut through their conversation. Probably a godsend as the words bubbling inside she couldn't take back once released. Hearing Riley's footsteps approaching, she forced a smile. "Time to go, Bubby." She grabbed his hand, ignored her mother's outstretched arms, and left without another word.

Chapter 31
Today's Special: Oven-Crisped Heartache Served over Torched Regret Pilaf

Holland peeked at Riley through the cracked-open bedroom door. The fear of losing him increased every second. Heart attack-inducing thoughts of Riley being dragged away, him running from Layla, an empty house, and missed therapy appointments overflowed Holland's system. She shoved her hands in her pockets and refrained from climbing into Riley's bed and snuggling until he fell asleep. If the routine wouldn't throw him off, she'd do it.

Three scattered, overwhelming days had passed since she met with Shane's parents and claimed a solid night's sleep. And three days of multiple ignored phone calls and text messages from Layla asking for a sit-down.

She adjusted the bedroom fan and tugged the weighted blanket to his chin. After whispering goodnight, she moved to the living room while massaging her temples.

A hurricane of paper and notes rested on the living room floor, and her stomach twisted into a knot. She considered Shane's dad's explanation of the options for court versus mediation. *Of course,* mediation would be easier. But mediation meant compromise, and she'd never give up on Riley. She gripped the pen, scoured her notes, and triple-checked every email, calendar, doctor, therapy appointment, and daycare record for the last five years to prepare for court.

She picked up her buzzing phone and read a message from Shane.

—*What are you doing?*—

—*Taking a ride on the midnight train to the land of obsession.*—

—*Glad to see you still have a glimmer of humor left. You up for a visit after work?*—

She smiled and typed a response.

—*Sounds amazing. Tell Amanda I'm ready when she is.*—

—*You're the worst. Want me to stop by and get chocolate crunch ice cream in case your current supply is running low?*—

—*I might be the worst, but you're the best.*—

Shane's patience was one for the record books. He sat with her every night, rubbed her shoulders, and forced her to eat whatever takeout he brought. He took notes and color-coded events on the calendar.

She was a self-centered girlfriend right now, but that behavior would change. She and Shane had time. Riley didn't.

Twenty minutes later, lights flickered in the living room window, and she dashed outside. The slight chill from the fall night popped a line of goose bumps on her arms.

Shane exited the car.

As she hugged him, she felt the tightness in her shoulders dissipate.

He folded his arms around her and kissed the top of her head. "Whoa. Can you hug me like this every time?"

"Yes." She breathed in his fresh-meadow shower scent. "How was work tonight?"

"You left around three, right? Your girlfriend did not love that she picked up a double, and a party of four came in five minutes before closing."

"Oh, no." She walked to the mailbox and pulled out a massive stack of letters. "That's the worst. She put salt in their water, didn't she?"

"Not that I saw." He chuckled and dangled a grocery bag. "Cookie dough tonight."

"No chocolate crunch?" She tucked the mail under her arm and followed him into the house.

"They were out."

"Unacceptable." She grinned. "Tell me it's chocolate."

He set the ice cream on the counter. "You think I'd make a rookie mistake like that? Of course, it's chocolate."

When she tossed the pile of mail on the kitchen table, an official-looking envelope with *State of Minnesota* printed in the left corner peeked from under the stack. Her heart stopped. She picked up the letter, then froze.

He threw the ice cream wrapper into the garbage. "What is it?"

The envelope shook in her trembling fingers. "I'm scared to open it."

"Everything will be okay." He put a gentle hand on her shoulder. "Whatever's inside, we'll handle it together. Want me to do it?"

She shook her head and slowly peeled the flap, convinced a live snake or poisonous vapor would seep out. She scanned the document, and the words blurred. *Child support...back payments...Riley Mulberry...Layla Mulberry...installment.* She flipped to the second page. A thousand-dollar check. *A thousand dollars!* This money paid for a month's rent—nearly the equivalent of a paycheck. Was this check a bribe or something? She pushed the letter against Shane's chest.

His gaze scanned the document. He furrowed his brows and then his face settled. "Looks like Layla is paying owed child support."

She grabbed the paper and tossed it on the table. "I don't want it."

He sighed. "Come on. The money can do a lot of good. And my guess is it'll keep coming."

"I'm not taking it." Her stomach turned sour. "This is blood money."

"The check is not blood money." He picked the document off the table. "The original judgment ordered Layla to pay you child support. Since she has avoided her responsibility, this probably means she has steady employment, and they're garnishing her wages."

How was he so calm? Out of the blue, a thousand-dollar check showed up from her sister, and he sounded like he was reading a page from an encyclopedia.

"Take the money, Holland."

She trailed a finger across the letter, evaluating every word while her throat turned sticky. "Accepting this feels so wrong. If I cash this, I'm saying everything was okay." She needed the money. She was a few hundred dollars over living paycheck to paycheck, and one unexpected bill could send her into a tailspin of debt. This money meant non-generic groceries, a blender, and a new winter coat for Riley.

He pulled two spoons from the drawer. "If you really feel bad about cashing the check, spend the money on sensory toys. Use it to take him to the zoo. Or go to the spa to get your nails and hair done. You deserve some pampering."

She lifted an eyebrow. "Is that your nice way of saying I look like a hot mess?"

"Stop it." He chuckled and picked up the ice cream tub. "You're beautiful."

"Even with split ends?"

"Yep, and funky toes."

"What!" She playfully smacked him on the arm.

"No, I mean, if you had funky toes…not that you do…just if you ever wanted a pedicure…you know what? I'm shutting up now." He stuck the spoon in his mouth.

She put a finger to her lips. "Don't wake Riley. Let's go sit on the porch."

On the swinging bench outside, she tucked her legs under her bottom and draped a blanket over her lap. The moonlight rays poked through the smattering of colored leaves on the trees. She shivered from the brisk air and nestled into the seat. She scooped from the ice cream tub, rolled the sweetened cookie dough on her tongue, and let her mind wander. Would the checks keep coming, or was this an isolated event? Would accepting the money compromise her morals? Surely, taking the funds had deeper implications—she just didn't know what those were.

He piled a heaping portion of ice cream onto his spoon. "How did it go tonight?"

The chocolate melted against her tongue, and she shrugged. "Not great. Mom won't drop our conversation from a few days ago. She called again to badger me into talking to Layla."

"Why don't you want to talk?"

Really? She stopped snuggling. "Because nothing Layla would say will change my mind. A conversation is pointless."

He swallowed the dessert. "What if she explained why she left?"

She stiffened. "How do you explain leaving your kid? The only excuse would be if she were in a coma or kidnapped—neither of which happened." She tried to ignore the fire igniting in her gut but failed. "She's selfish. She didn't care enough about Riley to even check in."

He dropped the empty spoon on the side table. "I understand why she wants to see Riley. Maybe a quick visit wouldn't hurt."

Shane, too? Her stomach hardened. "Are you kidding me? What if she kidnaps him? What if he has a meltdown, and she hurts him? Or leaves him because she can't handle the intensity?" She narrowed her eyes. "I have a hard enough time leaving him with my parents. The only people I trust alone with him are Amanda and his therapists. The hesitation I feel in allowing Layla to see Riley is not just about knocking him off his routine. Ask any person if they'd willingly hand over their kid to a stranger."

"But…" His voice was quiet, and he rested a palm on top of her hand. "He's not your kid. He's Layla's."

The fire that had ignited earlier in Holland was now fully ablaze. She leaped from the bench and slammed her hands on her hips.

He jumped up with the tub in hand. "I know you

love him like he's yours."

Too late. She tiptoed back a few steps and crossed her arms. "You say that, but do you understand that? No distinction exists in my mind or heart he's my child. If I could've adopted him, I would've."

He set down the ice cream and crept closer. "If he were my kid, I'd want to see him, too."

"You wouldn't have left your kid," she snapped. Was anyone on her side anymore? The open, starlit sky now closed in. She tried to inhale a calming breath, but the air around her felt heavy and thick.

"Holland, listen." He reached for her hand.

She yanked her arm away.

"A long court case with the stress and commitment along with the toll it'll take on you, on Riley—"

"Don't even pretend you know what's best for Riley." Shane was the person she thought was in her corner—the one who had her back. Logical or not, her disappointment nearly mirrored what she had for her parents.

"Whoa." His gaze hardened. He exhaled a shaky breath and retreated a few steps. "I don't pretend to know what's best. But you know how much I care, right?"

Her cheeks burned. "Could've fooled me."

His mouth dropped. "Unbelievable." He brushed his fingers through his hair and paused for several moments. "Anytime we're together, I make the time about him. We do the activities he wants—the baking, the trains, the screen time. I'm as accommodating as possible."

She dug her fingers into her sides. "I didn't realize he was such a burden."

"What?" He shook his head. "Why are you saying this? I love Riley. He's not a burden. I do whatever I can."

"Except protect him."

He stuffed his hands in his pocket. "I will *always* protect him."

"I'm the ONLY one protecting him." Hot tears filled her eyes, and her throat burned from swallowing back a scream. How does he not see how awful things would be by bringing Layla into Riley's life ? Not only would this be detrimental to Riley's growth, but Layla was unfit! No one was worried about Riley's safety or thinking about the aftereffects of what would happen when Layla leaves. No one cared Layla had an obvious pattern of skipping out on everyone she loved.

He tipped his head to the sky. "Maybe you're making this fight more about you and your sister and less about Riley."

"Shut. Up." She officially had enough. From here on out, her battles were her own.

He leaned forward and squinted. "Excuse me?"

She stomped to the edge of the patio. "I guess I can't expect you to understand not giving up your commitment to Riley. *Since you quit everything.*" The sarcasm spewed out of her mouth like hot lava.

His face paled. "I can't believe you said that." His voice was quiet, and he stood frozen. After several moments, his head dropped. "I'm leaving."

Everything about this conversation was terrible. Her internal pressure reached the max threshold. "Exactly what I said. *Quitting.*"

He walked off the porch with his chin dipped into his chest.

With her back to him, she clamped her lower lip between her teeth to keep from crying. When the sound of his footsteps faded into the distance and an engine started, she allowed herself to release. Confident he was gone, she ran into the house, flung herself onto her bed, and cried. As the tears flowed, she hardened her heart. If the people she were closest to weren't supporting her decisions, she'd navigate this like she'd done everything else in her life—alone.

Chapter 32
Today's Special: Best Friend Comfort Casserole

An hour after the blowup with Shane, Holland mustered enough energy to unbury her head from her soaked pillow. She rolled over on the bed and tugged the sheets to her chin. Feeling dusty-eyed and chalked-mouthed, she called the one person left in this world who was on her side.

"What's up, playa?"

Amanda's chipper voice boomed through the phone. "Shane left. I think we broke up. I'm going to lose Riley. Pretty sure my life is over." The words flew out in rapid-fire succession, and Holland choked back a cry.

"Whoa. Slow down," Amanda said. "Tell me everything."

Holland picked at a blanket thread and relived the events from the past day—the argument with her mom, the child support check, and the fight with Shane. Like a flourless upside-down cake, her life collapsed.

"Oh, Hol, I'm so sorry. This sucks so hard. But one, you're not losing Riley—even if we have to pack up and move to Mexico. Two, don't feel bad for a second about cashing the child support check. And three, Shane. Whatever. I never liked his Denver omelet, anyway."

"Amanda..."

"I know, I know. I'm sorry. I'm joking because I don't have any words. Sad thing is, I liked Grumpy-Butt. Seemed like a decent guy." Amanda whistled for her dog. "But my feelings don't matter here. You broke up. I take you in the divorce. I'm ride-or-die for life."

Holland used her sleeve to wipe away tears. Would it have killed Shane or her parents to have a sliver of this type of support? "You've always had my back."

"Remember when the school found my pack of smokes junior year? You said they were yours and took detention. How many times have I sobbed on your couch from nasty breakups? We got each other's backs." Amanda paused for several moments. "Let's talk about what we're doing. I don't want to egg Shane's house because he lives with James. Sneezing pepper in his apron? A fake cockroach in his pie? Mess up his berry pattern on a pancake?"

"No, I love you for offering, though." Holland stared at the popcorn ceiling. "I just don't know what to do. Too many things are happening, and my mind is fried. I'm literally running on fumes."

The sound of tapping on a surface sounded through the phone. "How about you take a few days off? I can pick up your shift tomorrow, and I'm sure James will cover the other days. Besides, it might be good not seeing Shane for a while, 'cause…uff. Awkward."

Amanda was the best, but all her positivity couldn't shake Holland's images of Riley crying, being forgotten at school, or getting forced to eat food he didn't like. Holland spoke for another hour, and her chest downgraded from boiling to simmering. "What am I gonna do about Layla?"

Amanda sighed. "That's a tough one. What do you

think you should do?"

Run away and never come back, bury herself under a blanket until the nightmare ended, or grab Riley and skip town. "She doesn't deserve to see him."

"You're right. She doesn't." Amanda's firm voice echoed through the speaker. "But does he deserve to see her?"

Itchiness rolled over her skin. She shifted to the side, then to the other, and finally scooted up and stuffed pillows behind her back. Every cell in her body fired at once, and she was simultaneously cold, hot, and thirsty. "I don't think seeing her will faze him. He's not gonna fully grasp the concept of who she is." She closed her eyes and tried to quiet the million negative scenarios bouncing in her head. "She could be dangerous and irresponsible."

"Definitely. Those are all things to consider." A long pause followed. "When you two spoke, did she seem unstable?"

Holland paused. "Besides showing up unannounced after five years and demanding to see her kid?" Her breath was as sharp as her words. "No, she seemed lucid. Spoke clearly, wasn't stumbling or anything."

"Almost would've been easier if she were seriously unbalanced, huh?"

Holland snapped a thread from the blanket and wrapped it around a finger. "A sliver of my dark place wished Layla was unhinged. I would've called the cops and had her hauled away, kicking and screaming. But, she had to be perfectly coherent and calm, and now I don't know what to do." A heavy breath sounded through the phone.

"If she asked for a social worker-supervised visit, you'd still say no?"

Holland rubbed her eyes with a knuckle. "Correct." Although admittedly, the only scenario in her mind involved Layla leaving with Riley.

"Why? I'm not judging, only curious. You say *no*, and I'm standing behind you with my dollar store karate *gi* and fake black belt and will help defend the heck out of whatever you want."

This. Amanda's support was the exact type she wanted from Shane. But he just left, like she and Riley weren't worth the effort. Of course, she probably shouldn't have said the things she did. *But still, he just left!* "Because…why should she be able to?"

"So, Riley is the means to punish Layla for her behavior?"

The words punched Holland in the gut. "What? I'd never use Riley."

"I'm sorry. Totally didn't mean it like that," Amanda interjected. "I've now got my *gi*, an economy size can of hairspray, and a lighter to defend whatever you say."

Even though Amanda's unintended accusation of using Riley to punish stung, she knew her best friend didn't mean to hurt her. Right now, she needed Amanda more than anyone. She shifted the phone to her other hand. "Why couldn't Shane be supportive like you?"

"I don't know. And I don't want to give the guy too much credit 'cause no one should be as cute as him, have emotional intelligence, *and* be kind—it messes with the balance in the universe." Amanda chuckled. "But, maybe, if you want to, rethink his words. If not, I got an extra toilet paper roll I'm happy to wrap around his car."

After Holland hung up, she brought her knees to her chest and dropped her head. Amanda left her with a ton to think about, but she had brain fog and a dry mouth. She lay back for what she assumed would be a fourth sleepless night.

Chapter 33
Today's Special: Sweet and Sour Revelations

In a huff, Shane flung the moistened paintbrush against the corner of his studio wall and clasped his fingers against the back of his skull. The piece he'd been working on for months was close to completion but now seemed pointless and uninspiring. Three miserable days had passed since he last talked to Holland. Every morning, he woke up tired, cranky, and more defeated than the previous night. Wasn't time supposed to heal things? *What a joke*—nothing was healed, and everything was worse.

Tonight was Tuesday. He should be baking cupcakes with Riley and then sneaking back in after he fell asleep to cuddle with Holland and watch a goofy rom-com he pretended to hate but secretly loved—not sitting in his studio wondering how it all went wrong.

Every free moment outside of Salt & Sugar, he returned to his workroom and attempted to get clarity on how things went south so fast, while also focusing on everything needed before the gallery opening. After years of dreaming, he was within finger-touching distance of his goal. But pricing inventory and working on his website sounded terrible while everything with Holland was in flux. He never meant to upset her, but she didn't even *try* to listen to his point. Following his dad's advice, he attempted to help her see a trial was not the best route. He *protected* her…and she acted like he hurt her.

"Dang it," he muttered and grabbed a water bottle. He leaned against the wall and scanned the room. So many dreams filled this space. When he first arrived, the plan for this place was always about him. But shortly after meeting Holland and Riley, *his plan* morphed into *their plan*. His future faced him, and he'd never been more excited. And now, that future was shot.

A replay reel spun in his mind of their interaction, and he cracked his neck to alleviate a stress headache. She used his weak spot against him, his fear of being a quitter, and her words stung. His bruised ego prevented him from reaching out. But the message didn't transfer to his heart.

Someone pounded on the door.

He flicked the blinds apart, expecting to see James, who'd acted like a neurotic mother hen the last few days. *What the…?* "Amanda?" Tightness restricted his chest, and he swung open the door.

She pushed her glasses higher on her nose and stood firm. "Can we chat?"

"Um, sure." His limbs felt like he stuck them in concrete. "How did you know where I was?"

She cocked her head. "I saw your car, and Holland told me you rent space here. Sorry, brother—we're a package deal. If there's something you don't want me to know, you have to tell her not to say anything."

He cracked a smile and moved back. "Good to know. Come inside."

After stepping into the space, she stopped. Her eyes scanned the hanging artwork. "Dang. These are yours?"

"Yeah."

"They're really good. I take back every crappy thing I said about you. Wait, no, I don't. I stand by those words." She walked a few more feet inside the studio. "These are beautiful. Someday, I'd love to see more. But right now, I'm not here for a social call."

He couldn't stop his stomach from knotting. "Is everything okay?"

"No." She flopped on the couch and draped her arms over the back. "My girl's not good."

Because of them breaking up? In general? Was she safe? He pulled on the rolling chair resting by his easel, and the wheels squeaked across the hardwood floors. "What's going on?"

"She's super-ticked at you."

He spun the chair and slumped into the seat. "Well, I guess you're getting right to the point."

She rested her elbows on her knees and leaned forward. "What were you thinking? I can't believe you said those things."

Heat seeped up his throat. "My dad explained how brutal a court hearing would be, and I protected her. Based on Layla paying her first installment of child support and retaining a lawyer, this situation could get ugly." He untwisted a water bottle cap. "I genuinely think the best scenario is to work something out with Layla. But Holland wouldn't even entertain the idea of a conversation. I'd understand the hesitation if Layla came in guns blazing and threatening to take Riley. But that's not what happened."

Amanda cocked her head and tapped her fingers against the sofa edge. Several long moments passed. "I remember Layla from when I was younger. She was a party girl, made some bad decisions, and got fired from every job she had. She was always surrounded by a cloud of drama, but she wasn't a *bad* person."

Hmmm. The information was surprisingly helpful. He set the water bottle on the floor and remained silent.

She stood and paced the room. "Holland and Layla stopped talking when we were juniors." She ran a finger across the bottom of the Maui painting's wooden frame. "Holland always brushed it off, almost like *good riddance.* She can be stubborn…if she thinks someone doesn't have time, then she won't have time. Probably more of a self-preservation tactic than anything. But I think deep down, for a while anyway, she missed Layla and was really hurt when she left."

Focusing so much on Holland's hatred for Layla, it never dawned on him her anger could come from a place of pain. He returned the chair to under the desk and joined Amanda pacing the room. "I don't want to sound like a jerk. I understand how hurtful Layla's leaving must've been. But I stand by what I said. Holland needs to talk to Layla before they go to court. Do you think you can bring this up? Maybe if this message comes from you, it will land better."

"Holland and Layla talking is not up for me to decide." She tilted her head and kept her gaze on an ocean scene painting. "My only job as her best friend is to be supportive in whatever decision she makes."

Amanda's words needed to soak in, and he was more confused now than when she first arrived. He dipped a paper towel in a water bowl and wiped off a brush. After several moments, he rested the brush in the container and leaned against the wall. "Why are you here?"

She faced him and pulled in a large breath. "She misses you."

He lifted his chest. "Really?"

"Well, yeah. Duh, Dude." She rolled her eyes. "It's been like three days. Feelings don't get turned off in a snap."

Amanda's words were hard to accept. She hadn't seen how Holland looked the night of their fight. In a blink, she swapped adoring glances and a soft smile with blazing eyes and clenched teeth. And, she sucker-punched him with her words. Amanda might be wrong—Holland might have snapped off her feelings in a day. Soon, he fell into a downward sulking spiral. "She hasn't called or texted."

"Have you?" She crossed her arms.

He flicked at the side of his water bottle and avoided what he figured would be a heated gaze. Finally, he looked at her and shrugged. "I'm giving her space."

She angled an eyebrow. "A.K.A., I didn't want to communicate my feelings."

"Not fair." He pushed himself off the desk and tossed the bottle into the recycling bin. "She was clear she didn't want to talk, and I'm being respectful."

"I defer to my previous comment."

Maybe Amanda had a point. All his life, he avoided hard conversations—Cherise, his parents, and now Holland. But Holland *told* him to leave. He stared at his hands and clicked a finger against his palm.

Amanda wandered the room.

A few seconds passed before he recognized where she stood—and what she was looking at. "Wait!" he said. *Too late.* She saw the painting.

She dragged her gaze away from the canvas. "Wow. The painting's incredible. Has she seen it?"

He shook his head. "She doesn't know about it."

After several moments, she pulled in a large breath and exhaled slowly. "Riley had a rough night tonight. Holland called me before I came here."

His stomach knotted. "Today's Tuesday, Baking Night."

She nodded. "Seems that little guy has taken quite a liking to you. Maybe you should reach out."

Reaching out was terrifying. His heart swelled, then deflated. He wanted to be over there, baking. Last week, he found plastic cake toppers that lit up and couldn't wait to show Riley. "Thanks for coming by. You've given me a lot to think about."

She grabbed her purse from the couch and walked to the door. "You know, you're not half bad, Mr. Blackwood."

"Yeah?" He cocked his eyebrow and grinned. "The jury's still out on you."

She snorted and left.

He sat back on the couch and stared at the ceiling. Time to make a difficult decision.

Chapter 34
Today's Special: Slow-Roasted Reconciliation

After her blow-up with Shane, Holland followed Amanda's advice and took off a week, thankful she could now afford the leave. She slowed to a stop at a red light, peeked at Riley in the rearview mirror, and exhaled. All week she buried herself in anything that would take her mind off Shane. When her eyes felt like they would bleed from reading too many court documents, she hyper-scrubbed the floors, ripped up the garden to prep for the winter, and spent every second with Riley when he wasn't in school.

She eased into the school parking spot and guided Riley up the stairs. A sickening, pending doom erupted with each step, like her reality could crumble at any minute. Outside of the classroom, she knelt for a hug. "Love you, Bubby."

He pushed her off and ran to the corner by his preferred toys.

A new wound broke open. If Layla took Riley, then he could miss out on his school's incredible support system and second family. She choked back a sob and bolted to her car. On the way home, she clenched her stomach and detoured down Main Avenue, past Shane's studio. Maybe she could get a glimpse from afar— check if he had hunched shoulders or dragged his feet. Was he sad about them not speaking? Or did he bounce back like she and Riley never mattered?

He hadn't called—not once in five days. Not a text, drop in, nothing. He was just *done*.

His car wasn't parked out front. Not surprising for a Friday since he usually worked that shift at Salt & Sugar. She slumped into the seat and continued the drive to her neighborhood while she tried to ignore her screaming inner voice. Was she unreasonable? Maybe bringing up his past was a jerk move. *Maybe.*

The sunlight beaming through the front window did nothing to make her house feel any brighter. The time off work this last week helped provide the needed minutes to organize things for court. After multiple conversations with Shane's dad, she bought binders and tabs to color-code documents for an upcoming trial. She scoured every email for the last four years. She ignored her mother's phone calls and instead focused on drafting a statement about why she was Riley's best choice for a guardian.

Her noisy belly reminded her to eat. She popped a piece of bread into the toaster. Leaning against the counter, she checked the cell to see if, by some miracle, Shane had texted. *Nope.* She crunched into the buttered toast. A knock interrupted breakfast. She clapped the crumbs off and leaned into the peephole. *Layla.* Holland whipped open the door. "I said if you ever came here again, I'd call the cops."

"Please, Holland. Give me five minutes." Layla clasped her hands in front of her chest. "That's all I'm asking for, as your sister."

Her pulse rushed to her ears, and she felt dizzy. "You lost that title eight years ago after you left home and never talked to me again."

Layla pulled in her lips along with a breath. "Fair. Listen—"

"You're dang lucky Riley isn't here." Holland's cheeks flamed.

"Five minutes. Please."

"You get one." Holland slammed the door behind her and wrapped a sweater around herself to stave off the brisk air.

Layla glanced at the chair resting against the railing. "Can we sit?"

"You're down to forty-five seconds."

"Geez. *All right.*" She looked at her feet. "I just wanted to say how grateful I am for you."

Huh?

Layla stiffened. "And I don't want to go to court."

Double huh? The bomb inside Holland's chest partially diffused. She released her rigid shoulders, dropped onto the swinging bench, and jutted her chin toward the wicker chair in the corner. "You have five minutes."

Layla sat on the edge. "I want to tell you why I did what I did." Her gaze fell to her hands. She opened her mouth, closed it, then took several deep breaths. "I've never been responsible. You probably remember the horrible taste I have in men. I'm antsy and don't like keeping a job. But when I had Riley...man...I was *so* excited. The dad and I split up before I knew I was pregnant, so I did the single-parent thing. But raising a kid alone was really hard."

"You don't say." Holland did not hold back the sarcasm in her tone.

"Anyway, I couldn't manage everything." Layla shifted in her seat. "I had horrible credit, got evicted from multiple apartments, and was clinically depressed. Riley and I were verging on homelessness. And I just…couldn't. I didn't know what to do."

No chance was she about to let Layla off easily. "Why didn't you ask Mom and Dad for help?" She took a moment to observe Layla. Eight years changed someone. Layla still had the famous Mulberry red hair but chopped her formerly waist-length hair into a pixie cut. Wrinkling around her eyes and forehead made her look much older than thirty-two. She was thinner than Holland remembered. The Mulberry girls were always known for their healthy curves, but Layla looked more frail than strong.

Layla used a thumbnail to pick at a frayed edge of the wicker chair. "You know how they are. I only spoke to them a couple of times a year. And truthfully, I didn't know if they'd help."

Just like Holland, Layla had been on the receiving end of shoddy parenting. The breeze picked up, and she readjusted her sweater. "Why didn't you call me?"

"Humiliation, I guess? My self-esteem was shot. I thought I was a horrible human and an even worse mother. I worried you'd refuse if I asked you to help *both* Riley and me. But if I asked you to help *only* Riley, you'd more likely say yes." Layla eased back in the chair. "You were the responsible one. And you've always had a spark. I wanted that so badly for Riley."

Holland's firm belief Layla was an uncaring monster faded word by word, but she had nearly a decade of pent-up anger to counteract the soft feelings. A laundry list of icky things Layla did shuffled through Holland's mind. "I can't believe you didn't show up for court."

Layla cleared her throat. "I *did* show up."

What?

Layla flicked her fingers against a palm. "When you filed for guardianship, it gave me the kick in the butt I needed. I was in the parking lot when you pulled up. For hours, I sat there, waiting for it to open."

She was there?

"I watched you take him out of the car seat and bundle him up. He was giggling, and you were smiling and kissing his head. And...I disintegrated. My insides crushed. I saw your love and knew I couldn't return to his life. In that short time, you already gave him what I couldn't." She flicked at a tear with a thumb. "After you went inside, I sobbed in my car and finally drove off. That day was simultaneously one of the best and worst of my life. Confirming I made the right decision to have you raise him hurt more than you can possibly imagine."

Holland's core memory bank cemented almost every detail of that day—the judge's words, Riley's red sweater and new shoes, the stuffiness of the courtroom. But the parking lot was a fog. "Where did you go?"

"Various place—Texas, California, most recently Mexico." She tugged on the cuff of her sweatshirt. "I had an ex-boyfriend who lived there. I could live for cheap, work for cash, and fly under the radar until I pulled myself together, which clearly took years."

As a teen, Layla was a giant. Bigger than life and louder than anyone Holland knew. But now, she seemed small, almost childlike. Holland wanted to hug her and still kick her off the porch. She crossed and uncrossed her legs to relieve the spasms until she gave up and succumbed to bouncing. "You should've explained what happened or called and asked to talk to Riley. *Something.*"

"I know." Layla dropped her head. "In the beginning, I called Mom and Dad every few weeks for an update. And they said how amazing you managed everything. With each positive update, the more I thought I'd be harming Riley by being in his life. I convinced myself the best thing I could do was stay as far away as possible."

Holland raised an eyebrow but kept her mouth shut.

"Mom told me about his diagnosis and everything you did with the therapy and stuff. I've never been more blown away. And every day, I had less and less self-worth."

The vision of Layla Holland had been carrying for years was not this composed, regretful person. She dragged her hands down her face, then twirled her ring. Layla left all those years ago without a word. But she also sat in the parking lot crying, called Mom for updates, and was homeless? Holland's head pounded.

Layla's throat rolled with a swallow. "I made the right decision by having you raise him."

To keep from wringing her trembling hands, Holland shoved them under her seat. "So…you don't want to take him from me?" Her voice cracked.

Layla shook her head. "No, I don't."

Holland gasped. She bit back the request to have her repeat the soft words.

The wicker in the chair squeaked underneath Layla's movement. "I've been in therapy for over a year, and we both agree Riley's better off in a stable environment. And I don't have one, yet. To strip him away from everything he's known just because I'm working on myself is totally unfair."

Wait, does this mean...

"I want him in my life, though, and we'll need to figure that out." Layla stiffened her backbone. "I'm begging for us to come up with a plan. None of us wants to be dragged through that mess. The financial hardship, energy, turmoil—I think we can come to an agreement ourselves. But if I have to, I'll go to court."

Holland leaned back on the swing. Her tongue felt heavy and dry, and Layla's words collided in her brain. But one message was clear: *Layla was not taking Riley away.*

"And I'm committed to repaying the child support," Layla said.

"The money's the last thing on my mind."

"You're still entitled. You *deserve* it." She sighed. "And honestly, I owe it to myself to pay it."

Holland swallowed hard. The check she cashed a few days ago gave her much-needed breathing room. If those checks continued, she could stop picking up extra shifts or buy Riley a new train set.

Pink flushed Layla's cheeks, and she cleared her throat. "Can you tell me something about him?"

The timid voice caused Holland's body to involuntarily soften. Where would she begin with all the things she loved? "His favorite color is purple."

Layla lifted her brows. "Purple?"

Holland couldn't hold back a hint of a grin. "Yep. His room is purple. He has purple stuffed animals, purple blankets, and purple pillows. The place looks like a purple tornado ransacked it." She snorted. "He loves chicken nuggets and cookies. *So many cookies.*"

Layla raised her eyebrows. "He got the Mulberry sweet tooth, huh?"

"Sure did." Holland's insides warmed. "He's the best hugger, but the *worst* cheek kisser. He grabs my cheeks to kiss me but just slobbers all over them, makes tooting noises, then runs away laughing. He thinks he's hilarious."

Layla wiped tears with the back of her left hand. "Tell me more."

Holland tucked a leg underneath her bottom. "He's so smart. And, he loves trains so much. Oh gosh, he's such a good painter. He's gonna be in a museum someday. Oh! He hates monkeys. Like, what kid hates monkeys? I took him to the zoo once, and he was not having it..." She talked for an hour. Laughter tears rolled as she retold the story from when Riley was obsessed with a '60s singer for a year after seeing a video.

Riley had run around the house singing and hip-shimmed in a white jumper and gold belt for months.

The morning sun moved past high noon. After a few more stories, Holland checked her watch. "I need to run a few errands before I pick up Riley from school."

With a slight frown, Layla rose from the chair. "Thank you. You have no idea how much this talk means."

"I'm doing this for Riley, not you." One conversation did not make all forgiven.

"Understood."

"If you'll be in his life, it has to be on my terms." Holland squared her shoulders. "Or I *will* fight."

After a beat, Layla exhaled. "What are your

terms?"

Holland lifted herself from the bench and crossed her arms. "You need to meet with his behavior therapist, Amy, and learn about ASD and Riley's specific plan. Once she thinks you understand, then she'll sign off."

Layla nodded. "I read everything I could on autism this last year."

"Good. But you have to remember the diagnosis is not one size fits all. People with autism are as different as you and I. You still don't know him and his strict routine." Her pulse quickened. "All visits will be with me or Amy present. No exceptions."

Layla flinched and took a half-step back. "For how long?"

"For as long as it takes me to be comfortable leaving him alone with you." Holland held an assertive gaze.

Layla's mouth opened and closed. "That's awfully vague."

"Non-negotiable, Layla." Holland raised an eyebrow. "I'm doing this for Riley, truly."

She shifted her face to the sun and inhaled a deep breath. "Okay."

Holland inched a few steps closer to the front door. "And with his caretaking, you have to commit to following my lead. I've studied this child like a dissertation for the last five years. I know, *I feel*, when things will escalate. Something might seem like no big deal, but I know it's a meltdown trigger. If we're together, *I* make all parental decisions. *You're* a visitor."

Layla pinched the bridge of her nose. "Okay." She

laid a hand on Holland's arm. "Thank you for taking the time to talk." Her voice quivered. "Thank you for loving my son like your own. I could not have picked a better mom."

The life she'd known for the last five years was about to change. Holland's heart flew into her chest, and she swallowed a cry.

Chapter 35
Today's Special: Fried Ego on Burnt Toast

Holland scraped toast crumbs onto her plate, then brushed them into the compost. The Guatemalan, full-bodied dark roast aroma funneled into the air, and she leaned closer to the pot to inhale the scent. She filled her travel mug and added an extra scoop of sugar. "Five minutes to finish your cereal, Bubby. I'm setting the timer now."

Riley stared at the cereal box on the kitchen table and ran his finger over the maze printed on the back.

With the imminent threat of a court case disappearing, the tension in Holland's lower belly released. She dashed around the house and gathered items to bring to her parents, who'd be watching Riley for the day. Her phone blinked with an unread message from Layla. She stuffed the cell in her pocket. After speaking to her mom, Amanda, and Amy, they all agreed Holland made the right decision, and now she could be cautiously optimistic. She called Shane's dad, Ken, and thanked him profusely for his guidance on notarizing and filing a parenting plan with the state.

The timer beeped, and Holland squatted to Riley's eye level. "Bubby, we have a...friend visiting today for a few minutes before we leave for Grandma and Grandpa's place."

"A friend?" He set his empty dish in the sink and

bounced back to Holland with his arms stretched out.

Holland tugged Riley's rainbow dinosaur sweatshirt over his head. She wasn't sure what to call Layla. *Mom* felt weird. *Aunt* wasn't right. Holland would have to play this one by ear. And, until Layla could prove she'd be a constant in his life, her first name would have to do.

The last two days, Holland spent no less than five hours on the phone with Layla, who peppered Holland with every question imaginable, ranging from allergies to dentist appointments to the dip he used for his chicken nuggets. And last night, Layla begged Holland for a quick visit today.

Holland wanted to say *no*—Layla still needed to meet with Amy. And forty-eight hours was not enough time for Holland to process everything. But Holland didn't trust her parents or Layla to respect her wishes. Her flaky parents might allow Layla over when they watched Riley this afternoon. At least, this way, Holland could control the environment. "Yes, a friend. You saw her the other day when…" She gulped. "When Shane was here." Would the crack in her heart ever disappear when she said his name?

"Shane likes to bake." Riley gripped his toy car and followed her to the living room.

"He sure does." She forced a smile and prayed Riley would not notice a change in her facial expression.

The sound of knuckles rapping on the door echoed in the room.

Riley grabbed the doorknob and paused. "Open?"

Every day, every moment, Riley grew and learned and evolved. A few months ago, he would've whipped open the door without checking. "Yep, you can open."

Riley flung the door open. "One, two, three, eyes on me." He cocked his head.

"Hi, kiddo." Layla smiled. She stood at the door, shifting her weight back and forth between her feet. She gripped the top of her bag, looked at Holland with wide eyes, then moved her gaze back.

Riley's expression didn't change, but he moved behind Holland, and soon his little head buried into her lower back.

She flattened both palms against his back. "You're okay, Bud." She was torn between not forcing Riley to do anything he didn't want to and accepting reality. Layla seemed determined to be in his life. The safer Riley could feel now, the better for all involved. "Riley, this is Layla. My, um, sister." *Gah!* Facilitating this was so much harder than she thought. Her mouth parched, and her lungs felt tight.

Tears filled Layla's eyes.

After Riley eased his head off her back, he buried himself in the crook of her arm. "Your friend-sister?"

Holland bent to face him at eye level. "Yep." She motioned Layla forward.

Layla squatted and dropped her bag on the floor. "I like your hair, Riley. Same color as mine."

A brief moment later, Riley touched the top of her head.

Holland gently tugged on Riley's arm. "Riley, ask Layla if you can touch her hair."

He withdrew his hand. "Can I touch your hair?"

"Of course. Thank you for asking first." Layla sloped her head.

He patted her hair and then rubbed a lock between

his thumb and forefinger. "Red like me! Red like Mimi's!"

"Sure is." Layla's shoulders dropped a fraction of an inch, and she put her mouth to Holland's ear. "Can I give him a gift?"

For the last twenty-four hours, Holland had prepped for Riley and Layla's meeting. She thought she prepared herself as much as possible, but she was wrong. She pulled in a large breath and blinked back tears. "Sure."

"Riley...Holl—uh, Mimi—said you like to color." Layla opened the bag. "I brought you a little gift."

"I love presents. Say cheese!" Riley clapped and smiled wide.

Layla dug out a coloring book and crayons and handed them over with trembling hands.

"Train coloring book?" Riley snatched the items from her fingers. "I love trains!"

Holland exchanged a look with Layla.

She mirrored Holland's slightly curved edge smile.

Holland nodded.

Layla nodded back.

Not everything was perfect. Time, healing, and forgiveness needed to happen. But hope existed.

****

When Holland pulled into the Salt & Sugar parking lot after dropping off Riley and didn't see Shane's car, she slumped, her stomach dropping. Since he hadn't called after his dad told him about Layla, his silence clarified everything she needed to know. And even though she picked up her phone multiple times to reach out, she couldn't. *He* was the one who left. He needed to reach out first.

The searing of the grill and plates rattling in the kitchen usually jolted her into work mode, especially after being gone for a week. But not today. She eyed the prep station where Shane normally stood and mustered a smile at the line cook.

"Welcome back." James flicked his pen against the clipboard and scrunched his brows. "Everything okay?"

Where would she begin? She slept for the first time in a week because Riley was safe. But nightmares plagued her about Shane's absence. Everything was okay and not okay. She lived in a perpetual state of fogginess, and her heart broke and filled in a span of days. "Yeah, I guess." She shoved her purse in the locker and pulled out her apron and order pad. "A lot of changes this last week."

James' face softened. "Sounds like it."

"I'm sure Shane told you, but I let Layla see Riley. We won't be going to court."

He stepped back. "Wow. No, he didn't tell me. I, uh, thought you two haven't spoken."

Hearing someone else say those words was harder to hear than she thought. She wrapped the apron around her waist and exhaled. "We haven't, but his dad knew, so I assumed he told him."

"Hard to say." James tugged on his polka-dotted bowtie. "You know how much I love dishing, but gossiping's not as fun when I care for the people being dished about."

James—one of the good ones. "Um, is he coming in today?" She prayed her tone was cooler than her insides but was sure James could decode every syllable.

"Shane?" James rubbed the back of his bald head. "Sadly, no. He quit last night."

What? *No!* Her heart sank. *He quit?* If anyone should quit, it should be her. James and Shane were family. Thinking her actions had a trickle-down effect and left James in a horrible position killed her. "I'm so sorry, James. I had no idea."

James shrugged. "Ah, what do you do?"

He spun away before she had time to mutter another apology. Unforgivable words spewed from her mouth to hurt Shane. Why would she choose his vulnerable spot? She never thought of herself as a going-for-the-jugular type of person, and here she was terrible to someone she cared about the most. She gulped back disgust in herself and exited the kitchen without another word.

Her shift was a blurry, hot mess. She missed the refills at Table Seventeen, dropped a plate with a piercing screech, and spilled a drink on the tray. Every piece of this place reminded her of him—the prep station, the citrus-scented cleaner, and the booth in the break area. When a customer ordered a cupcake, she thought about Shane and Riley bonding during Baking Night. Even a chocolate shake was a reminder, and she dumped it out after a few sips.

By the end of the evening, a crushing realization pushed into her chest. She screwed up—and she needed to fix it.

Chapter 36
Today's Special: Sparkling Hope Lemonade

A loud, rapid-fire knock on Shane's studio door broke his minimal concentration. He plunked his paintbrush into the water bowl and opened the door.

James stood a few feet away, dangling a bottle.

Not that he minded his uncle dropping by, but whenever his phone beeped, or someone who wasn't Holland knocked on the door, he stilled, his heart dropping. A week without Holland felt like a lifetime. The pain increased—not decreased—every day since they last spoke. On the daily, he forced himself not to be a creeper and drive by her house.

"Sparkling lemonade." Shane leaned against the frame. "To what do I owe the honor?"

James lowered his arms. "Apparently, alcohol kills your creative mindset, so lemonade will have to do." He barged past Shane and scanned the room. "Wow, this place is really coming together."

"Sure...come on in." Shane chuckled and latched the door.

James wandered to a cherrywood framed, country setting painting and stared at the art with a cocked head. After several moments, he twisted off the lemonade bottle top and moved toward Shane. "Holland came back to work today."

Shane passed James a mug and said nothing. What

could he say? That the sensory toy he bought last week for Riley now sat on his desk, and he couldn't bear to return the item to the store? That eight days ago was the last time he slept?

"Court's off." James poured the beverage into each cup.

He lifted his head. Did he hear James correctly? "What? How?"

"She didn't give any details. She assumed you knew from your dad."

"My dad would never disrespect client-attorney privilege and tell me that information." He flopped onto the couch next to James and absorbed the best news he'd heard in months. He twitched his thumbs, wanting to reach for the phone. Was Layla gone? Or did they resolve their issues? "Is she okay? Does she seem relieved?"

James set the empty bottle on the desk. "You should call her yourself and ask."

He had a devilish twinkle in his eyes. "I'm giving her the space she obviously needs." Even though his heart was heavy, a lightness seeped in. *No court over Riley.* He hated seeing how Holland struggled since Layla's arrival. No matter how hurt he was over their broken relationship, he was also happy.

James cleared his throat. "Do you miss her?"

Heat grew in his chest. "Of course, I miss her." The fizzy bubbles burned on their way down. "I don't know. Maybe us being apart is for the best, you know?"

"Do you really believe that?"

"No."

James paused for several long moments before he meandered to the portrait of Shane and his grandma. He lightly traced the rustic, gray frame with a finger. "I always loved this painting of my mom. You do such beautiful work."

Shane focused on the mug in his hands.

"You know…" James voice was timid. "You never struck me as a quitter."

After hearing his trigger word, Shane jerked his gaze toward his uncle. "What do you mean? I quit everything—Cherise, school, my hometown."

"No, you didn't." James scratched at his chin. "You had the clarity to end a relationship you knew was wrong. And you didn't quit law school. You persevered as long as you could and followed your dream of art."

Shane had never viewed his past that way. Even with his newfound contentment, he couldn't shake the feeling he'd given up by leaving law school.

"So, what are you doing about Holland?"

No idea. Shane tapped the edge of the mug. "I'm gonna give her space."

James released a shaky exhale. "I'll never understand this concept. You and your parents didn't speak for months because you wanted to give each other space. Holland's parents never addressed Layla properly to give her space. Holland is probably not talking to give you space." James gripped the back of his chair, his voice less tender than usual. "How many more things will suffer because no one has the *cojones* to address them? If you let this relationship go, you'll regret it."

But she ended us!

"Well, I've said my piece and overstepped. Per usual." James rolled the chair under the desk and stepped toward the exit. "On that note, I'll leave. Love ya, kid."

The second James clicked the door shut, Shane rested his head on the couch. *What am I doing?* Was he really letting Holland get away because his ego took a hit? The intensity of his emotions grabbed him by the throat. He had something special with her, incredible even.

After stewing for several more minutes, he swallowed against the chokehold caused by James' words. James was right—he wasn't a quitter. Armed with herculean determination, he leaped from the couch and grabbed his keys. He would *not* give up on Holland or Riley.

A knock sounded on the door.

He hurried over to the entrance. "Seriously, James, did you forget—" His heart lodged in his throat. "Holland." The air in his lungs vanished, and the misery of the last seven days faced him.

Holland stood, shifting her weight between her feet, and tucked a piece of hair behind an ear with a shaky hand. "Have you heard my boyfriend is a pickle? He's kind of…a big dill."

Her voice was timid, almost uncertain. A ghost of an apologetic smile accompanied her furrowed brows. He shoved his hands in his pockets to avoid touching her. "I was just about to—"

"Can I go first before I lose all nerve?"

He nodded, and his pulse pounded in his ears.

"I'm so sorry for what I said." She twirled her ring. "I don't even know why I said those awful things. You trusted me enough to share this piece of you, and I threw those words in your face. That behavior isn't me."

Her crinkled eyes and pink cheeks killed him. "You were running on adrenaline—pure survival mode, and I kept pushing the talk with Layla." He gripped the inside of his pants pockets and forced himself to stay back, even though he ached to hug her. "I should've kept my mouth shut and trusted you to make the best decision for you and Riley."

She shook her head. "You thought you were helping me. And ultimately, you were right."

"Doesn't matter what I thought." He tiptoed closer. "My job is to listen and be supportive. And I overstepped."

She sighed. "You were looking out for me. And Riley." Her chin trembled. "And I love you for that."

"No, I should've been more—wait, what did you say?" His heart skipped a beat.

She cleared her throat, her face now matching her hair color. "I said I love you." She bit the edge of her lip. "Nothing like springing those words on you at the weirdest moment. I should've waited to tell you after I found out if we were still together or broken up or—"

He cupped her face and pressed his mouth against hers. His heart felt like it collapsed with relief and jumped in joy. She was here—at his studio, in his arms. *And she loves me.* Pulling back, he kept his hands on her face and lowered his gaze to meet hers. "I love you, too."

"Nope." She wrapped her fingers around his and shook her head. "Please don't say that now. You have to wait. I need to know this wasn't reactionary. Because if you say that, I'm all-in—one hundred percent, all the time. And I won't back down. I'll fight for us like I fought for Riley. So don't say those words until you know they're true."

He swiped his fingertips across her jawline. "The first time I came over and baked cupcakes, I knew."

She angled her head. "We weren't even dating then."

"I know." He dropped his hands from her face. "I left that night and wanted to capture the moment I fell in love with you. You inspired me with the love you showed Riley, with your cheesy jokes, and your smile. Do you remember what you texted me after I left?"

She squinted. "Probably a less-than-average dad joke?"

"And?"

She paused for several moments. "And the picture of you, me, and Riley in the kitchen?"

He reached for her hand. "Come here. I want to show you something." The warmth of her palm pressing into his filled him with a gratitude he hadn't experienced in his lifetime. His heart thumped in his ears, and he led her to his desk. He turned her to face the canvas and his photo for inspiration. The three of them, in pink chef hats and aprons, holding utensils, all saying, *Cheese!*

Her lips parted, and her eyes widened.

Did she hate it? Love it? Was it too much? He held his breath. Too late now to turn around and hide the artwork. She needed to know him, *all* of him—including how much she meant.

Slowly, she brought a hand to her face. Her gaze bounced between him and the canvas. "Oh my...you painted the picture from that evening." Her words were choppy, and she inspected his work.

"I've wanted to show you for months." He inched

closer. "But I didn't know if I was pushing our relationship too far or if the painting would freak you out."

With wide eyes, she shook her head. "I don't know what to say. The painting is…incredible."

He kissed her hand. His insides swirled and tangled, and he exhaled a heavy breath. "Being with you and Riley these past several months…you're the family I always wished for. You two have such a bond. My life has so much joy with you both in it." He paused, his mouth suddenly dry. "You're what makes me happy. Riley makes me happy. You *inspire* me. I don't see a future without you in it."

Her eyebrows pinched together, and she collapsed against the crook of his neck.

His skin turned moist from her tears, and he held her tight.

She pulled back, sniffling. "Did you quit the restaurant because of me? I think James is really upset and hiding it. Can you ask him to hire you back?"

Quit? He snapped his head back. "What are you talking about?"

She swiped her tears off with a sleeve. "James told me you quit."

He grinned. "Oh, he did, did he?"

"What?" She crunched her brows.

He dipped his head. "Holland, I didn't quit. Miguel asked if he could pick up an extra shift, so I gave him mine. I'll be back to work tomorrow."

She slapped a palm to her forehead. "That little sh—"

"Hey, hey, that's my uncle. Nice words only." He laughed and pulled her against his chest.

"He did that because he knew I'd panic." She exhaled with a deep sigh. "Well played, James."

Extremely well played.

She rested on him and lowered her shoulders.

He kissed the top of her coconut-scented hair and took a moment to breathe her in. A year ago, he would've never dreamed he'd be in Duluth, Minnesota, working at a café, on the verge of executing his dream of opening a small art gallery, and standing with the love of his life. And now, here he was, his insides warming at the present and dancing about his future. "Hey," he whispered, kissing her again on the forehead. "Want to get out of here, pick up Riley, and grab a chocolate shake?"

She stood on her tiptoes and pressed her lips against his. "Sounds perfect."

Chapter 37
Today's Special: It's Thyme! Infused Cheese Served with Excited Covered Strawberries

Holland sprayed the top of the display glass in the studio for the tenth time today and wiped the surface with a towel. Any more sprays from the meadow-scented cleaner, and she might need to call a fumigator. She glanced at Shane and smiled.

He straightened a hung painting, stepped back to review, and straightened it again. A speck of dust must've caught his attention because he grabbed a microfiber cloth and wiped the edge of the frame.

"You ready for this?" She tucked the cleaner away for good this time.

He dropped his arms and looked at her with a sparkle in his eyes. "Are *we* ready for this?"

She kissed him and took a moment to appreciate the surroundings. The whirlwind of the last three months flew past in a blissful fog. After devoting most of her free time helping him finish the studio remodel, setting up an area to sell her jewelry, and all the other logistics of opening a business, today was finally Opening Day. "Oh hey, I forgot to ask you something. Did you hear about the two artists who entered the art contest at the University of Minnesota?"

He stuffed the cloth into his back pocket and furrowed his brow. "No. What are you talking about?"

"It ended in a draw." She nudged her elbow into his ribcage. "Get it? *A draw*?"

He fake-scowled. "So bad, Holland. I can't even rate that one. You should return to the café full-time to perfect your craft again."

"I've lost my groove. Domestic life has stripped all my comedic powers." She twisted off a cap from a water bottle and sipped. "Replaced by nightly dinner with you and Riley. A perfect trade-off."

"Even if you lose all your comedic powers, promise me you'll never lose that smile." He folded her against him. "You know how much I love you, right? I couldn't have done this without you."

She laid her head on his chest. "Yes, you could've."

The gallery was open and bright, with track lighting and large potted plants. Two desks stood next to each other in the corner. One for Shane, one for her and Riley. She still made jewelry at night on her living room floor, but when Riley was with Layla, and Holland sat next to Shane at the studio and created in silence, her heartstrings tugged.

She peeked out the blinds at the waiting crowd, which had steadily grown over the last hour. She couldn't stop the back flips in her stomach. *All those people!* Her heart verged on leaping straight out of her body and onto the floor. She could only image how Shane felt, seeing his dream come to fruition. "I'm pretty sure your parents arrived before us to make sure they'd be the first in line." She smoothed her dress. "They're chatting and shaking hands with everyone like they're running for mayor."

"Classic Mom and Dad move." He kissed the top

of her head. "I'm happy to have their moral support, but they better stick to their word and not buy anything."

She respected his need to prove he could make it on his own without their interference. At the same time, his work stunned. She wouldn't be surprised if his parents wanted a piece of their own.

He reached for his buzzing phone on the desk and read a text. "Amanda said she finished handing out the gallery brochures, and the line is wrapped around the corner."

An undeniable spark layered his voice.

"She also said your mom and dad are cutting in front of people but keep getting blocked."

She giggled, picturing her mom elbowing her way to the front. "I'm a little jealous of you and Amanda. First bonding over football, then Division One hockey, and soon, she's gonna be your part-time employee." She nudged him. "What's next? Buying a pontoon together so we can all float around Lake Superior like retired folks?"

He smacked his hands together. "That's a great idea!"

She narrowed her eyes and gave him a light pinch on the arm.

"Ouch! Okay, just kidding?" He slid his phone back into his pocket and walked to the window. He pried the blinds open with his fingers and inhaled a sharp breath. A slow smile spread, and he snapped the blinds closed.

James stormed through the alley entrance with the catering crew. "The chocolate-covered strawberries, brie, crackers, and tapenade are all set. I popped half of the champagne, and the rest of the bottles are chilling."

He patted Shane on the back. "How are you feeling?"

"Better now that you're speaking to me again." Shane chuckled.

"Do you have any idea how hard finding a talented chef in this area will be? I'm gonna be forced to go behind the grill soon, and no one wants to see that. My mascara will run." James dipped his chin. "I'm really proud of you."

Shane's chest thrust out, and he turned to look at the canvases.

Holland checked her watch. "Okay, everyone, T minus ten minutes before doors open." Moving toward the case holding her pieces, she touched each one for the hundredth time, centering herself. *I'm not dreaming.* She fixed a glance at Shane. By some miracle, this gift of a man entered her life and rewarded her and Riley with more than she ever hoped.

With those beautiful dimples on display, he winked.

She'd never stop melting.

He grabbed her hand and led them to the door. "Ready?"

"Ready." She squeezed his hand.

He took a deep breath, and wrapped his fingers around the deadbolt.

All these years with just her and Riley, she had a fulfilling love and an inexplicable joy. Riley was everything and more than she ever needed. Her life was complete and worth celebrating. But with Layla back in her and Riley's lives, and Shane by her side, she had something else.

Abundance.

Epilogue
Today's Special: Macadamia Nut Pancakes
Swimming in Happily Ever After Syrup

Eighteen months later

The Maui-scented air surrounded Holland—an intoxicating mixture of sweet plumeria, salt water, and baked goods. She inhaled a full breath. Jade-blue waves crashed against the beach, and she stretched for a better view from the table at the outdoor restaurant in Kihei. The sun arched over the table, and she lowered her straw hat to shade her eyes. After a week in paradise, she still had three more days until she and her boys had to leave the white sandy beaches for the reality of the Minnesota winter waiting back home.

Shane cut into his rice, eggs, and gravy breakfast and waved his fork at her plate. "Seriously, how are you not sick of those by now?"

Holland shrugged, then bit into her macadamia nut pancake with coconut shavings—for the fourth morning in a row. Next to Shane and Riley, nothing existed she loved more than this sweetened breakfast. "That's like asking, how are you not sick of painting by now?" She pooled extra coconut syrup on the side to smother the gluteny-goodness.

He added a touch more creamer to his Kona coffee. "Even I take a break from painting once in a while."

She squinted in fake irritation. "What do you think,

306

Bubby? Good pancakes?"

"Yep!" Riley scooped another mouthful of plain pancake into his mouth and kicked his legs under the table.

Fortunately, Shane lived with her and Riley now because if she added this dish to the home menu, Shane would have to make it due to her lack of baking skills. For the first time in years, she might have a backup breakfast outside cereal and oat milk. *Better remember to tell Layla.*

Shane tousled Riley's hair and chomped into the breakfast.

"Chocolate monster!" Riley held up his hands and giggled.

She scrunched her nose. "Chocolate monster is right."

Shane wetted a napkin and wiped Riley's fingers.

Riley pointed toward her purse. "Screens, Mimi."

She grabbed the headphones and tablet from her bag. After taking a final pancake bite, she settled back into the chair and rested her head on Shane's shoulder. "Are you nervous about the gallery?"

"Nah." He sipped the coffee. "Amanda's got the store totally under control."

Good point. She squeezed his hand under the table and filled with pride. The gallery did extraordinarily well. He'd sold plenty of pieces to pay for their trip to Maui, another year's lease on the studio, and a lifetime supply of chocolate shakes.

Shane ran a napkin over his mouth. "Ready to go to the beach, Buddy?"

Riley beamed. "Turtles!"

Holland dug in her tote. "Oh, shoot! I swear I put

the sunscreen in here." She shook her bag and frowned. "Sorry, I have to go back to the hotel."

"No worries." Shane signed the bill and pushed back his chair. "I'll take Riley to the beach, and you can meet us there."

She scooted back from the table and smiled one last time before flipping the tote's straps over a shoulder. Shane and Riley had become extremely close this last year and a half, but this trip heightened their relationship to a whole new level. And her heart had never been so full.

****

Shane raced to the beach with Riley, his unknowing co-conspirator, and clasped his hand. The intensity in his pulse vibrated with every squishy step. He felt terrible pretending to be surprised about the missing sunscreen, but he took the bottle out of her bag before breakfast. He had to buy time, and that seemed the easiest way.

The salty breeze in the air counteracted the humidity and the nerves. He handed cash to a vendor for a bouquet and walked a few more yards to the perfect spot.

Riley dropped to the ground and dug his shovel into the sand.

"You're doing great, Riley." Shane dragged his foot across the sand and patted his pocket for the millionth time today to confirm nothing had fallen out. "When Mimi comes back, give her the flowers, okay?"

"Okay." Riley kneaded the wet earth in his fingers and plopped it on the ground.

Shane stopped to marvel at the child he loved as his own. Smiling, he continued working on his greatest masterpiece. Nothing in his art gallery came close to this creation. Beads of sweat formed on his forehead, and he swiped them with a forearm. He checked his watch and dug quicker.

Several minutes later, Holland headed toward him and Riley.

Shane's pulse hammered against his chest. She was so beautiful. So *perfect*. He couldn't stop his hand from trembling inside his pocket. "Riley, time to bring Mimi the flowers."

"Flowers!" Riley jumped with his chest out. He gripped the bouquet lopsidedly and bolted toward her.

As Shane hoped, she only focused on Riley, not on the ten-foot wide message written in the sand.

"Aww, Bubby. These are beautiful! Mimi loves them." She kissed his cheek.

The golden sun shone above her head like a halo.

Riley grabbed her hand.

She walked a few more steps while smelling the bouquet.

Only a moment passed—one, beautiful moment for squished eyebrows and a tilted head to shift.

She stared at the sand, frozen. As she scanned the sand, her eyes widened at the message: *Will You Marry Me?* She covered her mouth. The sun reflected the tears in her eyes.

He dropped to one knee and pulled the ring box from his pocket. "Holland." His love for her and Riley pushed through his central nervous system and came out verbally with a shaky voice. "You and Riley are everything I ever wanted. Everything I hoped for. I can't believe I'm lucky enough to know you, love you, and be part of your family." Right here, this moment, fulfilled every dream. He opened the box, held it up, and looked at her—the love of his life. "Holland Blue Mulberry. Will you marry me?"

She dropped to her knees and joined him on the sand. Cupping his face, she pulled him into her and burst into tears. "A million times over, yes."

Acknowledgements

First, I want to give a huge shout-out to my spouse. Pulling in extra parent duties while I finished my manuscript, along with steadfast support, has meant everything to me. You are my biggest cheerleader, and I am forever grateful for you. To my kids, Tanner, Kianna, and Joey, thanks for dealing with a distracted mom while I pursued my dream of publication. I love you all so much!

Amy Nielsen. This book would not have happened without your guidance, love, and support. Thank you for sharing your stories of being an autism mom, and for being open, honest, and vulnerable about the joys and struggles. You spent hours and hours helping me with this story, line by line critiquing, encouraging, and lifting me when I was at my lowest. I could not have done this without you.

Jennifer Gatewood. When you offered to read a few of my pages, I had no idea that would develop into such a beautiful friendship and partnership. Multiple stories later, you continue to share your knowledge and guidance. Thank you for sharing your gift and time with me.

To my parents, Dave and Esther, who introduced me to their love of sweet romance movies, which inspired this book. Your support and encouragement know no bounds!

Amanda Sauvageau and Erica Dusha—my first beta readers on ALL my work. Thank you for putting up with me. I love you both!

Special shout-out to my brother Dustin Dusha, who answered more questions about the restaurant business than he probably wanted to.

Katharine Bost. Thank you for your friendship and guidance, always.

Bryn Donovan. Thank you for all your help. I was so nervous for you to read a few pages, and you gave me the perfect amount of positive and helpful feedback.

To my editor, Leanne Morgena. Thank you for taking a chance on this story.

To my other helpers and supporters, Marnie Fischer, Addy Hammond, Jackie Freeman, Dana Green, S.E. Reed, I so appreciate you! You all lift me up and stand by my side, and I am forever grateful.

Thank you to everyone who believed in me and supported me for this project.
Dana

A word about the author...

Dana Hawkins is a caffeine-fueled mom of three humans and one Saint Bernard. Originally from St. Cloud, Minnesota, she has claimed Seattle, WA as her home for the last twenty years. When not chasing after humans (or dogs), she spends her time reading, enjoying the beauty of the Pacific Northwest with her family, searching for sea glass, and missing her mom's famous Minnesota hotdish. https://danahawkins.com/